Kay Louise Bowen recently took early retirement after being an adult education tutor for many years. She lives a lovely quiet life now with her husband and 5 cats and has a son and a lovely grandchild.

Secrets is her first book; it started as a bit of a hobby but she soon realised that getting into the characters minds and into the scenes she could write for hours at a time without even realising it.

She hopes you enjoy *Secrets* as much as she enjoyed writing it.

In memory of my lovely mum, loved and missed always.

Kay Louise Bowen

SECRETS

AUSTIN MACAULEY PUBLISHERS
LONDON * CAMBRIDGE * NEW YORK * SHARJAH

Copyright © Kay Louise Bowen 2025

The right of Kay Louise Bowen to be identified as author of this work has been asserted by the author in accordance with sections 77 and 78 of the Copyright, Designs and Patents Act 1988.

All rights reserved. No part of this publication may be reproduced, stored in a retrieval system, or transmitted in any form or by any means, electronic, mechanical, photocopying, recording, or otherwise, without the prior permission of the publishers.

Any person who commits any unauthorised act in relation to this publication may be liable to criminal prosecution and civil claims for damages.

This is a work of fiction. Names, characters, businesses, places, events, locales, and incidents are either the products of the author's imagination or used in a fictitious manner. Any resemblance to actual persons, living or dead, or actual events is purely coincidental.

A CIP catalogue record for this title is available from the British Library.

ISBN 9781037109195 (Paperback)
ISBN 9781037109201 (Hardback)
ISBN 9781037109218 (ePub e-book)

www.austinmacauley.com

First Published 2025
Austin Macauley Publishers Ltd®
1 Canada Square
Canary Wharf
London
E14 5AA

Thank you to my husband Stuart for his constant encouragement and support while I was absorbed in writing this book. He was left to his own devices a lot!

Thank you to Austin Macauley Publishers for their acceptance of my work and putting together the final product in such a professional way.

Table of Contents

Chapter 1 — 14
Haven Hotel — *14*

Chapter 2 — 19
Settling In — *19*

Chapter 3 — 25
Preparing for Work — *25*

Chapter 4 — 30
The Past Can Haunt You — *30*

Chapter 5 — 32
Neil — *32*

Chapter 6 — 34
Evasion — *34*

Chapter 7 — 39
Linda and Annabel — *39*

Chapter 8 — 45
Neil Goes Home — *45*

Chapter 9 — 49
Happy Days — *49*

Chapter 10 — 52
Date Night — *52*

Chapter 11	**57**
Revelations	*57*
Chapter 12	**67**
Annabel	*67*
Chapter 13	**75**
A Surprising Opinion	*75*
Chapter 14	**80**
Contemplation	*80*
Chapter 15	**88**
Reflection	*88*
Chapter 16	**96**
Edna	*96*
Chapter 17	**104**
Weymouth	*104*
Chapter 18	**112**
HMP Bristol	*112*
Chapter 19	**123**
Christmas Day	*123*
Chapter 20	**139**
Back to Haven Hotel	*139*
Chapter 21	**158**
No More Secrets	*158*
Chapter 22	**194**
Moving On	*194*
Chapter 23	**210**
Wedding Bells	*210*
Chapter 24	**234**

Two Years Later 234

Epilogue **248**

Secrets are a fundamental part of human nature, serving as both a source of power and a burden. People keep secrets for various reasons—some to protect themselves or others, some out of shame or fear, and others to maintain an advantage. Personal secrets can range from harmless, like a surprise gift, to deeply significant, such as hidden past mistakes or unspoken desires. While secrecy can offer a sense of control, it can also create emotional strain, leading to feelings of isolation or guilt. In relationships, secrets can act as barriers, preventing true intimacy and trust, yet in some cases, they may be necessary to preserve harmony or personal boundaries.

The impact of secrets often depends on their nature and the context in which they are kept. Some secrets remain harmless, never needing to be revealed, while others can fester, growing heavier over time. When a secret is finally exposed, it can bring relief or devastation, depending on how it is received. In friendships, families, and workplaces, secrecy can either protect or destroy bonds, depending on whether it is wielded with care or deceit. Ultimately, the decision to keep or share a secret is a complex one, shaped by the potential consequences and the weight of what remains unsaid.

Releasing a secret can be a powerful act of liberation, allowing individuals to move forward unburdened by the weight of hidden truths. Carrying a secret for too long can create emotional distress, fostering guilt, anxiety, or even a sense of isolation. When a secret begins to interfere with personal well-being or relationships, revealing it can be a step towards healing. Confessing a long-held truth—whether to a trusted friend, a loved one, or even through personal reflection—can provide a sense of relief and clarity. It allows for honesty to take the place of fear, making room for personal growth and deeper connections.

It allows you to move on…

Chapter 1

Haven Hotel

As the taxi pulled up at the hotel, Gina was surprised at how large the place was. She had read the brochure but the name Haven Hotel had not conjured up an image in her mind like the one she had before her now. There must be at least three acres of land surrounding the hotel and the gardens were truly magnificent. She could just see the path that led from the hotel straight down to the private beach; it really was lovely. She could feel a warm glow inside her and just knew she was going to enjoy her stay here. Although she was not spending her time here as a guest, she had originally applied for the receptionist job a few months ago, when she was at her lowest and desperately wanted to get away from home but had not heard until recently that she had actually got the job. She was now unsure if she still wanted to go ahead with it. She had considered it at great length and realised that she had nothing to lose. As she made her way up the hotel steps, she wondered to herself what exactly her future held for her now she had finally made the move.

 Gina did not have to start until Monday, so that would give her a couple of days to familiarise herself with the surroundings, having been told she could use all the hotel facilities in her spare time, it would give her plenty of things to fill her time in until she started work. This was something she was grateful for as time on your hands gives you plenty of opportunity to talk yourself out of situations and wonder if you have done the right thing. Yes, she realised keeping herself busy was definitely the thing to do.

 She made her way into the foyer looking for a porter to help her with her luggage; it was a most pleasant reception which she looked forward to working in. As there was no one at the desk, she wondered to herself if the previous employee had already left. Mrs Adams, the owner had told her at the interview that, Jane, the present receptionist, was leaving to have a baby and did not intend to return to work after the birth, so if Gina turned out to be satisfactory, the job would become permanent after a trial period.

Her employment package included her room, meals plus her salary and the hotel provided her uniform. It was a good package that had persuaded her finally to take the job, although she had reservations that she was doing the right thing.

Her thoughts were interrupted by the arrival of a man, who she thought was in his mid-thirties, and was enquiring about her visit to the hotel.

"Can I help you, Miss, have you got a reservation?" He asked.

Gina quickly told him who she was and he introduced himself as Neil Adams, the brother of the owner, explaining that he helped out around the place since his return. He did not say where he had returned from and Gina did not pursue the matter.

"I'll go and fetch my sister and she will sort you out. She knows better than me what you have to do and what room you are in. She's around somewhere, afternoons are usually quiet around here. People go out for the day or the older residents are resting in the lounge, you know how it is. I'll go and find her and send her out, see you around then eh, Miss, sorry, Gina."

"Thank you, Neil," Gina shouted after him quite breathless at his energy.

Abigail Adams appeared shortly after Neil had left. Gina put her in her late forties; she had worn well if she was older, stocky but not overweight, and had a smile from ear to ear.

"Welcome, Miss Taylor," she said with an energy that matched her brothers. "Glad you decided to join us, you'll be alright here with us. I suppose your parents will worry about you being so far away from home but they have nothing to worry about, we'll take good care of you."

Gina did not press the point that she was in fact twenty-six and had left home years ago; instead, she offered her hand out to Abigail, "Thank you, Mrs Adams," she said.

"Now we'll have none of that Mrs Adams rubbish; you must call me Abby when we're not on duty, only Mrs Adams when there are guests about. Are you hungry or would you like to see your room first and settle in?"

Gina plumbed for the latter. She was tired from the journey and although she was a little hungry, a short nap seemed more appealing right now. She could find out where she ate and any other questions she needed answering later when she came down to eat.

"I'll eat later if that's alright; I'd like to take a rest after the journey first."

"Of course, you would, dear," Abby replied and with that, she led her up two flights of stairs.

"Lifts are out of order, they are working on it now," she informed Gina. "Room 202 is yours, dear, always keep this one for staff."

The room was lovely; decorated in blue and cream, it gave it a feeling of relaxation and she was pleasantly surprised it was on the side of the hotel that overlooked the sea.

"Well, I'll leave you to settle in, come down to the staff kitchen when you're ready and they will rustle you up something to eat. If I'm not there, just tell them who you are and they will see you get your bearings around the place," said Abby leaving the room.

Gina sat on her bed, looking out at the sea and looking around her room taking in her new home. Yes, she was sure she had made the right decision. She would be happy here, she felt it, and hopefully, she would now be able to escape the past that still haunted her.

Gina woke with a start and looked at the clock, half past five; she had slept for over an hour. She realised she was pretty hungry now; she took a quick shower, changed and made her way towards the lift only to find it still out of order, she went downstairs where she found Neil on reception talking to the lift engineer. "Excuse me, Neil, could you tell me where the kitchen is?"

"Hang on a sec and I'll take you there myself, time for tea I think or should I say, my stomach does," he laughed.

Taking in the corridors and rooms around, Gina could not quite believe how well the hotel was decorated. When she had come for her interview, she had only gone as far as the reception, then a little office just behind and as she had had to catch a train home, she had declined the guided tour that followed the interview. She hadn't been bothered at the time; if she had not got the job she wasn't really interested in the hotel's layout anyway, but now following Neil, she took in the large lounge where a few guests were talking to each other waiting for their tea. She took in the magnificent views over the sea; even on rainy days, Gina thought that the view could not fail to stir your emotions. Being a city girl was probably what made it so breathtaking to her where others took it for granted but even so, whether it was rough or calm, it would always be a wonderful sight to her.

"Here we are," Neil said as he opened the door for her. "Let me introduce you to the others, Tracy, Carol and Sheila, all serve the tables."

Gina offered her hand and all three of them smiled back at her shaking her hand in turn.

"This is Gina, our new receptionist; make her feel at home, will you?"

Sheila beckoned to Gina to take the seat next to her. "And over there is Derek, Paul and Steven; they all work in the gardens and grounds and do maintenance around the hotel. Tea is a cold one for us and we get a hot dinner later on when the guests have been seen to, is that OK?"

"Yes, that's fine," replied Gina. "I'm sure I'll get the hang of all the routines soon."

Gina decided that after tea, she would take a walk down to the beach; it was summer and the nights were long. It had been a humid day and a walk later would be nice. She decided to explore the grounds and then stroll along the shore. Ah yes, this is what dreams are made of she smiled to herself, pure life of luxury at the moment, when would the bubble burst? She wondered.

After she'd eaten a delicious crab salad sandwich, Gina found herself taking the path to the beachfront. There were still families about, the hot weather made the days longer for their children, and even the beach was covered in fine sand and hardly any pebbles. She wondered if one of the lads she had met earlier at tea was responsible for keeping it in such a pristine condition. She strolled along, wondering where the private beach ended and the public one began. It seemed to go on forever but she had no worries about getting lost as long as she kept the hotel in her view.

"Found your way ok then?" Looking around, Gina could see Tracy. "I come down here all the time at night after my shift, it's nice and peaceful, isn't it? Helps you wind down after all the rushing about, do you think you'll like it here, Gina? Or is it too early to say, where do you come from?"

"A little town in Weymouth called Wyle Regis," Gina replied. "And you?"

"Oh, not far from here, my parents have always lived locally but most people who arrive here are trying to get away from their parents, striking out on their own or running from a rotten past. Any of them fit you, you're a long way from home, Gina?" Tracy asked laughing.

"Maybe," Gina smiled but she didn't expand on the answer.

"Shall we start back now?" Tracy asked. "It's starting to get a bit cool down here."

"Yes," Gina replied. "Then you can fill me in on the running of the hotel and what the guests are like."

"Oh, I only wait tables," Tracy said. "I don't know about much else, but what I can fill you in on is all the gossip about the other staff, that's far more interesting." She laughed.

"I can see you and Ire going to get on just fine," smiled Gina. And they started their way back to the hotel.

Chapter 2

Settling In

Gina was woken the next day by the sound of seagulls and thought how lovely it was. She also thought that, in time, the noise may become quite irritating, but for the moment, she would enjoy it and it made a change from the sound of traffic. It promised to be another lovely day, the forecast had said warm and sunny again on the Cornish coast, but it was still early. She had one more day to herself before starting her new job, so she decided she would go further afield today and explore the local area.

She showered and dressed, then went down to the kitchen. Oliver, the chef, was setting out breakfasts for the staff who ate before the guest surfaced. The guests were being served at eight thirty so now, at seven forty-five, all the staff were gathered in the kitchen.

Gina was surprised at the variety they had to choose from, it was surely the same standard as the guests' breakfast. You could not possibly get better food than what was set out before her. She helped herself to bacon and eggs, not her usual choice but today, she felt like spoiling herself. Oliver introduced himself and two other members of his team wishing her well in her new role and hoping she would be happy at the Haven.

The other two kitchen staff were Janice and Peter who didn't look much older than school leavers, but she surmised that if Oliver did all the cooking, *they were only probably needed to help not to actually cook, perhaps they were training*, Gina thought to herself. Oliver, like Neil, looked in his mid-thirties; he seemed very pleasant from what she had seen so far as did all the staff. Gina realised that Neil was not present for breakfast.

"Does Neil have breakfast with his sister and not the staff?" Gina asked Carol.

"Oh, no," Carol replied. "Mrs Adams has already had hers; she always eats early and Neil usually does as well but he went into town last night and spent the night at his girlfriend's flat. Mrs Adams is not best pleased that he's not back yet but I'm sure, he'll be here shortly to do his bit."

"Oh," Gina replied and then pulled herself up quickly as she realised that she had felt a pang of jealousy at the thought of Neil having a girlfriend. "Don't be so stupid," she reprimanded herself. "You hardly know him." But his rugged good looks and easy demeanour had not escaped her.

"Oliver's throwing a tantrum as well," Carol continued, "about him not being here; those pair have never hit it off. Oliver swears he would never get a job anywhere else with his bad record and this is the reason his sister gives him work. Oliver needs something attended to in his kitchen and, once again, Neil does a disappearing act, giving Oliver ammunition to go to Mrs Adams."

"Any chance that he gets to berate Neil he does; it's rumoured that a lot of it was over some girl or other that they both wanted when they were younger but that could just be gossip. Anyway, it was ages ago before Neil went away. He only came back a few months ago. Mrs Adams told us one day that he was returning and the next day, he just turned up like the proverbial bad penny, no one knows where he'd been or what he had been doing and so far, no one has dared to ask."

At that, Oliver came bursting back in asking if Neil had returned. "If he's not here within the next half an hour, I shall call someone in and then let's see how her ladyship likes that when she's paying her no-good brother to do these jobs; thinks he can come and go when he pleases and I don't suppose we've had a phone call from him?"

Silence from everyone answered his question for him. Gina tried to break the silence by asking if any of the others were on a day off like herself as she wouldn't mind some company and someone to show her around.

"I'm only working this morning," Sheila told her. "If you can hang around until after we have served breakfast, we can take the bus into town and you can take in sights on the way."

Gina thought that was perfect and decided while she was waiting for Sheila, she would take a stroll around the hotel grounds to familiarise herself with everything and get to know where everything was before she started the next day. She followed the corridor from the kitchen and made her way out front; guests were drifting into the dining room passing pleasantries with each other as they went. She wondered if there were many regulars who came back each year. The dining room was furnished with the same good taste as the rest of the hotel. She thought it must have cost Mrs Adams a fortune to get the place as good as this. She found herself wondering what had happened to Mr Adams, *had he died? Were they divorced? Was it because Abby was on her own that Neil helped her? Or was it true that he only worked here because he couldn't find work elsewhere?* She scolded herself for speculating on other people's lives, reminding herself it had nothing to do with her. Mrs Adams was her boss and Neil was just another member of staff. Her own life was a complete mess, so who was she to pry into others? She stood on the front steps, the mist had lifted and the sun had broken through. Yes, she smiled, it was going to be another glorious day.

Sheila finished at ten, so they headed off for the bus, which was just a five-minute walk from the hotel. She pointed out several places of interest on the way, Gina got on well with Sheila.

Alighting at the terminus, she guided Gina to the local market.

"Much cheaper than the stores; I and the other girls get most of our stuff from here," she told her.

It was very busy and many people were bustling around which surprised Gina, as it was Sunday morning.

"Holiday towns never close and Weymouth is always buzzing," Sheila added. "People come on holiday here for a week or maybe two. They don't want to find things closed, do they? Come on, let's go down to the pier, all the amusements will be open and I haven't been on them for ages. Living here, they tend to lose their novelty but it will be fun for you."

The sea air blew fresh on their faces as they walked down the never-ending pier.

"We'll take the train back," Sheila laughed.

"I thought that was for the kiddies," Gina replied.

"Oh, parents get on as well," Sheila said, "plus anybody who's knackered from the walk-up!"

The arcade was loud with music bellowing out and families having fun on the machines, the usual gangs of teenagers hung around and the young girls were made up far more than the girls back home would have dared. There were kids laughing and kids crying; all the usual things you get at the seaside and the seaside atmosphere could not fail to lift you.

Gina thought how strange it felt that in a week or two, this would be the norm to her and not just a day out.

"Fancy a hot dog?" Gina asked Sheila.

"Yes, please, onions and tomato sauce, the works!"

She left Sheila watching two boys playing the machines while she went to fetch the food. She stood in the queue when suddenly her attention was drawn to the sight of Neil in an office on a higher floor of the arcade, seemingly arguing with another man in there. She desperately did not want him to see her, for whatever reason she didn't know. She quickly paid for the hot dogs and hurried back to where Sheila was sitting.

"Look, up there, that's Neil, isn't it?" Sheila looked up at where Gina was pointing.

"Oh my god, you are right, what is he doing up there? He should have been back at the hotel ages ago. Mrs Adams will hit the roof, I think we'd better keep quiet about this one, Gina, don't you?"

Both agreeing, they took the train back down the pier, partly for the rest and partly to get away quicker.

After more exploring of the shops, they made their way back to the bus stop. "I'll stay with you and tell the driver where you need to get off. They are very helpful. They get used to holidaymakers who are not sure where places are, and then I'll see you tomorrow behind that desk. Don't worry about anything, you'll be fine, I'm sure of it. You'll take to it like a duck to water; you already fit in with all the staff, so you are halfway there already. I'm off to see my parents now and I shan't be back till late. I don't get to see them much with my long shifts but I make a real effort every couple of weeks to get over there. Oh, here's the bus now. See you tomorrow, Gina, enjoy the rest of your day."

Gina took in all the wonderful scenery on her way back; it was hard to believe that she had just left a bustling seaside town and now she was in the middle of nowhere. It was the best of both worlds and she was loving it already. She knew she was going to be very happy here; she could just feel it. Getting away had definitely been the right decision, away from all the unhappiness, the trouble and the scandal; no one knew her here. She could make a fresh start, unless, of course, some nosy reporter took a holiday here and recognised her. It was a remote possibility, so she felt pretty safe. Her only worry was that her picture had been in the paper but as her best friend pointed out, unless people were really involved, they didn't really take much notice. She hoped and prayed that Sammie was right.

Wherever she went in her life now, she would always have this fear in the back of her mind. She couldn't have gone further from home if she tried unless, of course, she had gone abroad but she had never been much of a traveller before and to go abroad on her own had seemed scarier than what she was running from.

She thought about Sammie for a moment. She had been the best friend anyone could have wished for. She had stood by her throughout and when Gina had told her plan, she'd cried at the thought of them not seeing each other. Gina had reassured her that when she was settled, she would get in touch and she could come to the hotel to visit. Sammie knew she had to do it and promised Gina that she would not tell a living soul where she was. Gina knew she could trust Sammie; she just hoped and prayed that no one else found out and spoilt things for her.

Her mind drifted back to Neil. She could have approached him and asked him for a lift back if he were returning to the hotel, but she could see from the two men's faces that it was not the time to interrupt them. She wondered what had been going on between them; it certainly didn't look as if they were exchanging pleasantries! What was it about him? There was definitely something, apart from the hassle he had caused at the hotel that morning. She was still apprehensive about him. Did she fancy him? Was that it? There was definitely something but she could not quite put her finger on it at the moment. She needed to put Neil firmly in the back of her mind. She was off men. It was, after all, a man who had put her in the position she was in today, and apart from that, she knew now that Neil had a girlfriend. No, their relationship would be strictly professional.

She made her way up the lane to the hotel, wishing now that she had not bought so much! When she entered the foyer, it was obvious that Neil still hadn't returned. Mrs Adams's face was like thunder.

"You didn't see him in town, did you?" She asked Gina.

"Er, no, Mrs Adams," Gina lied, immediately asking herself why she had covered for him, but then again, he hadn't seen her. Sheila was certainly not going to say anything and there was something about the scene at the arcade that didn't seem quite right. If she had said yes, she would have had twenty questions from Mrs Adams and she had had enough questions already to last her a lifetime.

She checked her watch, it had just turned two. Guests were still in the dining room finishing off their lunch. She was not a bit hungry having had a full breakfast and her hot dog, so she made her way up to her room. Later on, when her food had settled, she would take a dip in the pool which looked so inviting and then a sauna.

"I really must catch up with Abby later to get my uniform sorted before the morning and to find out what time my duties start on the desk in the morning," Gina reminded herself. Tired from the heat and the shopping trip, Gina lay on her bed and drifted into sleep. She found it easier to sleep these days, now it was over. She'd had so many sleepless nights in the past that she had wondered at the time if she would ever sleep a night through again, but time being the great healer that it is, she had found herself on the road to recovery and normality. She thought again about what had happened to her and wondered how on earth she had ever got through it. God only knows but she had, with the help of her family, Sammie and counsellors, and now she was concentrating on building her life again. She had been given this chance and she wasn't going to blow it for anyone.

Chapter 3

Preparing for Work

Waking at four, Gina set off to find Abigail Adams; she thought it may be a little quieter in the hotel now and that she would be able to discuss things with her. She found herself excited about starting in her new role in the morning; it would be a real kick-start to her new life. Calling for the lift, which was now repaired, she pressed the button for the ground floor where she entered the hotel's foyer. Abby was in reception filling in some forms.

"Mrs Adams, could we discuss details about tomorrow and sort out my uniform?" She asked.

Abby looked up from the desk. "Of course, we can, dear, come through into the office and we will run through everything."

Gina followed Abby into the office and sat down.

"Now," Abby began. "I believe you always learn more from experience, so I'll just give you a few guidelines for now." They chatted for a good half an hour, then went to fetch the uniforms. She was given a few sets and told that the hotel laundry took care of the washing and pressing of them, so Gina didn't have to worry about getting them cleaned at all. The uniform itself was very smart; navy skirts and jackets teamed with a nice white blouse.

When everything was sorted, Gina asked Abby for directions to the pool and sauna. "Oh, very popular with the staff and guests alike," Abby informed her. "It's just down the corridor and the first turning on the right, you can't miss it. I'll put Neil with you in the morning until you find your feet and know where everything is. It shouldn't take you long though. I have told him to meet you here at seven-thirty in the morning. Enjoy the rest of your day, dear and I'll see you tomorrow." Gina guessed that Neil had now returned and to her surprise and dismay, she found herself quite pleased by this.

The pool and sauna were up to the same standards as the rest of the hotel and Gina could see why it was so popular; everything here was so clean and fresh you couldn't fail to like it. She changed and jumped into the heated pool. This was sheer heaven and she couldn't wait for Sammie to visit so she could show her everything but that would have to wait a while. Oliver waved to her from across the pool; he was also taking a dip before the staff tea and the evening rush of dinner, probably left orders with his staff to start preparing everything for him, she thought. He came over to her as she was sitting on the side.

"Finding your way and settling in, alright?" He asked.

"Yes, thank you, Oliver, everyone is so nice here. I've settled in really quickly. I just hope I do ok tomorrow in reception," she replied.

"Oh, you'll soon have the run of that desk. I hear Neil's helping you in the morning, a fat lot of help he'll be but I suppose, he's better than nothing," and with that, Oliver bid her goodbye muttering that he would have to go and sort out dinner, so she made her way to the sauna.

Teatime was spent with staff who were all discussing the row between Abby and Neil earlier in the day. "She certainly told him a thing or two," Carol said. "Put him in his place good and proper. He'd hardly got his foot through the door and she pounced on him. Told him one more mistake and he was out; she hadn't taken him back in and given him his job back for him to repay her like this. There was a deadly silence between them for a while when she realised people were listening. I wonder where he'd been before he came back here."

"So do I," Oliver interrupted, "should be worth knowing."

It was clear to Gina that Neil's past had everyone wondering, including herself but she was sure no one was going to find out. She kept quiet about what she had seen earlier that day at the arcade, as she didn't feel it was her place to say anything.

After tea, Oliver offered a guided tour of his kitchen, which Gina accepted. Spotless was an understatement, but this didn't surprise her at all.

"Was there a Mr Adams?" Gina asked Oliver.

"Oh, yes," Oliver replied. "He passed away suddenly five years ago. Hadn't even been ill, then he was found dead in bed one morning. He was only in his late forties, but it seemed a funny business to me. One minute, he and Abby were selling up and moving on; then he was found dead. She used the insurance money to pay off the mortgage and do the place up and decided to stay put. We didn't think she'd stop. She'd been unhappy here for years but she did and she sank all her money into this place, must have been a tidy sum, mind you. It was a mess beforehand, and they had been really struggling, that's why they decided to sell but as I say, he died and she stayed."

"Young Neil was more upset at the time; he and Abby didn't see eye to eye for a long time, then suddenly they patched things up; he went away returning only recently. Her investment in this place certainly paid off though, always-busy here and it's worth a small fortune now. Harry was his name, Harry Adams."

"It is a lovely hotel" Gina replied, "but you really don't like Neil, do you?"

"Gina, it is bad blood over a girl from a long time ago, Linda Green. We both went out with her, the other not knowing at the time. She sort of played us off against one another. When we found out, we gave her an ultimatum to choose between us. We were both besotted with her and ready to forgive her if she chose us in the end. She chose neither of us and moved away with someone else, but it carried on for some time until she made up her mind and we had a few scraps along the way. Silly really, as it was so long ago, but it has sort of carried on, you'd have thought we could put it behind us by now, wouldn't you? But male pride and all that," Oliver said thoughtfully.

"But surely with you both working together again, you could try," Gina said.

"Yes," Oliver replied. "I've tried, but Neil is so different now. He's come back. He keeps himself to himself most of the time and always seems preoccupied, so now I've left it. He still annoys me to a certain degree and treats Abby badly which is a shame because they used to get on so well before Harry died. She brought him up when their parents died; he was still very young and she had been both a mother and a sister to him. Harry thought the world of him as well. They were inseparable, in fact, young Neil would tag around with them all day and now he treats his sister like this." With that, Oliver excused himself, said he needed to get on with dinner and suggested Gina go and sit in the lounge a while and get the feel of the type of guests they get here. She spent an hour in the lounge, watching television and chatting with the guests, who were middle-aged couples getting away for a few days, then she decided to go back to her room, take a bath and have an early night. She had a big day tomorrow and she wanted to be as fresh and alert as she could.

The next morning, Gina awoke at six thirty, took a shower, dressed in her new uniform which fit her perfectly and applied her makeup carefully. She wanted just enough to make her look fresh without overdoing it. She took up her post on the desk at seven-thirty where Neil was ready and waiting for her. She still felt that flutter when she saw him, which was now beginning to annoy her; she was off men and today of all days she didn't want any emotions getting in her way.

Gina soon got into the flow. She felt good in her new uniform and soon her confidence began to show. Guests were arriving today; she could see from the reservation list that all the rooms were full, so she guessed she would be busy all day today. Neil floated off as soon as he could see she was coping leaving her his mobile number in case she needed him but as yet she hadn't; she was coping fine by herself. All the girls came to see if she was ok and Abby came to tell her that she would cover her later, so she could go and get a bite to eat. She had been nervous earlier and had declined breakfast but now things were going, so well that she realised she was actually quite hungry.

Gina summed up the guests as they arrived in her mind, married, courting, retired, dirty weekend she giggled to herself, she made quite a game of it. Not that the guests would ever have realised, of course. She had got the greeting smile and warm welcome down to a fine art that even Abby had commented on. If they are happy, they can't be married; if they are indifferent to one another, they are, was what she surmised, although this may have been a little harsh as she was going from her personal experience and she was sure not everyone was the same. She thought of her own marriage, so happy to begin with, then the indifference and anxiety, and then finally, the acts that destroyed it and nearly destroyed her life along with it. Then there were the endless newspaper articles that made it nearly impossible for her to leave her house. How could anything that started so perfectly end so disastrously?

She had met David on a visit to her aunt's in the country following a car accident she had had; it was a nasty accident and she had been laid up at home for a long time afterwards. When she was on the mend, her mother had thought a change of scene would do her good, so she had contacted her sister and asked her if Gina could come and stay with them for a while. Gina had always been close to her aunt, so she agreed without hesitation. Aunty Pat and Uncle George had taken her out on a trip to some gardens and that is where she met David. They had hit it off straight away and he visited her at her aunt's often. When she returned home, they had written to one another almost daily. She really missed not seeing him regularly as he could only visit every other weekend due to work commitments. She had offered to go to his place but he had advised her against it saying his mother would give her the third degree and he wasn't sure she would want that so early in the relationship. She would, in fact, have done anything for him but she did not push the issue and left it with his fortnightly visits to her, which she looked forward to very much. They had shared fun when they were together; then tears when they departed. After only eight months, David proposed and Gina did not think twice; she knew she wanted to be with him forever. Her mother had thought it was too quick and that she was too young at only twenty but Gina reassured her that there was nothing she didn't know about David now and why wait any longer. How that had come back to haunt her!

Chapter 4

The Past Can Haunt You

"Ok, off you go and get something to eat," said Abby.

Abby's voice brought Gina back to the present with a start. "Take half an hour, I'll cover you, it will give me a chance to catch up on a bit of paperwork."

Sitting with her tea and sandwich, her mind drifted back to David. They had been married for five years in total and the first two were blissfully happy, setting up home together and David had got a good job almost as soon as he had moved down. At first, she had ignored the warning signs that their love life was on the slide, telling herself that the novelty always wore off after a while, but when it turned into non-existence and the rows had become more frequent, she tackled David about it. At first, he refused to face up to the fact that there was any problem at all but when Gina pressed the issue, he finally admitted that he was infertile. She had told him that they could get help together, but this only made him explode with anger saying he didn't want doctors messing about with him like he was a freak, so Gina had dropped the issue from then on.

She felt sorry for him that he had this problem and kept it locked up inside for so long and felt sure now that it was out in the open, the rows would begin to subside. She reassured him that it made no difference to her that she loved him with or without the lovemaking. She certainly believed his story and had no reason to doubt him. He never stayed out late and was, in fact, with her every evening, apart from his bridge night with the lads, so an affair never entered her mind. She resigned herself to the fact; she loved him for him and not for what he could do for her in the bedroom and if that's the way it had to be, so be it. She felt more resigned now the truth was out than she had done for a long time and she'd never been maternal enough to desperately want kids. So, life carried on and the subject wasn't brought up again, things seemed to settle back down and life resumed to how it was in the beginning until…

The knock at the door on that morning was to change her life forever. She had opened the door expecting to see a delivery man but instead found two policemen standing there; they had asked if she knew where David was. Yes, she did, he was watching TV in the lounge. Then she watched in horror as they explained to David that he was being arrested on the charge of rape. He was led away that night, and although Gina did not realise at the time, it was to be for good. Over the next few months, he was accused of several more rapes and a subsequent trial began. Then there was the guilty verdict, the life sentence handed down and the newspaper reports about the poor wife who knew nothing about it. Poor soul, everyone said but Gina was always sceptical about whether they really believed that she didn't know, which, of course, she didn't. Every time the news came on the television, her face was there leaving court, and when she arrived home after the verdict, she found the press camped out in her front garden! She didn't dare leave the house for weeks after and her mother had a nervous breakdown with the pressure; it just seemed to go on and on.

From the David she knew and loved, she now saw a monster standing in the dock before her. She would never come to terms with the fact that this man and the man she once knew were the same person. A year had now passed since the nightmare and here she was now trying to escape the past and start a new life hoping that no one would recognise her and spoil it all for her. She was still married to him, of course. She couldn't afford the divorce at the moment and anyway, it didn't really matter. He couldn't do her any harm now where he was and she never wanted to marry again she was sure of that. She would divorce him one day when she had the money. She wanted to be totally rid of him but for now, it would have to wait.

"Doing alright?" Tracy's voice interrupted her thoughts and brought her back down to earth which was probably just as well, it didn't do to keep dwelling on things that were best put to the back of your mind although never ever forgotten, she regained her composure quickly.

"Yes, yes, thank you, Tracy, so far so good," she answered.

Making her way back to reception, she realised that these thoughts that plagued her would never completely go away. It was such a traumatic time for her and her family but she had a new life now, so she needed to suppress them in her mind and start afresh; she only hoped it was possible.

"Come on, Gina, you can do it," she told herself and with that, she painted on her smile, slid behind the desk and got back to work.

Chapter 5

Neil

Neil unlocked the tool shed, made himself a brew and sat down on the makeshift stool, which was in fact an old beer crate that the brewery had left behind after a delivery. He felt like he was on his own, in front of him were Harry's tools and Neil remembered how Harry had looked after them. They were his pride and joy. 'Look after your tools, lad, and they'll always be there to help you,' he had said so often. Neil had never got over his death; he remembered his sister coming into his room the night before telling him they would be leaving the next day. Neil understood the marriage was in trouble and had heard their talk of splitting up.

He had told Abby that he would stay with Harry and help him. She was infuriated with this and harsh words had followed. The next time she came to his room was the following morning to tell him Harry had died; she seemed surprisingly calm which alarmed Neil. He knew they were splitting up but he had expected some sort of grief to show. He had been devastated; he loved Harry, his own mother and father had passed away when he was young and Harry had always been the replacement father that Neil needed.

Harry had taken his duties very seriously, teaching Neil rights and wrongs along the way. Now he was gone and Neil wondered if he could cope with losing someone else so close to him.

The days after Harry's funeral had been like a dream to him and he found for the first time in his life that he was not functioning as he should. Abby had noticed that he wasn't coping and sent for the doctor who had prescribed him some pills to help him through the bad times. Abby, however, had organised the funeral with military precision, still showing no emotion and no sooner as Harry was buried, she had collected the insurance money, paid off the mortgage, paid off all her other debts, moved the builders in and informed Neil they wouldn't be moving after all! He had stayed with Abby for twelve months after the death to help her out, then went away to try and sort himself out only returning to the hotel a couple of months ago. He was glad to be back although Abby had not looked ecstatic when he had just turned up, but she had soon gotten used to it.

He always wondered but had never said to this day, if Abby had helped Harry on his way rather than lose everything. After all, he had not been ill; he was in fine form and not that old considering. The post-mortem had revealed heart failure but what caused it Neil wondered. He never mentioned this to his sister, of course, he needed a job and a home and if his thoughts came out, he would have neither.

Finishing his tea, he selected the tools he needed and made his way down to the beach; some of the huts needed attention and it would be quieter now. He had spent many happy days down at the beach, felt liberated out in the open, hated being indoors just like Harry had, they really were soul mates. They had said the stress of selling the hotel had caused Harry's heart to fail but Neil knew Harry was not a worrier; he couldn't rest with these thoughts and knew that one day he would need to get to the bottom of it.

How he didn't know, he did not envisage his sister as a murderer but something went on that night, but what exactly had not yet been found.

He had so many unhappy memories here. He often wondered whether he had done the right thing in coming back, should he have stayed away and started a fresh life just like the new girl Gina had done. He thought about Gina for a moment; he liked her a lot but wondered what had happened so terribly that she had felt the need to run away. He would never ask her; it wasn't his style to pry, after all, he wouldn't want people prying into his life. Maybe one day, he would find out if he ever got close to her. He wanted to ask her out but thought he should wait a while; she was new and he may frighten her off if her bad past was anything to do with a man, which he suspected it was. He should give himself some time as well; he had only split with his Gemma yesterday and the scene that had followed in the arcade with her father had not been pleasant!

Chapter 6

Evasion

Gina woke early, got up, showered and dressed and then sat by her window in the sunshine for a while. She looked forward to her duties, and she really did love the job here at the hotel. She had been here a month now and she took a moment to reflect on things. She thought about Neil, in fact, she thought about little else just lately. He had come to her after the first week and praised her for the way she had settled into the job, telling her that anyone would have thought she had been with them years the way she ran the desk. She was pleased, only then he had asked her for a date; she was almost tempted to say yes but then she remembered the reason she was there in the first place. Wasn't she there because of a man and wasn't it now her choice to stay off men and think about herself only?

She had declined the offer of dinner, telling Neil that she did like him but could not possibly be anything other than a friend to him. He had looked hurt and said he understood but it was obvious from the look on his face that he clearly didn't, how could he? She could hardly understand her life herself. He had been nothing but a good friend to her ever since, that is until last week when he asked her again. She declined his offer once again with the same explanation as before, this time he confessed he didn't understand why.

"I thought we got on good," he had said. "And I've already told you that I'm no longer with Gemma."

"I know," replied Gina. "But like I told you last time, I cannot be anything other than a friend to you."

"Is it something that happened to you? Were you hurt before you came here? Is that the reason you're here in the first place?"

Neil was so persistent that she almost told him the truth but she stopped herself from doing so as she really didn't want anyone to know and anyhow, she may feel as if she knew Neil well but she didn't know him well enough to trust him with the truth.

"Well, I shan't give up." Neil continued. "I shall carry on asking you until you relent, the more time we spend together on this desk, the more you will be unable to resist my charms." He laughed.

Gina smiled at him; he was charming, funny and considerate, all the things that David was in the beginning and look, how that had turned out. Neil was true to his word; he spent lots of time on the desk with her, which didn't go unnoticed by Abby or Oliver.

"Be careful, he's a right charmer," they had both warned her. But she did feel herself being drawn closer and closer to him the more time they spent together and it was taking all her strength for her to resist him.

She made her way downstairs and went into the kitchen for some breakfast before she started. Neil was already there and so was Oliver. The atmosphere was tense as it always was when the two of them were in the same room. She got her plate and helped herself to some cereal and toast and sat down next to Sheila.

"Morning, Gina," Sheila greeted her, "how are you today?"

"Fine," Gina replied. "And you?"

"Oh, I'm great," Sheila said, "last shift today before my week's leave. I'm going away with Greg for a few days and I can't wait. We are like passing ships with us both working different shifts all the time and don't get away together very often so I'm really looking forward to it."

"Sounds great," Gina smiled. "Remember us slogging away while you're enjoying yourself."

"Oh, no way," Sheila laughed. "I shall give none of you a second thought!"

The two of them laughed together as they always did. Gina got on well with all the other staff. She could feel Neil looking at her.

"Ready for another day behind the desk?" He asked her.

"Of course, why wouldn't I be?" She replied with a smile.

"Oh, no reason." Neil smiled but she knew exactly why he was asking. He really didn't give up asking her out and she was nearly at the point of accepting. She wished he wouldn't put her in the position that he did; she didn't want to date any man but for how much longer could she resist him, she didn't know.

She took her place behind the desk at seven-thirty as usual and it wasn't long before Neil was also behind there with her.

"Please, come out to dinner," he pleaded within five minutes of them being together.

"I can't," she replied "and you really must stop asking me."

"Never," Neil said. "Never ever, I shall ask you every day and every night until you say yes." And with that, Abby came through.

"Neil, there's work that needs to be done in the garden, do you think you could manage to do some before lunch?" She said with a sarcastic tone in her voice.

"Of course, I can, sis," Neil said with a wink in Gina's direction.

"Good and Gina, can I see you for a few moments after your shift? There are a few things I would like to discuss with you."

"Yes, Mrs Adams, of course," Gina replied.

When Abby had left, Gina turned to Neil.

"You really must stop coming onto the desk every day," she said. "It looks as though I'm going to get a dressing down because of it now, she didn't look too happy and she probably thinks I can't cope."

"Rubbish," Neil said. "She was only saying to me the other day how well you were doing. Anyway, I'd better do my duties in the garden, I'll see you later." And then Neil was gone leaving Gina to worry about what it was Abby wanted to discuss with her.

"Sit down, Gina dear," said Abby as Gina entered her office at the end of her shift. "And don't look so worried," she laughed. "I'm not the ogre everyone tries to make me out to be."

Gina sat down and Abby began speaking, "Now then, I just wanted to ask how things are for you here."

"I love it," Gina replied. "I feel I know the job well now and everyone is so nice."

"Good," Abby replied, "because I think you are doing an excellent job and rather than wait three months to make your position permanent, I would like to do it now. You do the job very well, in fact, I would go as far as to say that you're the best we've had here on the desk so far. All the other staff like you and you get on with the guests very well."

Gina was thrilled; she really thought Abby was going to haul her over the coals about the time she was spending with Neil on the desk, thinking maybe she had asked him to be there because she couldn't cope and if there was anything that her recent experiences had taught her it was how to cope with any situation.

"That would be brilliant, Mrs Adams," Gina said.

"I've told you before, Gina, call me Abby when we're not in front of guests." Abby laughed. "Now I've got a new contract here, will you be happy to sign it today?"

"Yes, I'd be delighted," Gina answered. "Will everything remain the same like my accommodation?"

"The accommodation is yours for as long as you're here, Gina dear, unless, of course, you decide you want to move out of the hotel into your own property, but really while you're here, you have all your meals cooked for you and there's no cleaning and that must really be a bonus." They both laughed and agreed on this fact. Gina signed the new contract and Abby gave her copy; she was delighted that her pay would rise so soon after she had started. Abby had explained to her that she would be on a lower rate while on trial but when the position was made permanent, it would rise quite generously. Now it was here in black and white and Gina couldn't help thinking how lucky she had been to find this job and was glad that she had decided to go with her heart and take it.

"Now, there is one more thing, dear," Abby continued. "It's about my brother Neil." Gina's heart sank; she knew Abby had realised there was something, but could she really tell her that Neil was pestering her for a date because he wasn't really doing any harm and he wasn't exactly harassing her; he was just persistent?

"Is he bothering you? I know he spends a lot of time on the desk with you and it's not that I mind, as long as he does his work, he can be wherever he likes, but he does like a pretty face and I wouldn't like to think he is annoying you."

Gina was relieved; at least Abby wasn't annoyed at her. "Oh no, I don't mind Neil's company, we get on well and I enjoy talking to him."

"Well, that's ok then, but don't let him take advantage of your nice nature, dear. Neil's been through a lot in the past few years and he is a bit insecure, so he tends to latch on to people and they don't always want it," Abby said.

"I'm sure it won't get out of hand," Gina replied. "But if it does, I'll be sure to tell him, Abby. I'm not afraid to say what I think."

"Excellent," Abby said. "Well, I think that's everything; it will be nice having you on our staff, Gina."

With that, Abby got up from her desk and walked towards the door. Gina realised that their meeting was now over, so she followed Abby and bidding her goodnight, she made her way to the kitchen for her tea.

It's funny how things turn out she thought to herself, so many bad things had happened to her; now only good things were heading her way. If only now she could get Neil to stop asking her out, everything would be perfect because she truly felt that if she did give in and go out with him, her good luck would soon run out.

Chapter 7

Linda and Annabel

Neil was pruning the roses in the garden; they needed doing now before the winter arrived. *How different everything looked here when the weather changed*, he thought. All the plants retreated into their own warmth, waiting for spring to return them to their glorious selves. The beach was more or less deserted except for locals taking their daily stroll and a couple of families with their young children building sandcastles. They were taking advantage of the last bit of sunshine even though it was cold but he was sure that this would only last for another couple of weeks; after all, it was the middle of October. Then his mind turned to the hotel. Soon, it would just be the regular guests who came for a winter break, usually elderly people like Mrs and Mrs Overton. They never failed to show up each November for three weeks and then they were followed by the 'Christmas guests' as he called them.

Christmas was lovely at the hotel; all festive and happy; they usually put some shows on at Christmas for both the staff and guests. Everyone was so festive and jolly that you couldn't help, but get caught up in the atmosphere; he just wished he had someone special to share it with. He had decided to stop dating as it had usually landed him in trouble. The most recent being Gemma, of course, and the unpleasant incident with her father in the precinct, and a long time ago, a girl had caused him to fall out with his friend Oliver. Boy, had she strung them both along! Linda Green was a blonde with blue eyes and endless legs. She was gorgeous and Neil was besotted with her. He couldn't believe his luck when she agreed to go out with him although he thought it a bit strange that she wanted to keep it a secret. After all, they were both single.

So, he had told Oliver that he had met someone and how lovely she was but he didn't tell him who she was. Oliver really wasn't that interested as he had just met someone as well and was equally besotted with her. Neil wanted to spend every spare minute with Linda but she worked different shifts in her job, including some evenings, so he had to make do with three evenings a week and the odd afternoon. He would have done anything for her; he loved her and worshipped the ground she worked on. One afternoon, they were doing some shopping in town when they bumped into Oliver. Neil was delighted to be able to show Linda off at long last but when she saw Oliver, she looked horrified.

"What's going on?" Oliver had asked.

"Hi, Oliver, this is Linda, the girl I've been telling you all about," Neil said.

"I know exactly who this is," said Oliver. "And I'll ask you again, Linda, what is going on?"

Neil was confused. Oliver's face was like thunder and Linda was at a loss for words which was unusual as she always got on well with everyone.

"How do you two know each other?" Neil asked.

"Linda, I think you've got some explaining to do," Oliver said sharply. "Neil, this is the girl I've been seeing, the one I've been telling you about. I bet she wanted you to keep your relationship secret, didn't she? She said the same thing to me although I could never see why, but I do now."

Neil was distraught. "Linda. is this true?" Neil asked her, but she couldn't look him in the eye, so he knew it was. All she kept saying was how sorry she was to both of them. Neil couldn't believe what he was hearing, both he and Oliver had been telling each other about their new girl and it turned out to be the same one! Neil didn't want to let her go, how could he? He loved her, idolised her, and was besotted with her. Oliver interrupted his thoughts. "Well, you had better choose who you want to be with because you can't be with both of us," he said. It was obvious that Oliver didn't want to give her up either, and in a way, this annoyed Neil. He felt she was his and Oliver should just walk away, but Oliver wasn't prepared to do this. Linda had gone on to say that she needed time to make her mind up and had left them both standing there in the shopping precinct.

The atmosphere in the next few weeks was so sharp when Neil and Oliver were together. It could have been cut with a knife, both of them thought the other should have given her up but neither of them would give in and on one occasion, it had led to the two of them fighting in the kitchen, only to be broken apart by the other staff. Luckily, his sister had not got to hear about it, otherwise, he doubted either of them would have ever worked in the hotel again.

Eventually, Linda made up her mind; she was leaving with the waiter from the town's café. Neither Neil nor Oliver could get over her. They even blamed each other for her going, convinced if one had given her up she would have stayed with the other. They hadn't spoken again before Neil left and not a lot since he had returned; it was a shame because they had been best mates once and they both missed the laughs they used to have.

After this had happened and Uncle Harry had died, he tried to pick himself up to help his sister out in the hotel, but the strain got too much, so he decided to go away for a while and take a break from the people and surroundings that held so many bad memories for him.

When he left the hotel, he really wasn't sure where he was heading, so he just bought a train ticket and took it from there. He had a bit of money; some he had saved and some his sister had given him when she realised how badly he needed to get away. His first stop had been a little town just outside the South Sea. It was a nice little place, so he found himself a bed and breakfast and stayed for a few days before travelling on to the next town. It was nice to just get up in the morning, take a stroll before breakfast and then see where the day took him, instead of working to a routine that came with the running of a hotel.

After a few months, he realised his money wouldn't last forever, so when he reached Scotland, he decided he would need to look for a job. He found himself somewhere to stay, which was a lovely little guesthouse called Sunny Cottage with a landlady who made him feel so welcome. She had told him to get himself settled in his room, to come downstairs where she would fix him up with a meal. The room was lovely, overlooking acres and acres of greenery, which he gazed at for quite a while before realising how hungry he was. So, he showered, changed and made his way downstairs. A younger girl who introduced herself as Annabel greeted him. She too was lovely, and she had a welcoming smile and showed him the way to the dining room.

"Are you a guest here too?" He had asked her.

"Oh no, I live here," she replied. "It was my mother you saw earlier but she asked me to look out for you because she is preparing dinner."

They carried on talking for a while when the landlady came in.

"Here we go," she said placing a steaming plate of steak pie and vegetables in front of him. "The pie is homemade. I hope you like it. I see you have met my daughter Annabel. She helps out around here. By the way, my name is Edna and I'm usually always around if you need anything, are you staying long?"

"I'm not sure," Neil said. "I was hoping to find a job round here and settle for a while. I've been travelling around the country for the last few months which has been great but I really need to start earning again now."

"Well, I know Mr Pearson is looking for a gardener at his hotel in the next village. Are you any good at gardening?"

"Yes," Neil laughed. "It's all I've ever done. Could you let me have the address and I'll go and see him in the morning."

"I'll do better than that. I'll get Annabel to take you and I'll give him a call to let him know you are coming. It'll be nice to have you around, Neil and it will do Annabel good to have some company of her own age."

The next morning, after breakfast, he and Annabel had taken the bus to Mr Pearson'. True to her word, Edna had called him so he was waiting for them when they arrived.

"Morning, lad," he said.

"Morning, Mr Pearson," Neil said holding out his hand.

"Call me Alf, lad, can't be doing with that Mr lark. Now what experience have you had as a gardener?" Neil told him all about Haven Hotel and all the time he had spent with his uncle, learning the trade.

"That sounds good enough to me," said Alf. "You obviously know how hotel grounds should look. When can you start?"

"Whenever you want me to," Neil answered.

"We'll say eight in the morning then, shall we?" Alf said. "There's a bus at seven-thirty that should get you here by then, been nice meeting you, Neil. See you in the morning." And with that, he was gone.

Annabel explained that Mr Pearson was a lovely man with a heart of gold, but he didn't waste much time on conversation. Neil didn't mind that at all, after all, conversations usually led to you telling people about your past and he wasn't quite ready for that yet.

Neil enjoyed working at the hotel for Mr Pearson and he also found himself enjoying Annabel's company as well. They had gone to the cinema together a few times and she had taken him on sightseeing trips. She was a good companion; they got on well but Neil found himself more and more drawn to her which wasn't good as he wasn't sure he was ready for another relationship so soon after Linda. He knew it had been months since it happened, but his heart still felt raw from the pain of it all. He could sense that Annabel felt the same way about him. She had even dropped little hints to him, but he hadn't pushed the issue. He'd kept it purely on a friendship basis; after all, he didn't even know how long he would be here.

A few weeks after he had arrived at Sunny Cottage, Annabel asked him if he would like to go out for dinner to a nice little restaurant she knew in the village. He wasn't sure at first. Was she trying to push their relationship along by taking him out on a date? Then he reminded himself that they were good friends and it was only dinner, after all. Edna hadn't been bothered about them not eating at the guesthouse, in fact, she'd almost seemed pleased that they were going out together.

"Don't worry about offending me. You two just go and have a good time," she had said to them when they had told her, so they had set off.

When they arrived, the place was thriving, but Annabel had booked a table for them. The head waiter had greeted Annabel like a long-lost friend.

"This is Neil," she said. "And Neil, this is Tommy." The two shook hands then Tommy showed them to their table.

"Do you come here regularly?" Neil had asked.

"Oh, no," Annabel laughed. "Tommy and I were at school together and in a small village, you tend to remain friends."

They ordered their meal and drinks. Neil was amazed at the choice on the menu and opted for fresh salmon. Why not? He didn't go out to dinner often these days; they both had wine with their meal which flowed like a river, as soon as their glasses were half empty, Tommy was there to refill them. If he didn't know better, he may have thought that Annabel had had a word with Tommy beforehand to hatch a plan to get Neil drunk! But he thought he knew her better than that. They chatted easily throughout their meal and they were both quite tipsy at the end of the evening.

"Would you like to go to a club? It seems a shame to end a wonderful evening quite so early," Annabel asked him.

Neil looked at his watch; it was only ten forty-five and he had really enjoyed the evening. He could quite easily carry on for another few hours.

"Is there one close by?" He asked.

"It's not far, about 10 minutes' walk if you're up to it," she said.

"Lead the way," Neil replied.

They stayed in the club until two thirty; it had been great. They had laughed, danced and drunk plenty.

"We'd better get a taxi," Neil said. "I don't think either of us is up to walking up that hill back to Sunny Cottage."

"No problem," said Annabel. "I'll call one from that phone booth over there."

She called the taxi then they waited outside the club for it to arrive. Annabel was shivering with the cold, so Neil offered his jacket. He wrapped it around her shoulders and was reluctant to let go. She was petite and when she looked up at him with her big brown eyes. He suddenly felt very protective towards her. Perhaps he had deeper feelings for her than he realised or was it just the drink making him feel that way? He wasn't sure, but he kept his arms around her shoulders until she suddenly turned towards him and kissed him. He didn't resist her; it felt wonderful so he gave in to all temptation. They were silent in the taxi on the way home until they got to the guesthouse and Annabel led him to her room. He followed her easily; he wanted her; she wanted him more than anything at that moment. So, they both fell onto the bed and made love for hours until they both finally went to sleep.

As soon as he woke, Neil knew what he had done was wrong. His head throbbed both with the drink and from the guilt of what he had done. He remembered everything, every wonderful moment and now when he looked at Annabel sleeping, his heart ached. He didn't love her; he knew that and it was wrong of him to lead her on; he wasn't staying here forever and what then? He knew he would return to the only family he had got when he was ready and that, he knew, would be soon. What should he do now? They couldn't carry on as before, just friends. Annabel would want more than that and he knew he couldn't give her more. There was nothing else for it. He would have to leave, but he couldn't tell Annabel that he was going or she may want to come with him and how would he explain that to Abby?

"Oh, hi, sis, this is Annabel, someone I picked up along the way."

No, he would have to leave in secret. He would leave a note explaining that he was sorry for hurting her but it just wouldn't work out. He would also leave any money that he owed Edna, cowardly he knew, but what alternative did he have? He hoped she would understand although he doubted she would. He would see Mr Pearson before he left and tell him he had been called back home urgently. That is where he would go now, home. He felt ready to face the past, put it behind him and carry on with his life.

Chapter 8

Neil Goes Home

When he reached the drive at the bottom of Haven Hotel, he took a moment to take a look. All the old memories came flooding back, but somehow, they didn't feel quite so raw. He hoped Abby would be pleased to see him and also the rest of the staff including Oliver.

"Oh, look what the cat dragged in," Oliver cut in behind him. "You came back then, worse luck." And before Neil could answer, Oliver strode off up the drive.

So much for hoping Neil thought. He just hoped Abby's welcome would be warmer, which it was, just. Oliver must have told her he was on his way up because she was waiting for him.

"Hello, Neil," she said. "It's nice to see you back."

"Is it?" Neil asked.

"Yes, of course, it is, come on in and let's get you settled. I take it you are staying and that you want your old job back," she answered.

"Is it still available?" Neil said somewhat surprised. "I thought someone else would be doing it now."

"I knew you'd come back sometime," Abby said. "So, I only took on temporary staff, but I don't want any more funny business like you had with Oliver. He's a valued member of staff and I won't automatically take your side."

Neil looked confused; he didn't think she knew about that incident.

"Oh, don't look so bewildered. There's not much goes on here that I don't know about," Abby cut into his thoughts "I let it pass last time, but I won't stand for it any more, do you hear me?"

"Yes, sis," he said following her to his old room.

"Did you manage to sort yourself out and stay out of trouble while you were away?"

"Yes," he replied hesitantly briefly thinking about Annabel, then pushing it firmly to the back of his mind. "I'm ready to settle down and take more responsibility here now."

"Don't think you are coming back and taking over, Neil," she said. "This is my hotel and you work for me; you may be my brother, but that's the way it is."

"Anything you say, sis," he smiled. "Anything you say."

"As long as we're straight, we'll get along fine," she added with a little grin that he couldn't see. Secretly she was glad he was back, at least now she knew he was ok.

He settled back in quickly. All the staff except Oliver were pleased to see him, asking him where he'd been and what he'd been doing. He didn't really feel at liberty to tell all, so he didn't which kept them wondering all the more. He didn't even tell Abby about everything, only telling her he'd travelled around doing this and that. He couldn't tell her about Annabel, who he still felt guilty about when he thought of what he had done to her. He'd been back a couple of weeks when he started dating an old friend, Gemma; it was nothing serious, just someone to go out with, share dinner with now and then and he'd stayed over at her place a couple of times. He didn't really feel easy with the relationship as she was starting to get heavy. What was it with women? Couldn't they just have a bit of fun without all the heavy stuff?

Then a new girl started at the hotel, Gina. She was the new receptionist and boy, she had knocked him for six. She was a stunner, but he'd kept his distance at first, even though he wasn't a two-timer, he'd had that one done to him and it was no joke. No, he'd made friends with her at first but had felt himself intrigued by her. She was obviously running from something in her past but she wasn't letting on to anyone what it was. She kept her private life very private, discussing it with no one. After a few weeks, he thought about nothing else but Gina and decided if he thought so much about this woman, it was time to part company with Gemma. After all, it wasn't really fair on her either. He wasn't proud of his track record with women; he seemed to do nothing but hurt them but he felt sure if he could date a woman like Gina, it would change his ways forever. He may even go as far as to say he could love againwhich is something he once felt he could never do again after Linda. No, his playing around days were over; this was serious and he needed to free himself when he asked Gina out.

Gemma was not happy when he told her, saying that she had been good to him letting him stay at her place when he felt like it, feeding him and her family had accepted him readily, inviting him to everything that took place even though most of the time he declined their offers. She said her parents had taken it for granted that they would marry one day! *Where was this coming from?* He thought. It was a bit of fun, nothing serious now they were marrying him off after just a couple of months, jeez, no way could he cope with this! He knew now that he was doing the right thing, even without Gina, he knew he couldn't spend the rest of his life with Gemma. If she was this possessive now, what would she be like in a couple of years?it didn't bear thinking about.

He had broken the news to her at the arcade that her dad owned, and after about an hour of nonstop rowing, her father had turned up, by which time Gemma was in tears. When he heard what had happened, Bill was none too pleased either. Neil explained to him that whatever Gemma had told him, he had never intended on marriage. Bill exploded and told Neil never to set foot on his arcade again or he would have him escorted off. It wasn't a pleasant scene but one that Neil was now glad was over. Now he was free again he could concentrate on Gina.

She was proving to be a tough nut to crack. He had asked her out so many times and she had refused saying that it wasn't him, but she couldn't get involved with anyone.

"Are you married?" He had asked.

"It's not as simple as that and I'm not prepared to discuss it. I can't go out with you, so can you please let it drop," she had said.

Neil had been gutted and was determined never to ask her again after the first refusal. His resolve lasted about a week when he realised he couldn't just let her go. So, he had asked her again and again, and again and again, she had refused, so he had informed her that he would continue to ask her every day until she relented, and he had kept to his word.

He spent a lot of time on the desk with her; he didn't push her to talk about her past. She would tell him when she was ready he was sure. He didn't make life uncomfortable for her. He knew if he did, this would push her further away, in fact, they got on really well and he was sure that soon, she would say yes and go out to dinner with him at least, and when she did, he would make sure she would never regret it. He had plans for them. He knew this was the woman he wanted to marry and settle down with. He knew he would do anything for her and he also knew the feelings he had now far surpassed anything he had felt for Linda.

He thought about Oliver again. He always did when he thought about Linda; he wished they could be friends again; when he came back, he was ready to try and patch things up with him, but after the welcome he got from Oliver, he decided it was perhaps not yet time. Oliver hadn't spoken to him since he had returned, only to berate him in front of the other staff and Abby, of course, he never missed that opportunity, but perhaps if he could prove he had changed and settled down, then he would come around. He could only hope as he really missed his friend.

Chapter 9

Happy Days

Gina joined the others at the dining table and told them the good news.

"Seems I'm here to stay," she said with a huge grin. "Abby has just given me my permanent contract."

"Three months haven't gone past yet, have they?" Sheila said.

"No," replied Gina, "but Abby says I'm doing such a good job already she can't see the sense in waiting until the end of the three months, so she has given me my new contract now."

"That's fantastic, Gina," said Sheila. "I'm really thrilled you are sticking around. I would have really missed you if you hadn't, we've become really good friends now." And with that, she gave Gina a hug so tight she thought she would stop breathing.

Neil was at the table and Gina could see he was also smiling at the news and she knew why, this would give him more time to keep working on her! Not a thought she relished.

"So, she didn't haul you over the coals as you suspected," Neil said with a laugh.

"Not quite," Gina replied trying not to look him in the eye.

Gina ate her dinner, made her excuses and went back to her room. Once there, she thought about Neil again. He really wasn't going to give up, was he? But then, she had come to realise that if he did, she would probably feel a bit disappointed. She was enjoying being chased again, it was flattering. If he could have seen how she looked twelve months ago, she thought to herself with a smile, it would have definitely been a different story. After all the terrible business with David, she had let herself go quite shamefully. She didn't leave the house for a couple of months in case the press were lurking and she had come to the conclusion that if no one saw her, why should she bother with her makeup and hair?

Sammie had been the one to snap her out of it, "You're not the guilty one," she had said to her. "So, why are you the one doing the hiding away? Get yourself together, girl and start living your life again." When Gina thought about it, she realised that Sammie was right. Why should she hide? She had done nothing to be ashamed of. She had booked herself into the hairdresser and had a complete change of style; she had gone for a nice sophisticated bob that suited her more than she would ever have imagined. Then she went and bought a new set of makeup, completely different from what she would have normally worn, and with the new wardrobe that she had purchased, her transformation was complete. Not that she had changed so much that no one would recognise her but just enough to make her feel a whole lot more confident.

After this, she decided to get herself a job. David did not like her working, he liked her to be there when he got home from work with his tea on the table, so she had given up shortly after they had married. She would never do that again but she was so besotted with him that she didn't think twice about it. She wondered now if he just wanted her home so he knew where she was when he was up to his wrongdoings. She had been a sales rep, sent all around on different trips, and on reflection, could have bumped into him anywhere and he wouldn't have wanted that, would he?

She didn't want to go back into the sales environment; she had scoured the papers for something different when this job had caught her eye. She could change her job and move away at the same time; it seemed the perfect solution a fresh start in every aspect, not that Sammie agreed. She was horrified to think Gina would be alone after such a terrible ordeal, but Gina had put her case forward so convincingly that Sammie had no choice, but to agree with her. She never imagined she would get the first job she applied for and when she hadn't heard anything after a couple of months, she had just taken it for granted that she hadn't got it. Then out of the blue, Abby had called her and asked her if she was still interested, and the rest is history.

She knew she had made the right decision in coming here; she hadn't been so happy for a long time. In fact, if it weren't for Neil, she could honestly say she had never been as happy even when she had met David and she never thought she would say that!

Neil was just a blip she would have to deal with; maybe she would go out with him just once to pacify him. It may stop him hassling her and if she made it clear that there were definitely no strings, she may actually have a good time. It had been ages since she had a good night out and she felt it was about time she did. All the girls had boyfriends, so Neil may be her only choice. Yes, the next time he asked her, she would shock him and say yes, but also lay down the conditions that went with the 'date'.

When she went down to work the next morning, Neil was already behind the reception desk. "Morning," he said brightly. "You're looking as gorgeous as ever."

"Oh, you're such a flatter, Neil Adams," she said with a laugh.

They made small talk, and then Neil said he needed to go and do some work in the garden.

"Marvellous," she thought after he had gone. "No sooner I make up my mind to accept his offer of dinner, he doesn't ask me." She had to smile to herself about how typical this was.

She got on with her work, several new guests were checking in today, so she set about getting the paperwork ready for when they arrived at the reception. She was so busy and involved in what she doing she didn't see Neil come back into reception with the bunch of flowers that he just cut for her. When she looked up, he gave her a start.

"I didn't see you come in," she said. "Who are the flowers for?"

"You, please please, go to dinner with me tonight," Neil begged.

"Ok then," she said and began to laugh when she saw the shock on Neil's face. "But there are conditions, it is only dinner, there will be no strings attached whatsoever and it will probably be a one-off," she said.

Neil laughed. "Ok, ok whatever you say," he said.

"Neil, it probably will only be a one-off. I am only going out with you to stop you hassling me all the time." Although she realised now that she was quite looking forward to it.

"You'll enjoy yourself that much, you'll want to go out with me again, I'll make sure of that," Neil said with a wink. "I'll see you here a seven-thirty tonight, then." And with that, he had gone.

She had wanted to ask where they would be going so she knew what to wear but he had disappeared, so she thought she would go for her plain black dress; it looked nice on any occasion.

Chapter 10

· Date Night

Neil couldn't stop smiling all day. Gina had finally agreed to go out with him and he was going to make sure it was the best night out she had ever had because he wanted her to want to go out with him again. If he played this right and didn't push her into anything and didn't pry into anything, it may turn into something more than friendship. He had to be careful; she had been hurt in the past he knew that, but to what degree, he didn't know. He would play it however she wanted it played. If she ever wanted to tell him about her past, she would in her own good time but he would never ask. No, he had waited long enough for Gina to accept his invitation and he wasn't going to blow it now.

Still smiling, Neil set about making reservations for dinner at the finest Italian restaurant in town. He booked a table at 8:30 pm, which would give them time to have a drink first and break the ice. Then, if the evening went well, he would suggest a drink back at the hotel. He didn't want to go on to a club because he didn't really want to share her with anyone. He had waited a long time for her to agree to go out with him and now he wanted her to himself. He thought about what life would be like with Gina and liked what he envisaged. He had never come across anyone like her; she was stunning with a great personality; she had obviously been very hurt in the past, but she had picked herself up and moved on. OK, she had moved away from home to do so, which took guts, but she had still done it, and after all, he ran away himself, not so long ago.

They had built up a great rapport at work and he only hoped it would spill over to their social life, he so wanted tonight to be a success. If all went well, they might even become an item. Abby may not agree with the relationship at first because they worked together, but he knew she liked Gina and would soon warm to the idea. Anyway, she wanted him to settle down and once she could see how serious he was, she would perhaps even give it her blessing.

He knew his thoughts were running away with him; they hadn't even had one date yet, but he was already besotted. He knew Gina would be the making of him. He wouldn't even look at another girl if he had her, he knew that for sure, however, he was determined to take things slowly and not rush her. He couldn't believe how he was acting. In the past, if he wanted a girl, he set out to get her, no matter what and if they weren't interested, he would simply move on to the next without a second thought, but this girl had really got to him and if being patient was what he had to do to spend the rest of his life with her then so be it, that is what he would do.

When he walked into reception at 7:35, Gina had not yet arrived. He hoped she hadn't changed her mind; he would be gutted. He sat on one of the sofas and waited. He had really gone to town on his appearance tonight, bringing out his best Armani suit for the occasion. It was his only decent suit; he didn't really dress up that much. He had bought it for a friend's wedding a few years back and this was only the third time he had worn it. He teamed it up with his best white shirt and grey tie, if anyone walked through now, they would surely have laughed, Neil thought. He was only ever seen in jeans and a white t-shirt, and here he was, dressed up to the nines waiting for a girl. This in itself was unheard of as he usually waited for no one; in fact, he was usually the one who turned up late and kept them waiting, but tonight was very different. He had put on his best aftershave and his hair was slicked back neatly; he wondered if she would even recognise him. He smiled to himself at the thought of her walking straight past him as he looked at his watch, 7:35! Panic began to rise in him when he suddenly saw her coming down the corridor.

"Wow," he said out loud, she looked fantastic.

She wore a sleek black dress and black shawl draped around her shoulders and her hair was pulled up on top of her head; yes, she would make any man proud to be with her and he was ecstatic that tonight he was him.

"Hi, Neil," she said as she approached him. "You look great, very different to what you usually look like."

"Yes, well, tonight is special," he replied. "And you look absolutely fantastic." She blushed slightly; it had been a long time since she had made such a great effort and she wasn't sure why she had done so. It was only one date; a date she had agreed to only to stop him hassling her, but she had taken ages getting ready because deep down, she was excited about tonight. She really had a strong attraction to Neil but she was determined to stop her feelings from surfacing. She was annoyed with herself now for putting in so much effort, wasn't she supposed to be deterring him not encouraging him? But he did look great and he had put in a lot of effort also she could see that. She was so confused in her head that it hurt, she wanted him, and she didn't want him. She knew the only reason she was holding back was because of what David had done and was that really fair on her or Neil? Should she carry on punishing herself for what he had done to her, on the other hand. she found it very hard to trust anyone now. She decided there and then that she would see how things went later. She was going out and she was going to enjoy herself, if they didn't get on out of work then they would both know; he may never want to take her out again anyway. But for now, she wasn't going to waste the chance of having a good night out; they would just have to see how things went. What else was there to do?

The taxi ride was strained, both of them not quite knowing what to say to each other. He didn't want to say the wrong thing and she felt a bit awkward. Gina eventually broke the ice by asking where they were going.

"It's a surprise," Neil answered.

"Well, I hope I'm suitably dressed."

"You are suitably dressed, believe me," Neil said with a wink.

They pulled up outside the restaurant and Gina was pleasantly surprised. She had seen this place when she had come into town shopping but never thought she would be able to afford their prices on her receptionist's wages, but as this was Neil's treat, she was sure she was going to enjoy sampling the Italian cuisine.

They went inside at 7:50 and because they were early for their meal, they decided a drink in the lounge would be nice. Neil ordered a glass of white wine and Gina asked for a gin and tonic. They sat down with their drinks still not quite knowing what to say to each other.

"Nice place," Gina said. "I noticed it when I came to town shopping, but I've never been here."

"Nor have I," Neil said. "But I've always wanted to; only I've never met anyone before who I'd want to bring."

Gina took a sip of her drink and looked down.

"Gina, you can take a compliment; I'm not going to pounce on you, you know," Neil said.

"Sorry, I'm just a bit out of practice, that's all," Gina said.

"Look," said Neil. "Let's just relax, we're two friends out having a meal together. You know how I feel about you. I've never hidden it, but I'm not rushing you into anything. The last thing I want is for you to be tense all evening, so let's enjoy our meal and drinks and see how things go."

"That is fine by me," Gina said relieved and then she began chatting about the hotel. After they both relaxed, time passed quickly. It was 8:20 and Neil suggested they go and book in for their table. They made their way to the restaurant foyer and waited for someone to show them to their table. Gina had a look around; it was dimly lit by candles; the tables were covered with lace tablecloths and there was a single red rose in the centre of each one. Obviously, a romantic place, she thought which put her a little on edge. She wasn't here for romance; only for a meal with a friend, but the atmosphere was calm and restful. They were shown to their table, a little table for two in a secluded little alcove. Had Neil requested this table? She asked herself. No, he said he hadn't been here before, how could he know the layout; he could have asked for somewhere private.

They sat down and looked through the menu. "What do you fancy?" He asked her. "Have whatever you like." She decided to skip a starter and played safe by ordering a lasagne and salad. Neil ordered the same saying he wasn't keen on all the fancy stuff as he really liked plain English food best.

"Why did you book here then?" She asked.

"Thought it would be more special, maybe next time, we'll go English."

"Next time?" She grinned. "You sure there'll be a next time, are you?"

"Well, I mean, if there's a next time," he laughed.

They had both relaxed now and she was enjoying his company and he hers. She realised she had been hard on him as he really was a nice guy although, she realised he may have been putting in extra effort as it was their first date; the real him could emerge later. She hoped things would work out. She really enjoyed his company and they had lots of things in common; well, the things they had talked about anyway, neither of them had approached their pasts yet.

After dessert, which was plain ice cream for both of them, they decided they would return to the hotel and have a drink in the bar; it was 10:30 when they left the restaurant and hailed a taxi to go home. Abby was serving the bar this evening and gave them a strange look when they walked in.

"Been somewhere nice?" She asked briskly.

"Yes," Neil replied. "We've been to the Italian in town and had a very nice meal." He grinned at Gina as they both knew now they would have probably enjoyed fish and chips better.

"Very nice," Abby said. "What's the occasion?"

"Oh, nothing special," he answered, "just two friends having something to eat together."

"Well, you certainly both dressed for it," she said eyeing them both up and down. "I'll look forward to seeing how you both look when there is a special occasion!" and with that, she walked off.

They both laughed as they sat down with their drinks, which Neil had poured himself, as it had become obvious that Abby wasn't going to do it for them.

"I don't think she likes it," Gina said.

"Oh, don't worry about sis, she'll be ok. She likes you and doesn't trust me, that's all. Probably thinks I am going to break your heart."

Gina looked at him seriously, "And are you?" She asked.

"Am I what?"

"Going to break my heart."

"Never," he said. "You are too special to hurt and whoever hurt you in the past was mad."

"How do you know I've been hurt in the past?"

"It shows, Gina, but if you never want to talk about it, that's fine by me, if you do, I'll listen and never judge, I promise."

"Maybe one day," Gina said. "And maybe one day, you will tell me about your past."

"Maybe," he replied. "When you're ready to listen."

He walked her back to her room and when they came to her door, she didn't really know what to do now. Did he expect her to ask him in because she didn't want to? Not yet anyway, it was far too early.

"I have really enjoyed myself, Neil," she said.

"Me too," he answered. "I'll see you in the morning," and with that, he turned to leave.

"Neil," she called after him; he looked back at her. "Thank you," she said and went into her room.

Chapter 11

Revelations

Neil was so happy that he thought he would burst. He knew she had enjoyed herself when she had relaxed and he had loved being with her, so much so that he never wanted to be with anyone other than her again. He had acted like the perfect gentleman at the end of the evening, walking her to her door and not pressing her for so much as a kiss. He knew when she called after him that she was warming to him and probably respected him for not trying to take advantage. Yes, he had played it differently this time. Gina was special and he knew that he would have to change his ways if he was to keep her. He got into bed happier than he had ever felt and couldn't wait for the next time they went out together, and he was sure after this evening that she would go out with him again.

Gina was surprised at how much she had enjoyed the evening and how much she liked being with Neil. *It wasn't supposed to happen like this*, she thought to herself. *I was supposed to be deterring him.* Then she realised she didn't want to deter him now. She liked him; she liked him a lot and she really would like to see him again. He had been the perfect gentleman all evening, buying her meal and drinks and opening the taxi door for her and when he walked her back to her room, he hadn't even tried to kiss her or press for another date. He just said goodnight and went back to his room; it was almost as though the night had not finished off properly, and that's why she called after him. What should she do now? Should she ask him out or should she just wait and see if he asks her?

She got into bed with a smile on her face. She hadn't felt this happy in ages. She thought about the irony of it all; she had really wanted to put Neil off. She didn't want a relationship but here she was, wanting more and he had not asked her. Oh, she hoped he did because she would readily say yes next time and who knows, perhaps they would even share that kiss.

The next morning, Neil got up with a spring in his step. He showered and dressed then went downstairs for breakfast. His good mood was soon blemished though when he walked into the kitchen to be greeted by Oliver.

"Abby wants to see you in her office," he said with a smirk. "Have we been a naughty boy again?"

Neil ignored his comments and went to find his sister. He knew what she wanted. She was going to berate him for getting mixed up with the 'staff' as she put it, but he would make her see how serious he was about Gina and then she'd change her mind, maybe.

He walked into her office without knocking.

"How many times have I told you to knock before you come in here?" She said sharply; *looks like she's in a good mood,* he thought to himself.

"Why, it's only me, your brother, we're not supposed to have any secrets, family and all that."

"Then you won't mind telling me what you were doing with Gina last night, will you? You know we're not supposed to get mixed up with the staff."

"Why not?" Neil asked. "You own this hotel. I only work for you. Remember, you tell me often enough and besides, I like Gina, so I asked her out, where's the harm?"

"I like Gina as well Neil but, as you say, I own this hotel and you are family, you shouldn't get mixed up with her."

"We had dinner together and I'd like to do it again and if you don't like it then I'll resign from my job."

"Now, you're just being ridiculous and childish," Abby said. "You'd resign over a girl."

"Gina's not just any girl," he said. "She is special. I really like her, sis, give me a chance at some happiness."

"I thought you said it was just a meal with a friend. Sounds to me like you are talking long term."

"I'd like it to be," he sighed. "I've just got to wait and see what happens."

"I can't say, I'm happy about it, Neil. With your past record, you'll just hurt her and I'll lose a damn good receptionist."

"People change, sis, and I believe Gina could be the one to change me if she'll give me a chance, she's really special."

"Well, just remember, she's running from something, something that none of us knows what it is. If you push her, you'll just push her away; if she wants to tell you, she will. Don't treat her like all the girls in the past; treat her with respect. She deserves that at least."

"I knew you'd come round," Neil said hugging her.

"I haven't come round," Abby said. "But I won't stand in your way if it means so much to you. I'll be keeping my eye on you, Neil. When are you seeing her again?"

"I don't know, I haven't asked her yet. I was waiting to see how she was today. If things seem ok, then I'll broach the subject of another date; if she's distant, I'll leave it a bit."

"Very sensible," Abby said. "I think, at last, you're learning."

Gina woke up with a slight headache; blaming the gin and tonics she drank to calm her nerves. Although there was no need, Neil had been great, she thought about the previous evening with a smile. It had turned out so different to how she had imagined; even now she had time to sleep on it she still felt the same. She was looking forward to seeing him this morning and took a little more time to get ready than she would normally have done. She made her way down to the kitchen for breakfast. She was hungry this morning and intended on having full English. As she was walking down the stairs, she wondered about Abby and what she would say to her. She needn't have worried as when she walked through to the kitchen, she passed Abby and she was most pleasant.

"Morning, dear, did you sleep well?" She asked.

"Yes, thank you, Abby," Gina said, a little surprised by the woman's change of attitude. Last night, she had been very abrupt and Gina wondered what had made her change.

She sat down at the table and poured herself a cup of tea when Oliver appeared next to her. "Have a good time last night?" He asked sarcastically. "Bet he made you go Dutch."

"Yes, I did thank you," said Gina, a bit annoyed at his tone. He'd never asked her out, so it wasn't like history repeating itself or anything. "And no he didn't; he paid for everything if it's any of your business."

"Oh, pardon me for asking," said Oliver and returned to his cooking.

"Well, come on spill the beans." Sheila laughed as she sat next to her with her toast. "Tell me all about it."

"It doesn't take long for the word to spread around here, does it? It was a very nice evening and Neil was the perfect gentleman."

"That's a first," interrupted Oliver again. "I suppose that's why old Adams was on the warpath this morning looking for him. He must have twisted her round his little finger *again* because she seems in a good enough mood now."

Gina ignored Oliver, in fact, he was starting to get on her nerves, and she turned to Sheila.

"Was Abby really after Neil this morning? Oh, I hope he's not in trouble because of me; it was only a meal with a friend nothing more. Oh, I must go and find him to make sure things are ok."

"Calm down, calm down," said Sheila. "Number 1, Abby is in a good mood now and Neil's already been to see her so things must be ok and Number 2, if it was only a meal with a friend, what does it matter if he is in trouble? It shouldn't really bother you, should it?" Sheila started to laugh. "Or maybe you'd like it to be more than just friends, you could do worse, he is a looker, but just take things slowly. Neil's not got the best past record with girls, but you never know, you could be the one to tame him!"

Gina started to laugh. "You are terrible, you know that. I told you we are just friends who had a meal together, although I must admit I'd like to do it again. I've surprised myself. I only went out with him to stop him hassling me but now I feel funny sort of all tingly inside at the thought of us together, and we didn't even kiss."

"No, really! He didn't try to kiss you," Sheila said amazed.

"No, I told you, he was the perfect gentleman; that's what makes it worse. I think I wanted him to kiss me and he didn't, he didn't even ask when we would see each other again."

"Oh well, that's easy, isn't it? It's probably in about 20 minutes when you go to reception." She laughed.

"That's not what I meant," said Gina. "I meant when we were going to go out again."

"Well, ask *him* then, he probably didn't want to rush you."

"I can't do that; it doesn't seem right."

"Well, you'll just have to wait and see if he asks you then, won't you?"

"I don't know, there's no pleasing some people." And with that, Sheila got up to sort out the guests' dining tables and Gina fetched herself some toast. She had somehow gone off the full English now.

By mid-morning, Gina was back into the swing of work, greeting guests, booking them in a sorting out their room keys. It was a hectic morning; Abby had mentioned this time of year when the regular old-age pensioners came for their winter break. They arrived the first week in November and stayed for about three weeks, but she hadn't imagined that there would be this many. They had arrived by coach and poured into reception. There must have been thirty or more of them. She booked them all in and gave them their room keys, then called for Derek, Paul and Steven to help them all to their rooms with their cases. The boys always doubled up as porters for the old folks especially when there were so many of them.

The crowd were very cheerful. They obviously looked forward to this break each year, and it was like a big reunion for them. Gina could see that the atmosphere in the hotel for the next few weeks would be uplifting if nothing else. Abby had arranged entertainment three nights a week for them and tea dances on Tuesdays and Thursdays; it would be a change from the usual guests and Gina was looking forward to it.

She was glad of the distraction this morning; it stopped her thinking about last night. She had really enjoyed it but now she was worried about Abby. This morning, she was more pleasant than she ever was yet Oliver had said she was on the warpath first thing. Where was Neil this morning? She wanted to ask him what his sister had said to him; only she hadn't seen him at all yet. Was he keeping away from her? Had Abby ordered that he keep away from her? Or had he not really enjoyed last night at all and didn't want the embarrassment of seeing her this morning?

Now the crowd had all gone, it started to play on her mind. She had almost convinced herself he was keeping out of her way when suddenly he was behind her.

"Morning, gorgeous," he said happily.

"Morning, Neil," she smiled, relieved to see him. "I thought you were avoiding me this morning and you shouldn't talk like that when we are at work."

"Stop worrying, will you? You'll put yourself in an early grave." He laughed. "Anyway, you don't look half as beautiful when you're serious and why would I be avoiding a lovely creature like yourself?"

"It's just that I haven't seen you this morning at all."

"I had to pop down to town to pick up some things for sis. Why, did you miss me?" He laughed.

"I wanted to see you and ask you if you saw Abby see you this morning, only Oliver said she was on the warpath and I've been worried."

"Take no notice of Oliver, he's just trying to wind you up. I did see her and she was fine."

"Really?"

"Yes, really, she warned me to behave myself and all that. I think she likes to see herself as a mother figure to me, but when she realised how much I like you, she seemed quite pleased and told me she would give us her blessing. That is, of course, if you would like to go out again," he looked at her questioningly. "After all, you said it would be just a one-off."

"Because I thought you would be all pushy and ask me things that I am not ready to talk about."

"And did I?"

"No, and I was grateful for that and yes, I would like to go out with you again. I really enjoyed myself. However, next time can we do something a little less fancy."

"We can have fish and chips on the beach if you like."

"Great," she smiled. "Let's say tonight at seven then."

"Wicked," he replied and with that, he punched the air and went back to his duties.

Gina was relieved now. Abby was fine and she had arranged to see him again, which was something that now put butterflies in her stomach. She found that she really liked Neil, the *real* Neil, the one she was with last night. He tended to put on a front to people; perhaps it was his barrier from getting hurt after the Linda incident. She didn't really know what it was; maybe she would find out more about his past one day, but maybe he would only tell her when she was prepared to talk about hers and that would be a long way off yet, she knew he would never push her and that was another point in his favour.

For now, she was just going to enjoy herself; enjoy being with him. It was about time she started dating and enjoying herself again, she thought. Her life had been on hold too long. She couldn't keep hiding away because of what David had done to her.

She thought of David again briefly, how was he and how was he coping in jail? She knew he must have written to her, tried to get in touch via her family and friends but they didn't know where she was still. She spoke to her mother and father on the phone once a week to make sure they were ok, but she still didn't let on where she was. If she did and David pressured them, they may be tempted to tell him. It would only be to get back at him by telling him how well she was doing and how she had got her life back and was managing without him but she couldn't take that risk. It was best they didn't know for now, then they couldn't possibly tell him, because if she did get a letter or communication from him, she wasn't sure how she would handle it. She knew she would never have him back when he got out or even contemplate seeing him at all but the episode had made her quite ill and the only way she coped now was by blanking out as much as she could. One day, she knew, she would cope better with it and then she would tell her parents and Sammie where she was.

She was due to go home at Christmas to see everyone and had been looking forward to it immensely. Now that it was drawing nearer, she wasn't so sure. Would it resurrect old memories too painful to bear? She realised she would miss not seeing Neil for two weeks. She had to go; she hadn't seen her parents for months and she knew she needed to, so she could see they were well and they could see she was. Maybe if things worked out between her and Neil, he would like to go with her. She knew her parents and Sammie would like him and they would be pleased she was moving on. Was she moving on a little too quickly? She asked herself. She had only been on one date, a reluctant one at that, and now here she was planning to take him home for Christmas! *Slow things down, Gina girl*, she thought to herself, *otherwise you could be heading for another very big fall.* Anyway, Neil would want to spend Christmas with his sister, so really her thoughts were futile.

Neil was waiting for Gina when she arrived in reception at 6:55.

"Are you always early?" She laughed.

"When I'm waiting for a beautiful lady, yes."

Gina smiled at him. "Always the charmer."

She took a look at him. He looked gorgeous tonight. He was wearing blue denim jeans and trainers, with a sports jacket, scarf and basketball cap.

"Ready for that walk on the beach?" He asked.

"You bet I am," she said. She had dressed sensibly too; a walk on the beach with fish and chips was going to be great, but in November, it was also going to be very cold!

They fetched their chips and walked down to the beach. Neil opened his jacket and fetched out a blanket. Gina burst out laughing.

"I thought you looked a bit bulky."

"Well, I didn't think you'd want to stand to eat your meal or sit on soggy sand," and he placed the blanket down and gestured for her to sit.

"You thought of everything," she said sitting on one side of the blanket.

They ate their fish and chips in silence, just watching the waves from the sea lap up onto the shore. It was a lovely calm night and the sky was so clear that you almost felt as though you could reach out a touch the stars.

This was more her kind of night out she thought to herself; she wasn't really into fancy, she was more homely and down to earth.

As if reading her mind, Neil turned to her. "It's lovely out here tonight. Isn't it? Much better than sitting in some fancy restaurant eating food that you don't really enjoy."

"I couldn't agree more," she replied. "We have more in common than I imagined."

"Seems we do," he said. "Are you warm enough?"

"It's a bit chilly, but I'm fine."

He put his arm around her shoulders. "Not getting pushy, just warming you up."

"That's ok," she said and turned to look at him. At that moment, she had an overwhelming urge to kiss him, so she did. He responded as though he had wanted it so much for so long.

The next few weeks passed quickly; Gina hadn't felt this happy since she had first met David. She hoped that wasn't a bad omen; after all, things had been wonderful when she first started dating him and she envisaged being with him for the rest of her life, and she was so sure of this that she had accepted his proposal after a very short time. Oh, how she wished she had listened to her mother and waited, but, what's done was done, she thought and she had learnt by her mistake. She was adamant that she would take things more carefully this time with Neil. They were very much an item now; in fact, everyone at the hotel knew about them and were all surprised when they knew that Abby actually approved of the relationship. Oliver had done his best to put her off, but then he would wouldn't he, he just didn't want to see Neil happy.

"He'll hurt you, you just wait and see," he had said to her one morning.

"I'm a big girl, Oliver; I can take care of myself and my own affairs," she replied a little too abruptly.

"Well, we'll see," he said. "We'll see."

She wished they would patch up their differences. She knew Neil wanted to but Oliver was having none of it. Perhaps in time, he would come to realise that life is too short to hold a grudge.

They were going to the pictures tonight. They had done a lot of things in the past three weeks; nothing too fancy, just walks on the beach, trips to the pictures and one night, they even went down to the funfair that was passing through town. It had been great. She only hoped it would stay that way. They were going to see a film she had wanted to see for ages and she was really looking forward to it.

She met him in the reception early as they were going to walk into town. It was a nice evening for a walk, crisp as it was now November but dry and she had wrapped up well with her big coat, scarf and gloves.

Neil looked as handsome as ever when she saw him and she proudly took his arm as they set off. They chatted all the way into town. They always found things to talk about, which was one of the things she liked about him, they got on so well.

When they arrived at the cinema, there was quite a queue. It was the opening night for this film here and it was quite a biggy. They joined the end of the queue and waited.

"I hope we get in," she said. "The cinema only holds 150 people and there must be that many here already."

"I'm sure we will," he said. "But if not, we'll go and get a burger and come back tomorrow."

They did get in which pleased Gina. She had really looked forward to it and she would have been disappointed if they hadn't. She wasn't let down either; they both enjoyed the film very much.

It was 9:30 when they came out and decided to go for that burger. They sat in the burger bar watching people go past wrapped up against the cold before they decided to head back to the hotel. They would have a drink in the bar before heading back to their rooms. They hadn't spent a night together and Neil was not about to push her to. When she was ready, she would, he had thought and until then, he was just happy to take her out and spend time with her. He knew this was a complete change of direction for him and he was quite proud of himself. Usually, if they hadn't slept with him by now, they would have been history but Gina was different. She was very special to him and if he played it right, she would be with him for the rest of their lives so there was plenty of time.

It had crossed Gina's mind about them separating at her door each evening and wondered if Neil was getting ready to take things further. She knew it wouldn't be long but as yet he hadn't asked her, so she hadn't pushed it. She had wanted to wait a while. She didn't want to rush things, but she was beginning to think about it more and more now so perhaps she was ready. She would leave it a little while longer then maybe she would invite him back to her room one evening and see how things went.

They walked back to the hotel taking in the clear sky and the stars that shone so brightly up there.

"It really is a lovely night for the time of year," she commented.

"Yes," he said. "But then any night that I'm with you is beautiful," and he turned and kissed her very slowly. "I think I'm falling in love with you."

She smiled at him but didn't reply. She did feel the same but felt it was too early in the relationship to be declaring undying love. Look where it had got her before, but she was thrilled when he said it.

He hoped he hadn't upset her by what he had just told her; she didn't look upset and she had smiled at him when he had said it. He wouldn't say it again, however, until he felt she had the same feelings. He thought she had and perhaps he was right and she just didn't want to say so at this stage. He looked at her again and she was still smiling; no he hadn't upset her, thank god, and at least now she knew how he felt.

They continued their journey back in silence. When they reached the hotel, Abby was waiting at the door, not looking best pleased.

"Hi, sis, what's up?" Neil said brightly.

"There's someone here to see you," she replied sternly. "Your secrets are coming back to haunt you, dear brother."

He looked past her to see who was waiting for him and suddenly the colour drained from his face.

"What's the matter, Neil?" Gina asked, looking concerned.

"Annabel," he said, "what the hell are you doing here?"

Chapter 12

Annabel

Neil had hardly slept a wink. Annabel turning up was the last thing he needed, especially now. Everything was going right for him at last and now this. What did she want? He had left her a long note explaining to her how things wouldn't work out, so why had she tracked him down? Why go to all the bother? It must have taken her ages to find him.

They had all gone into the bar last night as Annabel said she had some important news for him. She had asked to be alone with him but he said anything she had to say to him, she could say in front of Gina; boy, he regretted that now. If Gina hadn't heard what she had to say, he may have been able to resolve it without her knowing anything at all. He could have made up some other excuse for her being here like she had come to tell him some news about her mother or something, but no, thanks to him, Gina had heard the shocking news that she had come to deliver.

He thought back to the conversation that had taken place.

"How did you find me?" He asked Annabel.

"It took a while," she replied. "But I remembered you said that your sister owned a Haven Hotel and that is where you grew up. I knew it was in Dorset somewhere, so it was really a process of elimination."

"You travelled to all the Haven Hotels in Dorset, in your condition?" He asked amazed, as it was obvious from just looking at her that she was very heavily pregnant.

"No, she said, I called first," she said. "But there's not really that many in Dorset, so it didn't take that long to find you."

She looked at Gina. "Are you Neil's girlfriend?" She asked.

"I suppose you could say that," Gina replied uncomfortably. "I take it you are one of Neil's ex-girlfriends."

"Well, I was," she replied with a grin. "But when he hears what I've come to say, I'm sure he will have to think again about me being the 'ex'."

"Hold on a minute," interrupted Neil. "What are you talking about? You weren't really a girlfriend. We only went out a couple of times when I was staying at your mother's hotel."

"Oh. I think we did more than just go out, Neil. I can't believe you just left like you did, did you really think that a note would suffice after what we had been through together?"

"Annabel, I think you are blowing things out of proportion. I left a note explaining that I couldn't get involved with anyone. I knew you were taking things too seriously, so it was best for me to leave before you really got attached, I didn't want you to get hurt."

"Well, it was a bit late to think about that, wasn't it?" She said bitterly. "How could you just leave after we had had the best night?"

"I think I've heard enough," Gina said getting up to leave.

"No, stay," Neil said, holding her arm. "We should get this sorted out once and for all, I've got nothing to hide."

"No," Annabel cut in laughing. "He has nothing to hide."

"Get to the point, Annabel," Neil said losing his patience "Why are you here?"

"To tell you, Neil, that you are the father of this child I am carrying."

He hadn't seen Gina since then. She had fled to her room. He couldn't blame her really it must have been a shock for her had decided to leave her alone; it may give her time to calm down however he seriously doubted it.

He couldn't believe what Annabel had said. He had only slept with her once and he thought he had been careful; he had used a condom, so how had she become pregnant? Perhaps she was lying about him being the father. The thought flitted through his mind briefly then he realised she wouldn't have travelled halfway around the country to find him if it wasn't true, would she? Perhaps she was just obsessed with him. Perhaps she couldn't stand the fact that he had left without saying goodbye; perhaps the real father didn't want to know. Oh god, wait until Abby found out. Why had she turned up? She had ruined everything.

"Are you sure?" He had asked her.

"You think I'm lying, you can surely see I am pregnant," she laughed.

"No, but are you sure it is mine?"

"How can you ask me such a thing; do you think I sleep around? Do you really think so little of me?"

"I don't think anything of you," Neil said frustrated. "We had a brief fling; we only slept together once, for god's sake, and I did use a condom."

"Then it must have been spilt," she shouted. "I can't believe you are doubting what I am saying."

Then she burst into tears; this was all he needed: tears and tantrums.

"It's just a bit of a shock, that's all," he said trying to calm her down.

"I understand that, but when we get back to Sunny Cottage and you get used to the idea, and you see our baby born, you'll soon change your mind."

"Go back to Sunny Cottage?" He said outraged. "I'm not going anywhere with you; my life is here and that's where I'm staying."

"You've got to come back with me, Neil. You are the father and I'm due to give birth in three weeks and I want you to be there, you've got to be there."

"No way, Annabel. You come here, spring this on me and just expect me to drop everything and travel back with you. It's not going to happen, never, If the baby is mine as you say, and I mean if, because I want proof, I'll support it financially but that's it. There is no you and me and there never will be."

"Well, she won't want you after this," Annabel spat at him.

"Maybe not, but that doesn't mean I am going to want you."

Things were starting to get heated and at this point, Abby had walked in to see what all the shouting was about. Neil decided that it would be a good idea to sleep on things after all it was now nearly midnight and tempers were getting frayed. He told Abby he would explain everything in the morning and that Annabel was just tired after the journey.

"It's no wonder she's tired in her condition," she said eyes her bulging stomach.

They found her a room and got her settled then he went to his own bed.

He had tossed and turned all night. His head was full of questions. How was he going to sort this out? Could she prove it was his and what about Gina? He felt sure she would have nothing to do with him now and who could blame her really?

If he was the father, he would have to take responsibility but he wouldn't be getting it together with Annabel. Oh no, he would take his responsibilities as far as his child was concerned but he didn't want to spend the rest of his life with her; if he couldn't have Gina then he didn't want anyone.

He suspected that he was going to be very lonely from now on!

Annabel was pleased that she had got to Neil and she felt sure she had ruined things between him and that whore. She knew that girl was no good for Neil. Oh, she was very pretty and very smart but she knew what Neil liked and she wasn't it.

"Good," she said out loud to herself, "that'll teach him to walk out on me, nobody walks out on me like that."

She thought about how life would be with Neil; she liked the feel of the hotel and all right his sister had been a bit hostile to her last night but she would soon come round and accept her when she realised that Neil was going to stand by her.

She could work here. She guessed the whore did, but if she drove her out, she could have her job perhaps. Yes, that would be good; she would be working close to her Neil and she could keep an eye on him. She could make friends with all his friends around here. She had never really had many friends so that would be nice. They could go for long walks along the beach, strolling hand in hand.

Yes, it would be perfect. She was glad she had decided to track him down and now she had found him, he wasn't slipping away again. He would soon come around to the idea. She would make him fall in love with her then he would never want anyone else again, and after the baby was born, she would have the perfect hold on him even if it wasn't his, he would never know that, would he?

When she had woken up the morning after they had slept together and found Neil was gone, she was angry. At first, she had thought he had gone out for a paper or something; only then she had found the note.

I don't want to hurt you, Annabel, it read. *It's just that I can't get involved with anyone right now, I need to go home and get my head sorted, I'm really sorry.*

"Doesn't want to hurt me," she shouted. "It's a bit late for that. Well, if he thinks he's getting away that easily, he can think again."

She was determined to find him, but just where to start she was unsure. She would think about it and plan it carefully, but one thing was for sure, she would find him; he wasn't getting away that easily.

She went downstairs to help her mother with the breakfast.

"It's a shame about Neil having to leave so suddenly," Edna said as they were laying tables. "Did he say anything to you last night while you were out?"

"No," said Annabel. "Not a thing."

"Strange," Edna mused, "he said in his note that he had a message from home that his sister needed him and he had to go straight away, but he did leave me all the money he owed, so that's something."

"Oh yes, very commendable," Annabel said bitterly.

"Is something wrong, my dear, did you and Neil fall out last night?"

"Nothing wrong," she replied. "Just think it was wrong of him not to say goodbye after we took him in, that's all."

"Well, we hardly took him in, did we?" Edna said. "This is a guest house and he did pay his way. I know you will miss his company; we all will, but these things happen. It's not as if you two were an item or anything was it; just two friends who enjoyed a couple of nights out."

"Yes, you're right, Mother, but then you always are," she replied sarcastically; then she walked off into the kitchen.

Edna stared after her daughter. She didn't know what was wrong with her sometimes. She took everything anybody did personally. She hoped she hadn't become obsessed with Neil as she had done with Simon three years ago. She didn't want to go through that again.

She followed Annabel into the kitchen.

"I'll give Alf a call later to make sure he knows that Neil has gone home, but I'm sure he will have let him know."

Annabel raised her eyes. "Can we forget about bloody Neil?" She shouted. "He's gone now and that's the end of it." Although she knew it was most definitely not.

"Ok," Edna held up her hands. "I was just saying that's all. I don't know what's the matter with you today, is there something I should know?"

Annabel realised she might set off warning signals in Edna if she carried on, so she said, "I'm sorry, no, of course not. Where was his home, anyway, did he ever say?"

Edna was relieved that she had been able to defuse the situation as Annabel had a very bad temper and things usually got broken around the place when she started. She hoped she had taken her medication, but she didn't dare ask.

"No, I don't believe he did. I only know that he lived in a hotel with his sister, why?"

"Oh, no reason, just curious," Annabel answered and realising that she was going to get no information from her stupid mother, she decided she may pay Mr Pearson a visit later. After all, he and Neil worked together so they must have chatted. She would go on the pretence that she was just letting know that Neil had gone home and she would steer the conversation until she found out what she needed to know, and she would find out she always did.

"Morning, Mr Pearson," Annabel said breezily.

"Good morning, Annabel," he said seeming genuinely pleased to see her. "What brings you down here so early, why it's only 8:45?"

"I've just come to see if you knew that Neil had had to go home suddenly," she said.

"Yes, shame that," said Alf. "He was a good worker, still he must have had a good reason."

"Yes, I guess you'll miss him, won't you? Did you two get on well?"

"Oh yes, lass, we always had a good old chinwag at lunchtime, used to tell me about his brother-in-law and how good he was to him, how he taught him all he knew. He really misses him still by all accounts."

This was going where Annabel wanted it to and she was pleased, Mr Pearson was in a pleasant mood this morning and she knew she would be able to get some information out of him.

"Did he ever say where he lived?" She asked.

"Somewhere in Dorset," he replied. "But I'm not sure where, I know he lived in a hotel because he used to tell me about the gardens there."

"Can you remember what it was called?"

"Hovel, Shaven, no Haven Hotel, that's it. Why all the interest, my dear?" Alf laughed.

"Oh, no reason, just interested that's all. We shall all miss Neil, Mr Pearson, he was a good company."

"I know, my dear, but these things happen."

That was the second time she had heard that this morning and it still didn't make her feel any better but at least now she had something to go on.

She said her goodbyes to Mr Pearson and set off into town. She needed to get her hands on a telephone directory for the Dorset area and she wasn't really sure where to try. She decided to call into the little phone shop and ask them.

"I'm not really sure," the girl said. "But if you have the address directory, enquiries will find you the number."

"I know that," Annabel said impatiently, this girl was really dippy and she could see she wasn't going to get very far with her. "I don't have any address, that's why I need a book to have a look through. Is there someone else here I can speak to?"

"I'll get the manageress from out of the office," the girl replied, a bit huffily. "But I doubt if she'll be able to help either."

"Well, it's worth a try," Annabel answered sarcastically. "Now, if you don't mind, I haven't got all day."

The girl went to fetch the manageress who informed her that if she called British Telecom, they might be able to send her one in the post, but it would probably cost her.

"I don't care about the cost," Annabel said. "I just need to get one, thank you for your help, it is most appreciated." She threw the girl a smug glance and left the shop.

When she got back to Sunny Cottage, she called BT who advised her that they could send her one in the post but it would cost her £10 as it was out of her district.

"It doesn't matter," she said. "I'll pay."

She would have paid a lot more if needed; she wanted that book to track down Neil and when she did, it would all be worth it.

It took three weeks for the book to arrive. "There's a parcel for you, Annabel," her mother had said. "Are you expecting something?"

She wished sometimes her mother would just mind her own business. "Yes, just a book I ordered."

"Anything interesting," Edna said trying to peek at the parcel.

"Nothing you would be interested in," Annabel said and took the book to her room. *Now, Neil,* she thought, *it's just a matter of time before we are back together.*

She hadn't dreamt there would be so many Haven Hotels in Dorset but never mind, she would just have to keep phoning until she found the right one.

She would wait until tomorrow when her mother went into town and then she would start phoning, although it may prove a bit difficult to track him by calling as she realised she didn't even know his surname. Damn, it was so unlike her not to get every last detail about someone, just in case, it was ever needed, but she had been so wrapped up by Neil that she hadn't wanted to scare him off by asking too many questions. She knew now, of course, that he would have been scared off because the first time things had become a little more serious between them he had done a runner.

She woke the next morning, quite excited at the prospect of the day ahead and the mission she was about to undertake. Now, if she could just contain herself for a little while until Edna went into town. She showered and dressed and made her way downstairs to help her mother when suddenly she caught sight of a man in reception.

"Are you being seen to?" Annabel asked.

"Yes," he replied. "But I wish I'd have been a few minutes later than I could have had you sort me out, I'm James." He winked at her and held out his hand which made her blush but she shook his hand.

"Annabel," she offered thinking how very attractive this man was.

She took in his features; he wasn't unlike Neil in build, very athletic-looking body and he was most definitely flirting with her.

"How long are you here for?" She asked him.

"Just a couple of days," he said. "I'm working on the construction site in town, don't know what I'm going to do with myself in the evening though, any suggestions."

She knew exactly what he was hinting at and why not, a little distraction wouldn't do her any harm. She would definitely track Neil down, there was no doubt about that. She wasn't going to let him get away with what he had done but why shouldn't she have a bit of fun along the way?

"There are a couple of local clubs and restaurants," she said.

"Hmm, not much fun on your own though, eh," he said with a smile.

"I could show you," she replied coyly. "That's if you would like me to."

"Great," he said. "Can't think of anyone who I'd rather spend the evening with; I'll see you in here at eight."

"I'll look forward to it," she said.

She decided she would wait until James had left the guest house before she pursued her phone calling. After all, she had the rest of her life to look forward to with Neil when she had found him but for now, she was looking forward to a bit of fun.

Chapter 13

A Surprising Opinion

Over the next few weeks, Annabel had more bits of fun than Edna dared think about. What was the matter with her daughter? Every man that stayed at the guesthouse Annabel was onto them like a rash; it didn't seem to matter what they looked like or what colour their skin was; if they were male, she seemed determined to have them. She took them all out on the town and she knew that she had been sleeping with them. *Please, Annabel*, she thought, *please make sure you are being sensible*. She was sure she would be but she wasn't going to ask her; no she was wary of her daughter, she knew what she was capable of.

Three years ago, a young man called Simon had moved into town. He was a nice quiet lad but Annabel had set out to make him notice her and before long, they were going on a few dates. Edna knew that Simon wasn't ready to settle down yet. He was still at college, but Annabel was smitten, so she had mentioned to her daughter that she shouldn't get too serious at this stage as she and Simon were still very young, and he had his studying to think about. Annabel had bitten back at her telling her to mind her own business, that she and Simon were made for each other and they would end up getting married and having lots of children. Edna was dismayed by her outlook as she knew she may be heading for disappointment, but she had never seen Annabel so angry, so she decided to keep out of it. If her daughter got hurt, she would just have to be there for her at the time.

As Edna suspected, the relationship came to an end. It got too intense for Simon, so he had thought it best to cool things for a while until he had least finished his education and had found himself a job. Then they could see if they still felt the same and could resume the relationship if they did, but Annabel wouldn't let it rest. She kept phoning Simon pleading at first and when this didn't work, she started sitting outside his house at all hours of the day and night waiting to see him and beg him some more to take her back. Simon tried everything to let her down gently but she wouldn't give up.

In the end, he and his parents became so freaked by her behaviour that they called the police saying that she was harassing him. She was taken away time and time again but she kept on sitting right outside his house. In the end, she turned so violent against the police that she was committed to hospital with manic depression and was put on such a cocktail of drugs that she hardly knew what day it was. After she was discharged, she had never been the same again and now here she was behaving badly again, sleeping with all these men and Edna had a feeling it had something to do with Neil leaving. She had changed when he had left and Alf had mentioned to Edna the other day when they were chatting that Annabel had asked questions about Neil after he had gone.

She only hoped that history was not about to repeat itself. Edna didn't know if she could cope with it again. She would have to keep an eye on her, but for the time being, she could only hope that she would settle down and stop sleeping with all and sundry that she came into contact with.

After a few weeks of having 'fun', Annabel decided that it would soon be time to resume her plan of finding Neil. She was tired of all these different men now; she was ready to find her man and stay with him forever.

She woke up one morning feeling a bit queasy and thought it must have been something she had eaten or drank the previous evening; she really must have had an early night. She looked at Trevor who lay next to her asleep and suddenly realised that all this must stop; what would Neil think of her if he found out, not that he would, of course. Her mother would never say anything to him. Edna knew when to keep her mouth shut and these blokes were just passing through, so they would never see them again.

She got up and went to the bathroom where she was promptly sick. *That's all I need,* she thought to herself, *a bug.* She showered and dressed then went to help her mother who gave her a disgusted look as she walked into the dining room.

"I don't have to help you, you know," Annabel shot at her.

"I never said a word," Edna replied.

"Well, don't."

Edna shook her head and walked into the kitchen. Annabel stared after her. *She wanted to look out*, she thought to herself, *she'll miss my help when I go off on my search.*

After the guests had finished breakfast, Annabel still felt sick so she went to lie down telling her mother not to disturb her. She fell asleep until late afternoon. When she woke, she was a bit annoyed with herself; she had wasted so much time and now Edna was back from town, so she would have to wait until tomorrow.

The next morning, she was sick again and the next few mornings after that, so she decided to visit the doctor. She needed this bug cleared up so she could concentrate on her mission.

"Hello, Annabel." Dr George greeted her. "What can I do for you?"

"I think I've got a bug, Dr George," Annabel said. "I keep being sick."

"Is it constant or just in the morning?"

"More so in the morning when I get up."

"Could you be pregnant?"

"Pregnant?" She said; she hadn't thought about being pregnant. She was always so careful, except that time with James when they had been so drunk they were not even bothered with a condom. *Oh god*, she thought, *that was all she wanted now, to be pregnant with a child by a man that she didn't have any feelings for*. But then a thought came into her mind. "Yes," she said. "I could be."

Dr George advised her that he would need a urine sample from her so he could do a pregnancy test and she arranged to drop it in the following day.

When she left the surgery, her mind went into overdrive. If she was pregnant, she would be about three weeks gone if she was right about the father, making it impossible for it to be Neil's as it had been seven weeks and two days since he had left, not that she was counting. However, he would never need to know that. Doctors were always getting dates wrong and if she left it a few months before visiting Neil, he wouldn't know how far gone she really was, she could tell him anything. First, she had to find out where he was and with all the entries in the phone book for Haven Hotel, it wasn't going to be an easy task.

It took Annabel three weeks to locate the hotel which she thought was the most feasible place Neil lived. She had had to call when Edna went out, so she didn't suspect anything and those times had been few recently. She had only been to town three times in the last three weeks which was unlike her. She usually went a few times a week if only to catch up on the gossip with her friends. However, she had stayed around Sunny Cottage most of the time and Annabel wondered if she suspected she was up to something and was keeping an eye on her. Perhaps she was being too pleasant with her mother in her attempts to hide her secret and this is what was making her suspicious. Anyway, she did manage a few calls on the times when Edna had to go out for groceries even though her mother had tried to persuade her to go with her.

"I still don't feel well enough to go into town," Annabel lied.

"If this bug doesn't clear up soon, Annabel, you really must go back and see Doctor George," Edna had replied concerned.

Annabel had not told Edna about the pregnancy. She would know it couldn't be Neil's and she would keep an even closer eye on her because if nothing else, her mother knew her well, and she also knew she hadn't got over Neil leaving. Even though Annabel had not said as much, Edna's little subtle comments made her realise that her mother was keeping an eye on her. Not that she would say too much, not after the last time. Annabel realised Edna was a little scared of her and although she was not really proud of the fact, it kept her mother from interfering too much in her life.

No, best keep it a secret and when she did locate Neil, she would slip off as soon as Edna had gone to bed one evening and by the time she realised she was missing, she would have plenty of head start on her journey. Edna wouldn't come after herself. She would be scared of any confrontation with Annabel but she would inform the police that she was missing, and because of her past history, they would almost certainly begin looking for her straight away.

The first few days of calling had proved futile. Some of them hadn't got a Neil living there or even working there; others were vague when they realised she didn't have a surname or know anything about him and said they couldn't give out information to just anyone about their staff. She had told them all the same story, that someone called Neil had boarded at the guesthouse recently and he had left something valuable in his room. The only thing she knew about him was that he lived in a Haven Hotel and he also worked there. She would like to find out where he was so that she could pass it on. One of the receptionists had told her that if it was that valuable, the Neil in question would surely be back in touch with them to claim it back.

Annabel realised then that she should change her story as the receptionist was right and on the third day of calling, three weeks into her mission she had struck gold. She was on her eighth call of the day when she called the Haven Hotel in Weymouth. The receptionist had a cheery ring to her voice when she answered and Annabel warmed to her instantly and felt she could cut this girl a story and she would listen.

"Hello," said Annabel. "I was wondering if you could help me. Recently, we had a visitor at our guesthouse who did some work for one of the local hotels; we are trying to locate him to give him some news. He grew close to Mr Tate who owned the hotel and he has been taken very poorly and we thought Neil would like to know. I have been calling around all the Haven Hotels trying to find him to tell him but all I know about him is his name and that he lives at the hotel with family, could you tell me if anyone there fits the description?"

Annabel knew it was low and also tempting fate lying about someone being ill, especially when they were old like Mr Tate, but she was getting desperate now.

"We can't really give out information about the owners or staff," the girl replied.

"I know," Annabel replied as sweetly as she could. "But I know this Neil would really appreciate being told about Mr Tate. I would hate for him to try and get in touch himself and find out that way."

"Well," the girl replied. "It really isn't the correct procedure for me to pass on information as I said, but under the circumstances, I will say that we do have a Neil here, and he has been away, if you give me your name and number, I'll ask him if he knows this Mr Tate and ask him to get in touch with you."

At this, Annabel replaced the handset with a smile. Bingo, she had found him; she knew it had to be the correct place; she could just feel it. She couldn't give her name to that girl. If she told Neil, he would never call her, and if she had given Mr Pearson's name, Neil would have got in touch with him and found out it was a pack of lies. No, when that girl told Neil someone had called regarding a Mr Tate, he would say he didn't work for anyone with that name and they would just conclude the girl on the phone had got the wrong hotel. She realised she would have to move quickly in case Neil did suspect anything, not that he should. He didn't know about her past or anything but he did leave in a hurry. She didn't want him forewarned about her visit. She wanted it to be a surprise. She was sure when he saw her again, he would be pleased, things would be easier for him in his own hometown and when he knew about the baby, he would have to stand by her, wouldn't he? Annabel smiled; her future was looking decidedly brighter, but with her long journey ahead of her, it was time to step into action.

Chapter 14

Contemplation

Gina was still in shock from the news she heard the night before. She had spent most of the night crying. She really thought Neil could be the one for her; the one to help her get over her past and she had really started to see a future for them. It wasn't the fact that Neil had slept with Annabel that bothered her so much, after all, they hadn't even met then. But where did it leave them?

She thought back to Annabel's behaviour last night. It was weird, really weird; almost manic in fact, but there was no denying she was pregnant; that was plain for all to see. She was certain Neil would return to Sunny Cottage with her and they would live happily ever after on just her say-so that the child was his. She could understand Neil being sceptical. He had said he used a condom and if Annabel had slept with him after only knowing him briefly, surely she could have done the same things with other visitors to their B&B? There was definitely something not right but she just couldn't put her finger on it.

This could really change their future. If he did stand by Annabel and return with her, then she would be distraught that she had lost him so quickly after they had got together. If the child was his, he would surely need to do that very thing. He had to find out for certain she knew that, but did that mean Annabel would need to stay here until the baby was born? She didn't know if she could stand to be around them both while that happened, she had to decide what direction to go in now. She had planned to go home for Christmas and ask Neil to go with her. She knew now that she wouldn't be asking him along. He had things to sort out here. She needed time to think, so she would go home to her parents alone for a few weeks over the festive period and try to work out what she would do, she decided.

Neil was also still in shock; how could this girl just turn up and say he was the father of her child? He hardly knew her, yes, they had shared a few nights out together but it was hardly a long-lasting relationship, more of a friendship. He thought back to the night he slept with her, it must have been seven or eight weeks ago. Surely, she knew before now, so why she was only just turning up unless she had been tracking him for weeks? He had used a condom when they slept together, how could this of happened? He had been so careful! Her behaviour last night was really weird; she was convinced that Neil would return with her to play happy family forever and that was definitely not going to happen.

He had liked Annabel as a friend but nothing more. She was really just a means to an end, a bit of fun along the way. He felt bad for even thinking like that now. Gina had changed him so much and he felt sure he was going to lose her over this. He would happily take responsibility if it was his child but financially and access only; he was never going to go back to Sunny Cottage even if Gina didn't want to know him now. No, he was never doing that—ever! He was devasted that Gina had heard what she heard the previous night. He was stupid for telling her to stay. He could have maybe come up with a different story as to why Annabel had turned up, then dealt with the problem secretly. That would have been difficult, but better than losing Gina which he felt sure he had now this had happened. He would have to fight very hard to win her back now, he knew that. He had to make sure that the child was his and that would probably mean Annabel sticking around until the baby was born to get the DNA tests. Would Gina stick around while that was happening? He doubted it very much. "Oh, hell," he said aloud. "My tainted past is finally catching up with my big time." He put his head in his hands, "I really need to work out what to do."

Abby walked into Neil's room and asked, "Are you going to tell me what's going on, Neil? Who is that girl and why has she come here to find you?"

"Morning, Abby, ever heard of knocking," he said sarcastically.

Abby just shot him a look and repeated her question, "What's going on, Neil, and what does she want?"

Neil looked at her and suddenly broke down in floods of tears. "Everything is ruined," he said to Abby. "Everything is ruined."

"What on earth do you mean? What did she want?"

Neil told Abby the whole sorry story about Annabel and the baby and now he was convinced he'd lost Gina for good.

"Oh my goodness, something doesn't seem right. Why has she left it until now to tell you, you've been back weeks!" Abby said.

"She said she's been trying to find me, and it took her a while," he replied.

"What did Gina say?" Abby asked.

"She ran off to her room when Annabel told me I was the father. I was stupid and said Annabel could say what she wanted in front of Gina, if I hadn't said that, I could have maybe kept the truth from Gina until I was certain."

"Honesty is the best policy, Neil. Gina would have found out eventually and that would have been worse. After all, that girl is still in the hotel, how long is she planning on staying?"

"I don't know. I really need to get proof that I am the father. I'm not convinced it's true."

"No, me neither," replied Abby. "Something is definitely off. I suppose we could give her a room until the baby is born so the tests can be done, but I don't think that is very fair on Gina. I don't want to lose good staff over this. We don't know if it's true or if she's just looking for a father for her baby. You did leave her abruptly with a note, she could have a vendetta for that."

"Oh god, Abby, what am I going to do?"

"I need some time to think, Neil, this has all been a shock!"

"No need to tell me that, Abby," Neil replied with a huge sigh.

"Let me have a think, Neil," Abby said as she got up and left his room.

Annabel woke the next morning after a good sleep. *That's the best sleep I've had in ages*, she thought to herself and she knew why. She had been so wrapped up in finding Neil that it consumed her every moment of every day and night. Now she had found him and told him the good news, everything was going to be ok.

They would move back to Sunny Cottage, get married and then become a perfect little family after the baby was born. She couldn't wait; it was all she had ever dreamt about. Yes, the men she had slept with along the way had been fun but it was different with Neil. She had never met anyone so fit and handsome and now he was going to be hers for the rest of time.

Life was good; Annabel smiled and got out of bed. She showered and dressed, then went down for breakfast with a spring in her step. She couldn't wait to see him.

When she arrived downstairs, the whore wasn't on reception. She was a bit disappointed because she wanted to rub it in how Neil was now hers and there was nothing she could do about it.

She was met at reception by Abby who glowered at her.

"That's not a good way to greet your guests," Annabel said laughing.

"Are you a guest?" Abby asked, "Or are you here just to cause trouble?"

"How am I causing trouble? who are you anyway and what right do you have to talk to me like that?" Annable asked a bit more sharply. She didn't like being spoken to in such a manner. She was used to people respecting her, although deep down, she knew they were all scared of her kicking off. This woman was downright rude. She was just a receptionist, who was she to say these things to her?

"I am the owner of this hotel and Neil's sister," Abby responded. "I will talk to you however I please. You turn up at MY hotel and inform MY brother that he is the father of your baby! How far gone are you? How do you know it is Neil's baby? We shall want proof of dates and a DNA before you get a penny out of us and Neil will definitely not be returning home with you!"

Annabel could feel her anger rising, how dare this woman speak to her like this? "Neil is the father; whatever you think he will step up to his responsibilities. I will not be bringing this child up alone, that's for sure. A child needs a father and Neil will be there."

"We'll see about that," Abby said. "As I say, we want proof so I have booked you in with our family GP, so he can examine you and confirm the date of conception. He may even be able to arrange a DNA before the baby is born."

"You've done what?" Annabel shouted. "How dare you book an appointment for me? I have my own GP who has confirmed I am pregnant."

"And how many weeks did he say you had gone?" Abby asked.

"As many weeks as I slept with Neil," Annabel retorted.

"How many is that?" Abby asked.

Annabel was getting irate and couldn't think straight; she didn't answer Abby in case it all went wrong. She turned to go to the dining room for breakfast.

"Your appointment is on Monday morning at 9:30 am," Abby shouted after her. "Meet me in reception at 9 am and I'll go with you. You can stay here until then and then you'll be on your way back home—ALONE."

Annabel kept walking. "How dare that woman speak to me like that? Take me to the doctor herself, ha, we'll see about that," she said out loud. "I will get even with that bitch before I leave. And the whore will have a shock too!"

She didn't realise Oliver was following her down the corridor and heard every word…

Oliver had heard what had happened and he actually felt sorry for Neil. He knew how he'd feel if one of his many conquests turned saying the same thing. How did she know it was Neil's baby? She seemed very sure and had tracked him down across the country to tell him. Something didn't feel right and now he'd heard her cursing in the corridor, he knew there was definitely something amiss.

He walked into the dining room behind Annabel and took his place behind the serving area.

"Good morning," said Annabel. "I'll have the full English please, I had a really good night's sleep last night, the first one in ages and now, I'm ravenous."

"That's great," said Oliver. "I'm glad you found the hotel comfortable."

"Oh yes, very," said Annabel. "Everything is looking good for my future now at last."

Oliver looked at her; she had a funny look in her eyes almost frenzied. Something wasn't right with this girl; something definitely wasn't right.

He would speak to Abby later and tell her what he had heard. He somehow felt both her and Neil would need allies at this time and he might need to swallow his pride with Neil. This was going to be a bumpy road for them he just knew it.

Edna was concerned when she looked in Annabel's room and she wasn't there. It wasn't like her to be up and out so early. She looked around the room and realised her brushes off her dressing table had gone. She looked in the wardrobe and realised with horror that the suitcase and some of Annabel's clothes had gone.

Oh my god, where has she gone and what has she gone to do? She knew it was not going to be good. She had been acting very strangely over the past few weeks. She had kept asking her when she was going to town; she had spent a lot of time in her room doing something, however, when Edna had asked her what she had been told, not so politely, to mind her own business.

She hadn't been right since Neil had left suddenly and she really hoped Annabel hadn't gone out to do something stupid.

"That bloody girl will be the death of me," Edna said wearily. Life had been hard with Annabel; she'd always been different and when things had gone wrong with Simon, everything went very wrong.

After she was discharged from the hospital, she had become nothing less than a slapper. She slept her way through men like there was no tomorrow, and they were only ever passing through, so they would never amount to a relationship. Annabel thought every one of them would stay just to be with her, and they would live happily ever after. Did the stupid girl not realise they were only using her for sex while they were away working or on a stag do?

She couldn't say anything to Annabel for fear of her kicking off. Oh yes, she'd been on the receiving end of that once or twice and was in no hurry to go there again anytime soon. She realised, however, that she needed to find Annabel before she did something really stupid. She had a horrible feeling in the pit of her stomach and Edna's gut was rarely wrong. She didn't really know where to start, so she thought she would go into the village and see if anyone had seen her, and then take it from there. She'd got to call in the doctors to pick up Annabel's prescription anyway.

Edna made her way to the doctor's surgery and when she arrived, she was greeted with a cheery smile from Jenna the receptionist.

"Good morning, Edna, how are you? Have you come to pick up Annabel's prescription?"

"Yes, please," replied Edna.

Jenna went off to get the prescription and when she returned, she informed Edna that Dr George had put some anti-sickness pills on for Annabel to help her through.

"Help her through what?" Edna asked. "I didn't know she was being sick and now she's disappeared, I'm just down here to ask if anyone has seen her."

Edna's mind was whirring now. Annabel had visited the doctors and not told her; now she was missing. A nasty feeling crept over her; something was definitely wrong.

"Let me see if Dr George is free to talk to you," said Jenna, who could see that Edna had gone very pale all of a sudden, "take a seat for a moment."

Dr George came through into the reception and called Edna into his consulting room.

"Did Annabel not tell you I had been in to see me?" He asked Edna.

"No, not a word, doctor, and now she has gone missing. Something in my gut is telling me something is wrong."

"Well," said Dr George. "She came to see me a few weeks ago. I'm not supposed to divulge what about but with Annabel's history, it's probably best that you know, she is going to need your support."

"Support for what?" Edna asked, still not realising what was wrong.

"Annabel came to me as she thought she had a sickness bug, but it turns out she was pregnant. If I had to guess, she was about 3/4 weeks gone but when she attends her first-week scan, it will give us a better indication. How long has she been missing, Edna?" Dr George asked.

"Pregnant! Oh my goodness, this is not good news, doctor, what with Annabel's history. I'm not sure when she went, but when I got up this morning and when she didn't get up, I went into her room and some of her things have gone, so sometime during the night," said Edna growing increasingly concerned. With Annabel on her own and her mental health issues, she was really worried about her. Where on earth could she have gone?

"I need to keep looking for her and asking around," said Edna suddenly getting up to leave. "Thank you for telling me, doctor. Finding her is more important than ever now."

"I'll ask my patients when they arrive if they have seen her. Try not to worry too much, Edna, I'm sure she won't have gone far."

"She packed a bag, doctor, and that really doesn't bode well with me, really doesn't bode well at all."

When she left the surgery, she asked at some of the shops to see if they had seen Annabel that morning. No one had and Edna was getting quite stressed now.

She walked up the street and bumped into Alf. "Good morning, Edna, are you ok?" Seeing that she obviously wasn't.

"No, Alf," Edna sighed. "Annabel has packed a bag and gone off somewhere. I'm really worried about her, you know her history and how she's acting up lately. No one has seen her this morning and I really don't know where to look now."

"Really," said Alf. "You don't think it's anything to do with the lad Neil, do you? She was up at my place last week asking lots of questions about him and if I knew where he had gone."

Edna had a sinking feeling; it was starting to dawn on her what was going on here.

"Did you know where he had gone, Alf?" Edna asked.

"Yes, I knew he lived in Dorset and his sister's hotel was called Haven Hotel."

"And you told Annabel this."

"Yes," said Alf. "I asked her why she was so interested but she said she was just curious; you don't think she's gone after him, do you, Edna?"

"I have a very bad feeling that is exactly what's she done, Alf, and it's not going to end well."

"Why?" Alf asked.

"Because she's pregnant, Alf, and I think she's going to Neil to tell him he's the father, but he can't be because she's not far enough along for that to be true. Oh, Alf, I really have to find that hotel and stop her before she does something that we'll all suffer for."

Little did Edna know she was too late but she was going to find that hotel and fetch Annabel home that was for sure.

She returned home and started in Annabel's bedroom; if she'd been tracking Neil, she felt sure she would find something in her bedroom. If not, she would call all the Haven Hotels in Dorset until she found the right one.

She had to get to Annabel and get her home, regardless of how she might kick off. This wasn't fair on the lad when he had done nothing wrong…

Chapter 15

Reflection

Gina had spent most of the weekend in her room; she really couldn't face seeing Neil at the moment. She didn't know what to say to him. She couldn't tell him everything was ok and would turn out well. How could it? A baby with someone else had thrown a massive spanner in their relationship.

Could it work? Gina thought to herself. Could we continue to be in a relationship and deal with what's happened? Neil had said in no uncertain terms that even without her, he wouldn't go with Annabel, but when the baby was born he could think differently. It was his child and there would be a bond. Annabel wanted him to go back to her place but that was halfway across the country. Even if he didn't go, it would be a difficult situation whenever he wanted to see his child. "How would I feel when he was visiting?" Gina said out loud. "Would I trust him when he was there?" She didn't know him that well yet; yes she'd fallen for his looks and charm and the way he treated her but that could be a front, would the real him slip back in? What was the real him? She knew nothing about his past just that he'd been away for a while and returned recently, she knew nothing else about him at all.

Oh, her head was all over the place. She was falling in love with Neil but this would change so much. She needed time away and going back to her parents for Christmas in Weymouth is what she needed, so she could get her head straight away from the hotel and away from Neil!

With that, she set off to find Abby to ask her if she would extend her Christmas break…

After the breakfast shift the next morning, Oliver went to find Abby. She was in her office doing her orders for the following week's menu. Oliver knocked on her door.

"Come in," said Abby. "Oh, Oliver, you've just caught me doing the menu orders, did you want to add something on?"

"No," said Oliver. "But I would like a chat with you." Oliver had hardly slept last night after hearing Annabel's outburst in the corridor when she thought no one was around. He felt something was amiss with this girl and this had confirmed it, she wasn't all sweet and nice like she portrayed in front of everyone, no, she had a very sinister side he could tell.

"What is it, Oliver?" Abby interrupted his thoughts. "You look very serious. Please, don't tell me you've come here to tell me you've found another job."

"No," laughed Oliver. "I love my job here and you are so good to your staff, Abby, I wouldn't dream of leaving."

"What is it then?" Abby asked.

"It's about that girl that turned up here, Annabel."

"Oh her," Abby looked disdainful at the very mention of her name. "There is something amiss with her and I can't quite put my finger on it, coming halfway across the country to say Neil is the father of her child. She expects us to just believe her!"

"Do you think it could be?" Oliver asked.

"Well, last year, I would have said a definite yet, but I have seen a change in Neil. He said he was careful and I believe him; he is absolutely distraught right now. Gina won't speak to him, not that I blame her; it must have been a very big shock when she heard. They were getting on so well," Abby sighed. "And she had definitely changed my brother for the better."

"Yes, even I have to give him that, he has been a different person since he met Gina, but why did he just leave Annabel's with a note?" Oliver questioned.

"I asked him the same question," Abby said.

"And?" Oliver interrupted.

"He said they were just friends; she took him to the local attractions when he was staying at their hotel, they had meals out, cinema etc. Then one night, they both had a bit too much to drink and they ended up sleeping together; he said he had used a condom. Even I know my brother is not so stupid as to get caught in that trap, so I believe him."

"Also," she continued. "It's been weeks since Neil came back, surely she would have known sooner and tracked him down. Something about her and this situation doesn't add up, Oliver."

"Well," said Oliver. "That's the reason I'm here. Last night, when I was walking to the dining room, she was a bit in front of me heading there herself. I could hear her muttering, so I caught up a bit closer."

"What was she saying?" Abby asked.

Oliver told Abby that he had heard what she had said about her and—who he presumed- was Gina also that she'd said she was going to get even with Abby before she left.

"Did she now?" Abby raged. "We'll see about that. I knew there was something with her; she putting on a good front of sweetness and light, I'll give her that. Oliver, we obviously need to keep a close eye on her while she's here and I really need to get to the bottom of this soon."

There was a knock at her office door; it was Gina.

"Come in, Gina, I think me and Oliver are done for now."

"Yes," Oliver said standing up to leave, "And, Abby, I'm here to help should you need it."

"Thank you, Oliver," replied Abby. "We'll talk again later."

"Sit down, Gina," gestured Abby. "How can I help?"

Gina hesitated before she spoke, "I want to go to my parents for Christmas," she said. "And in light of what's happened, I'd like to extend my Christmas break if that's ok?"

Abby knew this was coming, who could blame Gina? She probably needed time away to think. "How long were you thinking, Gina?"

"Well, I was initially going for two weeks, but could I make it four, please."

"It's not a problem as we are quiet and the other staff can help out, but are you ok, Gina?" Abby asked.

Gina's eyes welled up. "Not really, Abby. I had really fallen for Neil. I thought he was the person I could be with for a long, long time."

"Neil feels the same about you, Gina," replied Abby. "You have definitely changed him for the better."

"I just can't see a way through this. If he has a child on the other side of the country, how can that work for us, would I trust him when he goes to see it? Will he change his mind about being with Annabel when he sees his child?" Gina was really crying now.

Abby put her arm around her shoulder. "Firstly," she said. "Neil will not go with Annabel whatever happens; he hasn't got feelings for her. Secondly, if the child is his, he will have to step up and help her financially, I'll give you that but he would never do anything to hurt you. And finally, there's something very wrong with the whole situation, no one is doing anything for her until we have solid proof that Neil is the father."

Abby told Gina what Oliver had overheard, leaving the part about Gina out so as not to scare her. If Annabel was planning some sort of revenge, then it was probably best Gina was away at her parents for a few till they could sort things out.

Gina was shocked at what Oliver had overheard. "She said that!" She asked.

"Yes," replied Abby, that rage back in her voice. "She is not getting away with it, believe me, but I need to work out how to deal with her."

"I thought her behaviour was strange when she turned up that night; she had almost manic behaviour," Gina said. "One minute she was sweet, then she was in tears, then she was really nasty."

"I've dealt with bigger and better," Abby said. "And I will deal with her, being in this trade, you have to know how to deal with all types of people. I just need to work out the best way. I'm not convinced this child is Neil's, Gina, and I'm intent on proving that."

Gina really hoped that was the truth but she wanted to get away while it was sorted and get her own head straight.

"You can have the four weeks, Gina. You need it, please, tell me you'll be coming back though. It would be such a big loss to us if you didn't," Abby said.

"I have every intention of coming back, Abby," said Gina. "Hopefully, my head will be straight and I'll be in a better place."

"That's brilliant news, Gina," said Abby giving her a big hug. "When are you leaving?"

"Would tomorrow be ok?" Gina asked.

"So soon," laughed Abby. "You are in a hurry to leave us, of course, dear, that's no problem. I can sort out your shifts for next week tomorrow. Please make sure you find me before you go."

"I will," said Gina. "And thank you, Abby."

Neil was heading to Abby's office and saw Gina leaving as he was approaching. Gina didn't look happy to see him at all; who could blame her? Annabel was making him out to be someone who does a 'wham bam thank you, mam.' He had to show Gina this wasn't him at all now; it had been one day but not now and it wasn't even like that with Annabel. He'd left to save her from getting attached to him, although he realised now that she already had, he'd left with the best intentions and now here she was causing all these problems for him. What was the matter with her? She was almost deranged the night she arrived, shouting, crying them being downright evil in her voice.

"Gina," he called.

"Not now, Neil," replied Gina, "I don't want to talk to you, my head is mashed and I need some time."

"Please, give me five minutes for me to explain."

"No, Neil, I have to pack. I'm going home for Christmas and I'm leaving in the morning."

Neil was distraught; how could he explain things and make amends if she wasn't even there?

"How long are you going for? Can I call you? Please don't go, Gina, I love you." There, he'd said it. It was true, that was for sure but he wasn't going to say it yet in case it scared her off, but what the hell, he felt he was losing her anyway. He couldn't comprehend the thought of that at all; how would he cope without her? She was the first woman he felt he could settle down with and here she was leaving after such a short time.

Gina looked shocked. "You tell me that now!" she said. "What is this, emotional blackmail? How can we even work, Neil, if you have a child at the other end of the country?"

"We'll make it work, and that's if it is even mine. I want proof of that before she gets anything off me. I was careful, Gina. I just can't see how this has happened?"

"Well, it has happened," Gina replied. "And I'm not sure how we can go forward, that is why I'm going away for a few weeks to get my head straight."

"A few weeks!" cried Neil. "I thought you were going for two weeks."

"I've extended it to four with Abby. I need time away from this place and time away from you! And no, you can't call me, I need a complete break."

"Are you coming back?" Neil asked.

"Yes," she said. "I love my job and I love this place, goodbye, Neil."

Gina made her way up to her room to pack, leaving Neil in the corridor with tears streaming down his face. It had taken all her strength not to hug him, she loved him and she did feel sorry for him with the situation that had so harshly crashed into his life. However, if she'd learnt anything from her past, it was that self-preservation had to be her priority. No man would ever destroy her emotionally like David did, not ever!

Abby sat in her lounge Sunday afternoon with a cup of tea and reflected on the weekend. It had started off quite normally. She was in her office as always on a Saturday morning doing the food order for next week's menu and then it all changed. *What a mess,* she thought to herself, and once again, it is down to me to sort things out. Not that she was apportioning any blame, what had happened with Neil didn't appear to be his fault—this time. Yes, he had gone off and slept with Annabel, then left her a note when he left, which was foolish at best but there was something definitely amiss.

She had seen the way Annabel behaved and she seemed odd, one minute, sweetness and light; the next angriness in her voice when things weren't going her way. She really felt that she was making Neil a scapegoat claiming him as the father of her child and Abby was far from convinced this was true.

Oliver had knocked on her office door first, looking very serious. She had convinced herself in her mind he had come to tell her he was leaving. When he told her that he definitely wasn't, she didn't think anything else he could say would have been as bad as that. Boy, she was wrong, when Oliver disclosed what he'd heard the night before, Abby was almost floored. She knew there was something strange about Annabel and this confirmed it. However, she was realising that she was quite perturbing and obviously very sinister. Oliver had said he would listen out for anything else; Abby thanked him for letting her know. She would need more evidence to bring Annabel to light to enable her to catch Annabel out.

As Oliver was getting up to leave, Gina knocked on a door. "Could I speak to you, please, Abby?" She had said. And another feeling of doom washed over Abby.

Gina sat down and explained that she would like to extend her Christmas leave, so she could spend time with her parents and have time to think and get her head straight. The recent goings-on had really upset Gina, and rightly so, she and Neil were just getting really close and then the bombshell had dropped. They would be quiet over the Christmas period; well, quite enough for them to be able to manage without Gina for a few weeks, in light of what Oliver had just told her, she felt it was best for Gina to be away from the hotel while she tried to sort things out.

Gina wanted to leave the next morning for four weeks, which would take her over the New Year and give her space to think. She would really miss Gina. They had become close and once she came to terms with her and Neil together, Abby was quite excited. *Oh, how things can change in a blink*? She thought. She agreed to Gina's time off, also begging her to return as she was a valuable member of the hotel. Gina had promised her she would, so Abby needed to get this situation under wraps before she did.

Next to her office was Neil, who was visibly upset.

"I've just seen Gina," he said, "you had allowed her four weeks holiday so she can go home. Why, Abby? How am I going to talk to her if she's not here and she's told me not to even call her?"

"She needs some space, Neil," Abby replied. "What has happened with Annabel turning up has hit her hard, which should give you some indication of how she feels about you."

"I've fallen in love with her, Abby," he cried. "I can't lose her now."

"Then we need to get this mess sorted before she comes back, don't we?" Abby said. "I've arranged an appointment with the doctor for tomorrow morning. I'll go with Annabel; we might have some indication of how far along she is. I'm not sure I believe her story, Neil, there is something very odd here."

She told him what Oliver had heard and how he was going to listen out for anything more.

Neil was surprised. "Oliver is helping?" He said.

"Yes," said Abby. "So, that's a step in the right direction, isn't it?"

Neil was happy that Oliver was coming around but also still distraught about Gina leaving. He couldn't lose her, he really couldn't. She was the best thing that had happened to him and he was actually seeing a future for them. *Oh, what a bloody mess*, he thought.

Abby could see Neil mulling things over. "If you want my advice," she said. "Leave Gina be for a while, an absence will help and she'll have time to think."

"What if she thinks she doesn't want me?" Neil said.

"We'll cross that bridge when we come to it," Abby said. "I think you underestimate Gina's feelings for you. Let's get one thing sorted at a time. At least Gina will be safe while we do that. Annabel's threat left me uneasy, so I think Gina getting away is a good solution for now."

Gina had left early that day; she said she wanted to go on a Sunday as it would be quieter. She had found Abby to say goodbye but had declined Abby's offer to find Neil.

"No," she said. "It will be too awkward and he'll start begging me to stay. I need this break, Abby, and I don't want to leave him upset, please just let me go."

Abby did as she asked and walked her to her taxi.

"Goodbye, Gina," said Abby, "try and have a nice break and hopefully, things will be sorted well before you return."

"Thank you, Abby," replied Gina. "I really hope so."

"I'll keep in touch with you over the festivities," said Abby, "and I'll make sure Neil doesn't contact you, if you want to speak to him, you have his number."

"Thank you," said Gina and the taxi drove away.

Abby walked back into the hotel. She was feeling quite sad at Gina leaving but she would be back and everything would be good, she could feel it. She bumped into Neil on her way in.

"You're up early," she said.

"I didn't want to miss Gina," he replied. "I needed to say goodbye."

"You've just missed her, Neil. She didn't want the upset of seeing you, leave her be for now; we have other things to sort out."

Chapter 16

Edna

They walked back into the hotel together and bumped into Annabel. She was swanning around the hotel like she owned it. Neil glowered at her and so did Abby.

"What's the matter with you two?" Annabel asked in her sickly sweet voice. "Anyone would think Christmas was cancelled."

"It is," said Neil. "For me anyway, the only person I wanted to spend it with has just left in a taxi."

"She gone?" Annabel asked smiling.

"Oh, don't worry," Abby said. "It's only her Christmas holiday, she'll be back."

"When will she be back?" Annabel asked.

"Mid-January," said Abby.

"Oh, we'll be back in Sunny Cottage then, Neil. Won't we?" Annabel said.

"In your dreams, Annabel, in your dreams," he replied.

Her smile faded for just a second, then she turned to walk away. "We'll see," she said. "We'll see."

God thought Neil, *I have to get rid of this stupid girl once and for all.* When the tests were done and he was not the father, he'll be rid of her. The same thoughts were running through Abby's mind at exactly the same time.

"Who the hell does she think she is?" She asked Neil. "Walking round my hotel, talking to my brother like that. This girl has got to go. As soon as we've seen the doctor in the morning, I'm telling her to pack her bags and get the hell out of my hotel."

On Monday morning, Abby was in reception early to cover for Gina. Neil was coming to take over at 9 am while she took Annabel to the doctor. It couldn't come soon enough.

It was 8:45 and there was no sign of Annabel yet; she hadn't even been down for breakfast. Oh well, I told her to be here at 9 am, so there's still time, thought Abby, maybe she doesn't want breakfast this morning.

9 am came. Neil had arrived at the reception but there was still no sign of Annabel.

"Where is she?" Abby fumed to Neil.

"Give her five minutes, then I'll go knock on her door," said Neil.

"We will be late for the appointment, if she doesn't hurry up, I'll go now and find out where she is."

Abby made her way up to Annabel's room on the second floor. When she arrived, she knocked sharply.

"Who is it?" Annabel shouted.

"It's Abby. I told you to be at the reception at 9 am. Annabel, we will be late for your doctor's appointment, get a move on, so we can leave."

"I have my own doctor," replied Annabel. "Why would I need to go to yours?"

"I told you why," said Abby getting angry. "Before Neil takes any responsibility, we need to get you checked. The doctor would be able to give us an indication of the dates once he has done the ultrasound."

"I've already told you, it is Neil's baby," shouted Annabel. "If you don't believe me, that's your problem. I am not going to your doctor and that's final."

"Have you got something to hide Annabel?" Abby asked.

With that, Annabel flung open the door; she was red in the face and had evil in her eyes. "I have told you; this baby is Neil's. I am not going to your doctor and Neil will be leaving with me to go back to Sunny Cottage."

She slammed the door in Abby's face. Abby was fuming; this was confirming all her thoughts.

"If you don't attend this appointment, you can pack your bags and get out of my hotel," shouted Abby, "and if you don't leave you, will have a police escort, I want you out of here in the next hour."

She knew Annabel was in no way going to attend that appointment, so she made her way back down to reception to ring and cancel the appointment.

"What's going on?" Neil asked.

"I have just ordered that girl out of my hotel within the next hour," she said and told Neil about the altercation they had.

"Oh, my god," said Neil. "She is deranged, I can't believe this is happening."

"I've dealt with bigger and better than her, Neil. She will leave my hotel and if she thinks she's taking you with her, she can think gain."

Neil was left wondering what Abby had meant by 'bigger and better' when the phone rang.

"Neil, go into my office to call the doctor to cancel that appointment and I'll get this."

Neil made his way to Abby's office as instructed and Abby answered the phone on reception.

"Hello," said the voice on the other end of the phone, "is that Haven Hotel in Dorset?"

"One of them, yes," replied Abby.

"Oh, I know there are a few in the Dorset district. I've been calling them all, I'm trying to locate someone."

"Well, I am the owner of this hotel and will help if I can," said Abby.

"Do you have a Neil there, possibly a gardener?"

"Who is this?" Abby asked.

"I realise this may seem strange, let me explain," said Edna.

Edna explained about her daughter Annabel disappearing suddenly and how she thought she was tracking down a lad called Neil to claim he was the father of her baby.

"I've been asking around and I've put two and two together," said Edna.

Abby listened with her mouth open, "Oh my god, you could be the answer to our prayers."

She explained how Annabel had turned up the other night and claimed Neil was the father of her child and she told Edna about her odd behaviour.

"I've actually just had an altercation with her, something seemed off, so I wanted her to get checked by our GP but she's flatly refused," said Abby.

"She will do as it can't be Neil's; she's not far enough along. Our doctor told me she is about 3/4 weeks gone and Neil left us way before that; she has mental health problems you see," said Edna. "She gets infatuated with men, she thinks they are all going to settle down with her and be happy ever after."

"All?" Abby asked.

"Yes, unfortunately," sighed Edna and explained how she slept with most of their male visitors. "I don't know what to do with her, to be honest, but she does need to come home where her doctor is."

"Well, I have just ordered her to leave within the hour," said Abby.

"Please, don't let her leave on her own," cried Edna, "she will just hang around and pester Neil every time she sees him. She will stay close even if she is not at your hotel."

"What do you propose we do with her?" Abby asked getting irritated that his women wanted them to keep her there.

"I will come and get her, but I can't get a train ticket until tomorrow. Could you make up an excuse to keep her there until I get to you? It will be evening time though as it is quite a journey from Scotland."

Abby thought for a moment; if this was the only way they could get Annabel away without further harm then she really had no choice, did she?

"Ok, I will tell her that I have rebooked an appointment for Wednesday, it will buy us some time."

"Thank you so much," said Edna. "I will sort my ticket out today and I will be with you tomorrow. I am so sorry she has done this to you all. I'd have stopped her if I had known."

"I have had enough dealing with her to know how deceitful she is," replied Abby. "You can't be blamed for it but if you can get her out of my hotel, I would be very grateful."

"I'll be with you tomorrow evening," said Edna as she hung up.

This is getting crazier by the second. Abby thought as she made her way to Annabel's room to tell her that she could stay till Wednesday and that she had made another appointment.

She had told Neil what had happened and he had cried in relief at the news that the baby could not be his; he may have a chance with Gina now. If only he could call her to tell her but he couldn't, he would have to wait.

Annabel had no intention of attending the new doctor's appointment but it was buying her time with Neil, so she thanked Abby and said she was sorry for her early outburst. She wasn't, of course, but she had another two days to convince Neil he was the father. Things were looking up at last.

Edna arrived at Haven Hotel at 6:20 pm on Tuesday evening. She booked in at reception and was greeted by Abby.

"You look tired," said Abby. "Do you want to shower and eat first? We can deal with Annabel in the morning, she not going anywhere."

"That would be so great," said Edna, grateful she hadn't got to face Annabel yet. She was indeed scared of her, but she was her mother and she couldn't let her do this to innocent people.

"I'll show you to a room; you can get cleaned up and order room service so that she doesn't see you tonight," Said Abby.

With that, Neil walked in. Abby introduced Edna to him.

"No introductions needed," said Neil. "We have met."

"Neil, I am so sorry Annabel has done this to you. I thought it was a bit strange how she reacted when you left. She let on; she didn't care but I could tell it did, and then she wasn't in her room when I went in in the morning and some of her things had gone. When I started speaking to people, I suddenly realised what she was doing. It's taken me a couple of days to track you down."

"This is not your fault," Neil said. "I am just grateful you are here. Abby said the baby couldn't be mine, the doctor had told her the dates. Why do you think she has done this to me?"

"She has done it before, Neil, she gets infatuated," and she explained to him about Simon all those years back and said history was repeating itself.

Neil listened in shock. He was about to get a lucky escape; god knows what life would have been like if he had just accepted Annabel's word. He knew she was a little bizarre when he had gone out with her in Scotland but he didn't realise she was on this level. When he got Gina back, he was never letting her go, that was for sure.

Abby showed Edna to her room where she showered and freshened up. She ordered food and realised she was starving. She had been so stressed about coming down that she hadn't eaten all day. She devoured the spaghetti Bolognese that had been bought up to her and helped herself to a gain from the minibar. Dutch courage, she thought, and she was going to need it.

She dreaded seeing Annabel in the morning and could only hope she could convince her to come home with relatively little trouble, although she doubted that very much. She needed to sleep, if anything; she needed to be fully rested for the events that were undoubtedly going to unfold tomorrow.

Wednesday morning, Abby was covering reception when she saw Annabel leave the dining room. She had told her that her appointment was 11:30. Annabel wasn't hiding in her room today, no doubt she would be later, she thought dryly.

"Morning, Abby," said Annabel cheerily. "See you later," she smirked.

Abby could have smacked her straight in the face. Annabel didn't realise yet that Abby and Neil knew that the child could not be his; soon that smirk would be knocked right off her face.

"Morning," replied Abby. "Yes, you will."

At that, Edna came down the stairs, "What the hell are you doing here?" Annabel shouted.

"I've come to take you home, Annabel," replied Edna quietly, she was not a shouter like Annabel.

"Like hell you are! How did you even find me?" Annabel shouted.

"Annabel, you know the baby isn't Neil's. You couldn't have got pregnant until after Neil had left. Dr George told me how far you had gone and Alf said you had been asking questions about Neil's whereabouts. I put two and two together and did some calling round."

"You had no right, you have no right, this is Neil's baby whatever you say, Dr George is lying to you!"

"Why would he do that? He was concerned about you with your history, it is not fair to claim someone is your child's father if they are not, truth is, you probably don't know whose it is?"

"You're lying," Annable cried. "You don't care about me, you evil old witch."

"Annabel," shouted Abby. "Do not speak to your mother like that in my hotel."

"You can go to hell as well," said Annabel. "I'm not leaving here without Neil."

Neil had arrived by now. "I'm not leaving with you, Annabel; it is not my child."

"How do you know that for sure, Neil?" Annabel smirked. "You left me with a note, for Christ's sake."

"I did that before you got too attached, or so I thought, to spare your feelings. I knew I wasn't staying in Scotland and I didn't want you to get hurt. I didn't realise how you felt Annabel but I don't feel that way about you."

"Liar," she shouted.

"I'm not the one lying here, Annabel. You know I can't be the father, you need to return to Sunny Cottage with your mum."

"I'll never forgive you for this," Annabel shouted at Edna. "I'm not leaving and that's that."

"Annabel," said Abby calmly, "if you don't leave with your mum, I shall have no alternative other than to get the police to remove you."

"Annabel," said Edna. "if you're that convinced Neil is the father, we will have a DNA test done when the baby is born." She winked at Abby.

"Yes," Abby said. "We can arrange to get Neil's DNA to you when the baby is born."

"Really," said Annabel. "Do you agree to that, Neil and when we prove it is yours, you will come to Sunny Cottage and be with me?"

"Yes," said Neil, knowing full well this was never going to happen but he needed to get this girl gone.

"But you have to come home, Annabel," said Edna, "so that Dr George and the hospital can keep an eye on you and make sure the baby is ok. You want your baby to be OK, don't you?"

"Of course, I do," replied Annabel. "But there are doctors and hospitals around here."

"But Dr George has treated you since you were born. He knows everything about you. Wouldn't you rather have someone who understands you look after you rather than strangers?"

"I suppose," said Annabel. "But we do the DNA test when it is born and Neil comes to Sunny Cottage when it is confirmed because it will confirm he is the father."

"Of course," said Edna. "Now let's go and pack your things and leave these good people in peace."

Annabel stormed off up the stairs to pack muttering, "I still can't believe that evil witch has hunted me down. I'll get my own back one day."

Edna had heard here, as had Neil and Abby. "She no doubt will too," sighed Edna. "I am so sorry it came to this for you, hopefully, you will have a nice Christmas once I've got her out of here."

Fat chance thought Neil, no Gina, no Harry, it would be just him and Abby so nothing too special. Things should have been different; he should be with Gina at her parents or her there with him. He prayed that would be his future Christmas, he really prayed.

"Thank you for coming down," Abby said to Edna. "I hope things turn out ok for you."

"Life is always difficult with Annabel," said Edna, "but we cope, and now it looks like we have another addition to cope with, as long as it's nothing like Annabel." She laughed. "That would really finish me off, thank you for keeping her here for me, I'll get her home now."

Edna went off to pack her things. When she returned to reception, Annabel was already down. Abby called them a taxi; when it arrived, Neil took their cases out for them and made sure Annabel got in the car. They drove off, Abby looked at Neil as Neil looked at her. "Thank god," they both said at the same time. They went back in and back to work. *When Gina comes back*, Neil thought, *I'll make her realise that she is the most important thing in the world to me.*

"If she comes back," a nagging voice in his head said. *No*, he thought, *I have to think positively*; Gina not returning is an unbearable thought.

Chapter 17

Weymouth

Gina's train pulled into Weymouth station at 3:15 pm. She gathered her things and then began to make her way to the exit door. She stepped onto the station and immediately saw her parents Kathleen and Henry waiting for her.

Gina was so glad to see them that she beamed. It was the first time she had smiled in days but if she needed her parents now, it was more than she had ever needed them. They were always there for her; they stood by her side all through the David saga and tried to protect her from all that publicity.

Her parents had Gina late in life. They had tried for many years for a child with no success and just as they were giving up trying, Kathleen discovered she was pregnant. Gina had a good, loving childhood. She was an only child and her parents doted on her. She had all the latest gadgets and she had enough clothes to fill a department store. She wasn't spoilt though; she was taught right from wrong, how to be polite and also to be grateful for what she had.

Her mother often told her stories of children in other countries who were poor and their awful living conditions and that she had all these things because she was lucky. Her parents had worked hard all their life and because they were in their 40s when Gina arrived, they had savings behind them and Henry still had a really good job as a managing director of a construction company. Her mother was a teacher but had given up work when Gina was born to look after her full-time. They had waited long enough for her; they didn't want to leave her with a babysitter. *In fact,* Gina thought, I *don't think they even went out on an evening until I was 14.*

Gina's parents were coming towards her with big smiles on their faces.

"Gina," cried Kathleen. "It's so good to see you, I can't wait to hear about your new life and job."

"Oh, I have plenty to tell you," Gina said.

"Let's get you home first," said Henry taking her case. "You probably need something to eat and a freshen up. Your mother has gone overboard with the food shop again," he said raising his eyes and smiling.

"Sound good to me," replied Gina and they made their way to the car park where Hendry's Audi was waiting to take them home.

It only took them 20 minutes to get home from the station. Gina made her way to her room to unpack and shower. She would put her pyjamas on; she thought, she wasn't going anywhere today. Tomorrow, she would call Sammie tomorrow and arrange a catch-up with her. It felt good to be home and away from the hotel for a while.

She made her way downstairs where she smelled her mother's cooking. Her mother was a great cook and didn't hold back on the portions either. She was going to have to watch her portions. She had been good at the hotel and she didn't want to undo her good work. Her mother would encourage her to eat, of course, she could hear her now.

"You have to eat, Gina; your skin and bone and you need to keep your strength up."

Gina carried on down the stairs; her mother had always had a good appetite and she believed everyone else should too. She smiled to herself, yes, and it was good to be home.

She sat at the dining table that had already been laid with cutlery and wine glasses.

"Won't be long," shouted Kathleen from the kitchen.

"No rush," replied Gina.

Henry came in a poured them some wine.

"How are you, Gina?" He asked.

"Oh, I'm good," replied Gina.

"You sure?" Henry asked. "I can tell that look in your eye, I'm your father, I know you too well."

"I'll fill you both in after dinner," replied Gina, "how have you two been?"

"Oh, same old, same old," said Henry. "I keep working, mother keeps spending," he laughed.

Gina laughed with him. "Nothing changes then."

Kathleen came in with two plates.

"There you go, you two. I'll just get mine and we can enjoy the meal before we have a nice long chat after," she said disappearing back into the kitchen.

Gina looked at her plate and then looked at her dad.

"I know," he laughed. "But you know what she will be like if you don't eat it."

"I can't eat like this for the next month," Gina exclaimed.

"See, what you can do tonight and I'll have a word with her later," he smiled. "You look like you could do with a good meal."

Gina looked at her plate again; her mum had done a full roast dinner—Beef, roast potatoes, boiled potatoes, roast parsnips, cabbage, carrots and Yorkshire puddings!

"Eat up," said Kathleen, "there's a nice apple pie and custard for afters."

Gina took a gulp and sipped her wine. "Really, Mum." She laughed and started to tuck in.

It was actually delicious as was the apple pie; she did miss her mum's cooking, just not the portions. She felt positively stuffed when she'd finished. She got up to clear the plates away.

"No," said Kathleen. "Not tonight, you've had a long day; go in the lounge with your dad and when I've finished, we will have a nice catch-up, I can't wait to hear your news."

Gina went into the lounge with Henry and flopped on the settee, "I've missed you both so much," said Gina.

"We've missed you too," said Henry. "It is good to have you back for a while, is it four weeks you have?"

"Yes," replied Gina, although at the moment she wasn't sure if she would go back.

They sat in divine silence while waiting for her mum; she and her dad had always been comfortable in each other's company without feeling the need to constantly talk, it felt good.

About 20 minutes later, Kathleen joined them and poured herself some more wine.

"Gina," she said. "We weren't sure whether we should tell you but your dad says you should know."

"What?" Gina asked, suddenly worried.

"David has been sending letters for you here. I have kept them in case you want to read them but if not, I'll destroy them, we haven't opened them, of course," said Kathleen.

Gina was shocked. She told David in their last conversation that she wanted nothing more to do with him; she didn't want him to call or write to her. What did he want? Why was he sending letters? He knew it was over for them. "I'm not sure if I want to see them," she said. "Can I sleep on it?"

"I think that's for the best anyway," Henry said. "I don't want them upsetting you."

"I agree," said Kathleen. "Now, come on, tell us your news."

Gina started to fill them in starting with her first view of the beautiful hotel.

"When I got out of the taxi, I could not believe how big the place was," said Gina, "it was certainly not what I expected! There are acres of land around the place and has its own private path down to the beach!"

"Sounds wonderful," her mother replied.

"Oh, it is," said Gina smiling. "I knew right then that I had definitely done the right thing by going for the job."

Gina told them all about Abby, Carol, Tracy, Sheila, Oliver, Janice and Peter, deliberately leaving Neil out for the moment.

"They all made me so welcome," she said. "Every one of them, within a couple of days, I felt really like a team member."

"That's great to hear, Gina," said her father. "But I know you well, my darling and there is a reason you have extended your stay, is there not?"

Gina's dad knew her so well, probably better than she knew herself! She had always been close to her dad and she knew she couldn't keep anything from him.

"Is there something wrong dear?" Her mum asked.

"Not wrong as such," said Gina, "I just feel a bit of a fool."

"Whatever happened," exclaimed Kathleen.

"Well," started Gina, "after David, I vowed to remain very much single, but Abby's brother, Neil, was so persistent. He is very good-looking but I know he had a past but I don't know what it was. Anyway, I eventually agreed to go on a date with him and we hit it off so well I agreed to do it again."

"Has he hurt you?" Her father asked.

"No, nothing like that," replied Gina and proceeded to explain about Annabel turning up claiming Neil was the father of her baby.

"But that was before you met him, wasn't it?" Her mum asked. "Everyone at your age will have exes, Gina, but I understand a baby may make things complicated."

"Yes, it was before he and I met, but he left her with a note!"

"And what was his reason for doing that?" Henry asked.

"I didn't ask," said Gina, "all I could see was everything was falling apart."

"Well, maybe you should have asked," he said. "There may have been a good reason. What did his sister have to say?"

"Abby doesn't think the baby is his at all. She is trying to get Annabel to go to her doctor to find out how far along she is. Abby says Neil has changed so much since we met, but I don't know how we could carry on. If he has to travel halfway across the country to see his child, that is going to make things really awkward if we had a future together."

"You really like him, don't you?" Her mum said.

"Yes," sighed Gina. "And that's the problem."

"Seems to me, our Gina," said Henry, "that you rushed out a bit too soon. You should have given the lad a chance to tell his side of the story. There was probably a good reason he left her abruptly and if his own sister believes he may not be the father then maybe you should have stayed to find out."

Gina was shocked. She thought her dad would be up in arms about everything, but here he was, trying to say she had been too hasty. What was it with Neil, everyone liked him and her parents hadn't even met him!!

"Yes, maybe," said Gina, "but after David, I panicked and just wanted to come home to your two for a while to get my head straight."

"You're always welcome here, Gina," said Henry. "You know that; it will always be your home; it's just from what you've told me, there seems more to this Annabel than you've given yourself a chance to see."

"You can stay for as long or as little as you want, darling," her mother said. "It will give you a chance to think straight then you may go back with a different outlook."

Yes, Gina thought, *she may be right*. She had certainly got a lot of thinking to do. She didn't want to throw away a future but she didn't know whether that future could be with Neil after what had happened.

What had happened? She had been out on some lovely dates with a handsome, attentive and loving person who she had begun to fall in love with. She felt he probably felt the same as he treated her like a princess, everyone said he was a changed man since being with her and everything had been going so well.

Then a crazy girl turns up, yes, she was crazy, Gina thought, she was very odd in fact. She accused Neil of being the father of her child, which, when Gina thought about it, was a decent time after Neil had been in Scotland. Why had she left it so long? She had a manic look in her eye every time she spoke, yes maybe, just maybe, her father was right and there was more to this. Maybe she had been hasty by leaving before it was sorted one way or another.

She wondered what had happened since she left, if anything, but she had forbidden Neil to call her so she couldn't really call him could she?

I really need to sleep on this and then start to think afresh in the morning. Something told her though, that sleep wasn't going to come easy tonight. She poured herself another wine that may help. She wanted to wipe everything from her mind tonight and then take a fresh look at it tomorrow.

Gina was right. Sleep had not come easy that night. She had tossed and turned with all sorts of thoughts going through her mind.

She wasn't looking forward to looking through David's letters. She was in two minds whether to open them or not, but she wanted to see if he had finally realised they were over so she would have a look at them after breakfast.

She thought of the hotel and Neil, what had happened with Annabel after she had left? Had Neil decided he would do the right thing and go back to Sunny Cottage with her? How was Abby and the others? Questions, questions, questions!

She really wanted to ring Abby to find out what was going on but it was too early, she needed more time. She really missed the hotel and all her friends there; did they miss her? "Oh," she said out loud, it hadn't occurred to her that they may not miss her and they may forget about her real quick, she hadn't been there long, why would they miss her? She thought sadly. Then she remembered that Abby had begged her to return after her holiday, so hopefully, she would still want her back.

Do I want to go back? She thought. Gina had full intentions of returning but just thinking about the events before she left turned her stomach and gave her a sinking feeling. *What if I go back and Neil has gone off with Annabel?* She thought, *could I face the hotel without him now*? She wasn't sure she could.

Gina decided to get up and shower then make her way downstairs.

"Morning," called her mum. "How did you sleep?"

"Morning," Gina replied. "Not well if I'm honest."

"A lot going through your mind," said Kathleen. "You need time to digest and get your head straight, this time at home will give you that chance."

"Yes," said Gina. "I just can't help wondering what's happening back at the hotel."

"You really like him, don't you?" Her mum replied. "Just give it a bit of time then call Abby to see what's happening, then you will know but take some time first, it's still early days from when you left. Did you have a think about David's letters?"

"Yes," said Gina. "I was in two minds not to look at them but it would be good to see if he has finally realised he needs to let me go."

"There's a lot of letters," said her mum. "He seems pretty persistent."

"I'll look at them after breakfast," she said realising she was quite hungry.

"I've made scrambled eggs this morning, can I do you some toast?" Her mum asked.

"Yes, please," Gina replied and poured herself some coffee.

After breakfast, Kathleen went to fetch the letters from David.

"Oh my god," said Gina. "There's loads of them."

"I told you there were a few," said her mum. "He must have written a couple of times a week since he was sent there."

"There's more than a few," exclaimed Gina. "I'll never get through all those, I'll look at a few and see what they say."

Gina opened the first letter and her heart sank, David hadn't decided to let go; he was quite the opposite.

Gina, I know I hurt you and I'm truly sorry for what I did. I was in a bad place and I took a girl home and I thought what we did was consensual, I would never rape anyone. I know, one day you will forgive me and we will have a happy future.

Gina couldn't believe what she was reading. Is he for real? He's admitted to cheating and he thinks they have a future, what about the other girls he raped, did he think they were consensual too!

When I get out, we can build a future together and put the past behind us, please come to see me, I missed seeing you in court.

Gina couldn't digest it. How did he think they had a future after what he had done? He was jailed for 15 years and he'll still be on a sex offenders register when he is released. It was unimaginable that he could even think she would want him back after what he had done.

She opened a couple more letters and they were all pretty much the same dialogue.

"Oh, Christ," she said to her mum, "look at them, he's deranged."

Her mum looked at them and shook her head.

"How could he even think you would go back after what he put you through, the rapes, the press? He can deny the crimes to his heart's content but the evidence was there. I heard it in court and it doesn't discount the fact that he cheated on you as well."

"I know," said Gina, "it's bizarre, I went through enough at the time. I thought he would realise there was never any way back for us but it seems he's living on a different planet to me."

"Are you going to write back to him?" Kathleen asked.

Gina thought for a moment and then replied, "No, I am going to see him to set him straight. He needs to stop all contact and if he doesn't, I will take out a restraining order against him, I need to tell him face to face, I don't think he will accept it otherwise."

"Are you sure?" Her mum asked looking worried.

"I am more than sure," Gina replied adamantly. "I will ring the prison and ask them to tell him to send me a visiting order for next week. He's in Bristol and it's not too far, just a couple of hours. This all has to stop now!"

At that, Henry walked into the kitchen, "Morning, both," he said.

"Henry, you had better sit down," Kathleen said, "Gina has some news."

Henry listened to the letters and Gina's planned visit to David.

"Are you sure?" He asked.

"Perfectly sure," replied Gina.

Chapter 18

HMP Bristol

Gina had received her visiting order and she was on her way to visit David. She was very nervous; she had never been to a prison before and she hadn't seen David since his arrest.

She had borrowed her dad's car for the two-hour journey. He had wanted to take her and wait outside, but she refused his offer and the journey would give her some time to think about what she was going to say, not that it would go to plan, it never did.

It had been over 12 months since David's arrest and it had been a rough time. She had hidden herself away because of the press. They had camped in her front drive hoping to catch her for 'her side of the story' but she had not left the house. What was her side of the story, anyway? They were a happily married couple and she had no idea what was going on. Would they even believe that? She had often thought herself in the past that surely the wives would know something wasn't right, but she understood now how that was exactly the case.

David had never acted any differently. He went out once a week for a pint and a game of pool with his mates. He was never particularly late home. He went to work and returned at exactly the same time every day; just when he committed those crimes, she would never know.

She didn't go to court; she couldn't face it. She couldn't face seeing the victims who her own husband had hurt so badly and she definitely couldn't face David. She didn't want to hear all the details. What she did know was bad enough. She would never get it out of her mind if she heard any more. Her mum and dad attended the trial, so they could keep her updated with what was going on. They didn't give her the details. She asked them not to, but they told her the verdict and what sentence David had received.

The police had called her to tell her what prison he was being transferred to. He was charged and was no longer on remand. Initially, he had been in HMP, The Verne, which was only a few miles from where she lived, but that was a category C prison and the police explained that now that he had been charged with multiple rapes and had a long sentence he would be transferred to a category B prison, that being HMP Bristol which was much further.

Not that it mattered where he was. She had given up their rented house; she wondered if he knew. And moved halfway down the country for her new job. She was certainly not going to tell him about Haven Hotel and where she was living. She wasn't telling him she was staying with her mum and dad either as that would give him an excuse to start ringing their numbers. No, she would say that she had a job in Scotland with accommodation and at the moment, she was staying in a bed and breakfast near her parents for the holiday period; that should put him off her scent.

She really wasn't looking forward to seeing him, although she suspected he was looking forward to her visiting. It was going to be a confrontation she was sure; he was probably thinking she was visiting to say she'd forgiven him, but he was very wrong if he did think that.

She pulled up to the visitors' centre car park. The journey had gone quite quickly really and she was a bit early. She went to the ticket machine to pay for her parking and noticed a small café up the street; she would go and have a coffee while she waited for her slot. She put her ticket on the windscreen and started walking towards the café.

She had to walk past the prison walls; it looked very imposing. High walls with barbed wire on the top, and it looked very old. She had read that it was built in the 1880s, so it was doing well she supposed.

She entered the little café. It was quite busy with more early visitors she assumed. She ordered a latte and found a seat in a nice little alcove. The waitress brought her drink over and Gina took a sip. It was so nice; she thought, *they must have made it with cream*! It was warm in the café; everyone was chatting amongst themselves; it was a lovely atmosphere. Gina wished she could have just stayed there rather than face what was coming.

Gina looked at her watch. They had told her to be at the visitors' centre 30 minutes before her visit time to check in and get a locker. She finished her latte and made her way over to the centre.

When she walked in, she thought how uninviting it looked. There were children running around, and women talking. There were prison guards both by the doors and behind a counter.

"Excuse me," said Gina to the guard by the door, "this is my first time. Could you tell me what to do and where to go?"

"Of course," smiled the guard. "You'll need to put a one-pound coin in the slot of a locker and leave your bag, phone, coat etc. in there. The only thing you are allowed to take over to the main prison is some change in a bag for the vending machine in the visitors' room. Then go to the counter where they will take your fingerprints and your photo so you can be identified next time."

"There won't be a next time," said Gina.

The guard laughed. "I've heard that before but you still need it done on this visit. You'll need to be identified at your next stop over the road. Once that's done, the staff behind the counter will tell you what to do next and where to go."

"Thank you," said Gina and went off to get a locker to leave her things in. She was going to feel lost without her belongings but hopefully, it won't be for long. Her visiting slot was for two hours but she certainly didn't intend on being in there that long. *I hope they'll let me out before my time is up*, she thought, *I'm sure they will.*

She stood in the queue of women and children waiting her turn. She was getting more and more nervous. This was a world she never thought she would be in and she didn't like it one bit. She felt like the criminal going through all these checks and the people behind the counter had little patience. I suppose we are all criminals in their eyes, the fact that we are visiting them would give them that impression. She wanted to shout out that she was only here to tell her criminal husband to leave her the hell alone and not because she wanted to see him. What would be the use of that? She remained quiet and worked her way up the queue.

"Name?" The guard behind the counter shouted.

Gina was startled. "Gina," she replied.

"Gina what?" The guard asked.

"Gina Taylor," she said.

"Who are you visiting, have you got a visiting order?"

"Yes, I have, and I'm here to see David Taylor."

"Stand there and look at the camera," the guard ordered.

Gina did as she was asked and a flash told her that her photo was now on record.

"That's fine," said the guard. "Now put your middle finger on the electronic pad and roll it from side to side."

Again, Gina did as she was asked.

"Now the same with the thumb."

Gina put her thumb on the pad and rolled it as instructed; she was feeling really out of her comfort zone.

"That's it, you're recorded, have you got anything on you?" The guard asked.

"No," replied Gina.

"Ok, over the road, through the main entrance and wait to be called."

Gina could see why she needed to be there 30 minutes early! She walked over to the main prison. Another queue! She joined and waited yet again. When she got to the counter, she was told to put her middle finger on the pad. Her face flashed up on a screen and she was told to move forward. There was a scanner in front of her.

"Take off your shoes and belt if you have one on, put it in the box on the conveyor and walk through the scanner."

Again, Gina did as she was asked; when she emerged through the scanner, she was frisked by a female officer. She was told to proceed and collect her things and then wait by the gate.

She waited by the gate with a few others and an officer came over, unlocked it and told them to walk through. There was another locked gate which could only be unlocked when the open one had been relocked.

"We are really treated like criminals," Gina whispered to a woman near her.

"First time?" The woman asked.

"Yes, and the last," Gina replied.

The other gate was unlocked and they were led up some stairs to another waiting area.

"All, take a seat and you'll be let in when visiting time starts."

Gina looked at her watch. Her slot was due to start in 10 minutes, so she took a seat and waited, looking around at the old building and realising how cold it felt. *I wonder if it's this cold in the cells*, she thought, *or is it just the visitors who get the rough end of the deal?*

Ten minutes later, the two big doors opened and there were six chairs, all set out in front of each other in a single line. The first six people were called though and the doors shut. *What now?* Gina thought I thought we had had all our checks.

The doors opened again and Gina was among the next six to be let in.

"Take a seat on one of the chairs," an officer said.

When they were all seated, the sniffer dogs were brought in to smell around everyone. *Oh god*, thought Gina, *this is just awful, it's so far from the life I have, and I will never come here again.*

"Ok, everyone is clear, make your way through to the hall and take a seat, the prisoners are on their way up."

Gina entered the large visitor's rooms; it was laid out with small tables with one chair on one side and two chairs opposite. Gina soon found out that the one chair was for the prisoner when she was told to move to the other side when she first sat down.

"Sorry," she said. "I didn't realise."

"It's fine," smiled a female guard. "If you've not been before, you wouldn't have known."

Gina sat down and heard the clanging of keys. The prisoners were coming in. Gina felt very on edge, these were criminals and she was in a room full of them, she couldn't wait to get out.

Just then, she saw David enter. He was looking around for her. When he saw, her he had the biggest smile and tried to hug her before he sat down. She pulled away and he sat down opposite.

"Gina," he said. "Thank you so much for coming, I knew you would when you had read my letters."

"I only read a couple of them last week, David. I can't believe you think we can carry on where we left off," replied Gina.

"But when you requested a visit, I thought it was because you wanted to talk and discuss our future," said David.

"David," Gina sighed. "We have no future, once upon a time, my main focus was our future but you put a nail in that coffin."

"You only read them last week? I've been sending them for a few months after I got in here."

"They have all been redirected to my mum's house. I had it done with the post office for 12 months when I left the house. That will have run out now, so I won't get anymore."

"Left the house," David said shocked. "What do you mean, left the house?"

"David, I stayed in the house, literally. For the first few months, I had press on the front drive, so I couldn't leave without being harassed, and my name was in all the papers because of you. If I went out, I got stares and people trying to ask me questions which I couldn't answer anyway. When I pulled myself together, I got myself a job in Scotland and gave up the house, I haven't looked back since."

"Scotland," he said raising his voice. "You got a job in Scotland? Where does that leave us when I'm released?"

Gina sighed, "There is no us." *Why wasn't he getting it*? She thought. She needed to get a bit tougher.

"So why did you come today?" He asked.

"I came to tell you to stop writing, not to call and to leave me the hell alone. If you don't, David, I will get an order served on you whereby you'll be breaking the law if you do."

"I won't give up on us, Gina."

"Then I'll be calling a solicitor tomorrow."

She got up to leave and David grabbed her harm. "You're hurting me, David, let me go."

"Don't leave, you have to stay and sort things out."

"I've said everything I need to say and quite frankly, I don't want to hear any more of what you have to say."

A guard came over. "Let go, Taylor, now."

David let go and the guard asked Gina if she was ready to leave.

"Yes, please," she replied.

The guard signalled to another guard by the doors and Gina made her way over.

"You ok, miss?" He asked.

"Yes, I just need to get out of here."

"I'll take you," he said and took her elbow and led the way.

Gina breathed in the fresh air when she got outside; she had to walk back to the visitors' centre to collect her things. She could feel the tears starting to sting her eyes. Why was she crying? She had done what she came to do; she didn't feel sorry for David. He deserved to be where he was after the awful things he had done. She didn't feel anything at all for him in fact, no love no hate, so why did she want to sob her heart out?

She collected her things and made her way to the car. She had a two-hour drive home now and she couldn't wait to get there. It was starting to drop dark and she didn't like driving in the dark so she had better get a move on.

She arrived home around 6 pm. Her mum opened the door and asked how it went. Gina stepped into the hall and broke down in floods of tears.

"What did he do?" Her mum asked.

"Nothing," replied Gina. "He's still delusional about us and thinks I'm going to wait for him but I told him I'm going to take an order out on him if he doesn't stop contacting me."

"I think that would be a good idea," her dad said coming into the hall. "Come and sit down and I'll pour you a drink, it looks like you need one."

"Yes," said Gina, "I'll phone the solicitor in the morning and get the ball rolling, we don't know how he's going to be in the future."

"So why the tears?" Her mum asked.

"I'm really not sure," said Gina. "The whole experience was a bit traumatic; it may be that or just relief that I have David where he belongs—firmly in the past."

Gina woke up the next morning and called the solicitors her family always used. Mike Johnson was a friend of her father's so she was sure he would help her.

"Yes, Gina," he said when she'd explained what she required. "We can put a non-molestation order in place which means he will break the law if he tries to contact you in any way. We will get it drawn up and issued to him at the prison within the next week."

"Thank you, Mr Johnson," she said. "I'll call into the office to pay you tomorrow, that is such a relief."

Gina put the phone down and smiled at her mum. "Now, it's time to concentrate on my future, whatever that may be, but I feel a huge weight has been lifted now that I've told him to his face and the order he is going to get."

"Everything is going to work out fine," said her mum.

"Yes," Gina replied, and for the first time in a while, she believed it might.

She decided she would give Abby a call on Monday, which would be a week and see what had happened after she left. Whatever Abby said would determine her next steps, but for now, she was just going to enjoy the time she had with her parents over Christmas.

Christmas day was in two days and she really wanted to catch up with Sammie. It had been so long and she loved her so much. Sammie always told her as it was and that's what she needed right now.

"Hello," said the voice on the other end of the phone.

"Sammie, it's me," Gina said.

"Oh my god, Gina, how are you? Where are you? I've missed you so much."

"I'm at Mum and Dad's for Christmas. Fancy a few drinks and a catch-up?"

"You bet I do," said Sammie. "I need all the gossip and find out about your new job, is there a new man? Have you heard of David?" "Sammie has so many questions."

"I'll tell you everything when I see you," laughed Gina. "There is so much to tell."

"Oh my god, I cannot wait," Sammie almost screamed. "I am babysitting tonight but I'm free tomorrow if you have no plans for Christmas Eve?"

"No, I have no plans for tomorrow; shall we meet in town and get some food?" Gina asked.

"Yes," let's do that and make a night of it.

"We may need a few hours," laughed Gina.

"I am so excited to be seeing you, Gina, I really have missed you."

"I know," Gina said. "I have really missed you too."

They arranged to meet at a restaurant they both adored for 6 pm the following evening. Gina made the reservation.

"You're lucky," said the manager of the restaurant. "Christmas Eve is a busy one but we've just had a cancellation for 6 pm literally a few minutes ago."

"Oh, brilliant," replied Gina. "We'll see you tomorrow, thank you so much."

Gina was first at the restaurant, arriving at 5:45. She was always early and Sammie was usually late but tonight Sammie was there a few minutes later.

"Not like you to be early," Gina laughed as she hugged Sammie so tight Sammie thought she might break.

"Hey. Not so tight," she laughed. "You'll break me in half. I'm early because I'm eager to hear all your news."

A waiter came over and showed them to their table. They ordered a bottle of Merlot to share and looked at the menu.

"Come on," said Sammie. "Let's hear everything."

"Let's order our food," said Gina. "At least it will be on its way then we can get going."

"Good idea," replied Sammie and scoured the menu.

They both decided and ordered their food when the waiter returned with the wine. He poured them a glass each, took their order and left.

"Ok, where to start," said Gina.

"Right from the day you got there," said Sammie. "I need to hear everything!"

Gina told her all about the hotel and Abby, how lovely it was there and how she loved her job. She told her about the other staff and how welcoming they all were with her.

"I love it there," Gina sighed.

"So, why the sigh, you'll be going back after the holidays, won't you?" Sammie tilted her head; she could sense there was more.

"Well, that's just it, I'm not sure," said Gina.

"Why on earth not?" Sammie said.

Gina told her about Neil, how lovely he was and how he spoilt her and treated her like a princess.

"Sounds divine," Said Sammie, "and just what you needed after David, that son of a bitch."

"Yes he is," Gina said, but there was more and proceeded to tell her all about Annabel.

"Oh, I see," said Sammie, "but you say, Neil says it can't be his baby and the girl sounds crazy if you ask me."

"Well, yes, she was a little bizarre, refusing to go to the doctor's appointment that Abby arranged and sometimes she could look positively manic!" said Gina.

"Look," said Sammie. "You obviously like this Neil a lot; he swears the baby can't be is. His sister has very big doubts too and it's not like he cheated on you, it all happened before you even arrived at Haven."

"I know," sighed Gina. "Abby and the other staff keep telling me he's a changed character since we got together but it was just such a shock with her turning up like she did. She said he left a note when he left her which made me uncomfortable."

"And his reasons for that?" Sammie questioned.

"He said sleeping with her had been a huge mistake. He had been drunk so when he realised what had happened the next morning, he knew he had to leave in the kindest way as he knew he couldn't commit to her. That's what he said, anyway."

"Sound quite admiral to me, he didn't want to lead her on and he probably didn't even know she was a psycho that was going to stalk him!"

"Sammie, you can't call her that, we don't know."

"Sounds like one to me. Look, Gina, you had strong feelings for him, he didn't leave with her I'd guess as it sounds like he has it bad for you."

"I don't know; he didn't leave with her."

"Because you've not picked up the phone to find out," Sammie said, getting a bit exasperated with her friend.

"I thought it was a little early, I was going to give Abby a ring next week."

"Well, do that then and stop worrying. I'm sure everything will turn out fine and don't forget your friend here has never been a bridesmaid," Sammie laughed.

"I think it's a bit premature to be talking wedding bells," Gina said, also laughing although her heart had just done a flutter or two at the thought.

"Right," said Sammie. "Now we've sorted that problem, put it to bed for a few days, so it doesn't ruin your Christmas with your mum and dad."

"I will," said Gina. "But I have more news."

"More," said Sammie. "Oh my god, spill, Gina."

Gina told Sammie all about David's letters and her visit to the prison.

"Is that man for real?" Sammie shouted. "He puts you through hell and he thinks it's all going to go back to normal when he's released in god knows how many years. Jeez, the man's deranged if he thinks you would go back to him after what he did to those women!"

"I know," said Gina. "He wasn't too happy when I told him I'd moved away, given up the house and got a job."

"You didn't tell him where, did you?" Sammie asked.

"Yes, I told him it was at a hotel in Scotland."

They both laughed. "That'll take him in the opposite direction," Sammie said. "Well done, Gina, that's possibly the most sensible thing you've said since we sat down."

"There is more," Gina said. "I have a non-molestation order being issued to him next week and I have started divorce proceedings. I feel so much better now I have actually done it."

"Hallelujah, praise the lord," Sammie shouted out. "My friend has finally found some gumption."

"Yes," said Gina. "Finally, things are looking brighter."

"I'll drink to that," Sammie said clinking Gina's glass. "You deserve some happiness after what you have been through."

"Yes," Gina smiled, "I believe I do."

Sammie looked at her watch. "Oh lord, it is 10:30, we have been talking for over four hours."

"We had a lot to catch up on," Gina said. "What are your plans for tomorrow?"

"Working," said Sammie. "The joys of being a nurse."

They asked the waiter for the bill, paid and got up to leave.

"Make sure we have another catch-up before you go back," Sammie said.

"If I go back," replied Gina.

"You will," Sammie winked at her. "Nothing can get in the way of true love."

Sammie got into her taxi and Gina waved as she left. Her taxi was just pulling up. She got in the back and smiled to herself. She really did think things would be ok; she was going to enjoy Christmas more than she thought. She half wished she let Neil come but she wouldn't have been able to think so clearly if he'd been around. No, she had made the right decision in leaving him at the hotel; these past few days had done her good.

When she arrived home, Kathleen and Henry had gone to bed. She decided she would head there too. It was Christmas day tomorrow and she wanted to enjoy it with her parents. She smiled; she felt like a little kid again waiting for Santa to come.

Chapter 19

Christmas Day

Gina woke the next morning and looked at the clock, 8:30 am. Christmas morning, Gina smiled to herself. She could hear her mum and dad pottering around downstairs just like in the old days when she was younger. Kathleen was probably cooking up a storm for breakfast and Henry would be getting the log fire going. The log fire wasn't used that much because it was too warm with the central heating but Henry always had it roaring on Christmas morning. "Adds to the atmosphere," he would always say.

Gina checked her phone and could see she had had a message from Sammie.

"Merry Christmas! Enjoy your day and think about us workers☺," it read.

"Merry Christmas," replied Gina. "What are your plans for after your shift?"

"Just home," Sammie replied with a sad emoji.

"Why don't you join us for dinner? We don't have it till late and you know mum always cooks way too much."

"Really," text Sammie. "I'd love that, see you around 5:30."

Gina smiled; it would be nice to spend Christmas night with her parents and Sammie. Sammie could always stay over if she wanted to.

Gina got up and put her dressing gown on. She would shower after breakfast. She made her way downstairs and could smell the bacon cooking.

"Morning," smiled her mum. "Merry Christmas, how was your evening with Sammie?"

"Merry Christmas," replied Gina. "It was lovely, we talked for over four hours!"

"You had a lot to catch up on," laughed Kathleen. "Breakfast won't be long; your dad is just stoking his fire."

"I hope you don't mind but I invited Sammie for dinner this evening; she's at work today and was just going home alone."

"Of course, I don't mind," said Kathleen, "it will be lovely to see her and there will be plenty to go around."

Gina laughed, when was there ever not enough to feed the five thousand?

The doorbell rang. "Gina, will you get that please?" Henry shouted.

"But Dad, I'm in my dressing gown, can't you go?"

"No one will take any notice of you in your dressing gown on Christmas morning," Henry replied. "Now, go answer the door, please."

Gina sighed and went to the door; she only opened it a little way until she could see who it was.

"Aunty Pat, Uncle George," she squealed. "No one told me you we coming."

"We thought we'd surprise you," Pat laughed.

Gina threw her arms around them. "You have certainly done that but what a lovely surprise it is, are you here all day? Are you staying over?"

"We are going back the day after tomorrow. I hear we have a lot of news to catch up on, but first let's have breakfast, we are both famished."

They made their way through to the kitchen and exchanged hugs with Kathleen and Henry then they all sat around the big table.

"This is so lovely," Gina said. "All of us together and my best friend joining us later; this is going to be the best Christmas."

"So far," said her mum with a wink. "You have plenty of Christmas to come yet."

"I know," said Gina. "But I'm going to savour every moment of today."

"Let's eat, then we can exchange presents," said Kathleen and started to place plates in front of everyone. As usual, the plates were stacked with food and Gina tucked in as though she had never eaten. She was happy with her family on this special day and she was going to enjoy every moment and every mouthful.

Everyone was reasonably quiet; they were savouring the wonderful breakfast they were eating. If nothing else, Kathleen was an amazing cook and everyone was enjoying her breakfast delights. When they finished, Henry poured them all a glass of Buck Fizz and they moved into the lounge.

"Present time," Kathleen smiled. "Gina, you open your first, then we can all open ours after."

"What about clearing the table?" Gina said.

"It will wait," said Henry. "I'll give your mum a hand later while you catch up with Pat and George."

Gina sat on the floor by her pile of presents. There were quite a few from her mum and dad, one from Sammie, a couple from her aunt and uncle and another one that just read Gina on the tag but no sender's name.

"That one arrived yesterday," said her mum. "When I took it out of the cardboard box, that's all it said."

"I'll open that one last," said Gina. "Let me open yours first, it looks like you've spoilt me again."

The first one she opened was a beautiful cashmere coat. "Oh my goodness, it's beautiful," she squealed.

"We thought it may keep you nice and snug on the Cornish coast," smiled Kathleen.

"I absolutely love it," she said hugging her mum and dad. "Thank you so much!"

She opened the rest of her parent's gifts and she had her favourite perfume and a beautiful necklace with a diamond-encrusted G as the pendant.

"You really have spoilt me, thank you," she said tears filling her eyes.

"You deserve it," her parents answered in unison.

She opened the rest of her presents except the one with no sender's name. She had the usual of her aunt and uncle, fluffy socks, body crème and hand lotion.

"Thank you," she said. "I love them."

Sammie had bought her a lovely charm for her Pandora bracelet; she laughed as she opened it.

"What is funny?" Her mum smiled.

"I have bought Sammie a Pandora charm," she laughed. "great minds."

Lastly, she looked at the present with no sender. "Well go on, put us out of our misery," said Uncle George.

She opened the present; it was a gorgeous watch which was inscribed with the words 'I love you' on the back. Inside the box was a handwritten note.

I love you, Gina, please come back to me
Neil xxxx

Tears rolled down her face until she started to sob.

"Whatever is it?" Aunt Pat asked.

"I'll fill you in later," said Gina. This had sent her mind into overdrive. Neil had taken the time to buy and send this gorgeous watch and had told her he loved her which meant a lot to her. But what about Annabel, the spanner in the works, how could they move forward with that over them? She really needed to call Abby on Monday. She had to find out what had happened. This gift had rocked her world all over again…

All the others opened their gifts then they sat around chatting.

"Come on, Kathleen, let's go and clear the table while Gina fills Pat and George in on all her news," said Henry getting up to go into the kitchen.

"Yes," said Kathleen. "We'll leave you to catch up while we clear up."

Gina started with David; she told them about the letters he'd sent and her visit to the prison.

"I rue the day we took you to those gardens," sighed Pat. "He caused you so much heartache and the crimes he committed were—well—hideous."

"I know," replied Gina. "But it's no one's fault. I was the one who fell in love with him, married him and lived with him. I had no clue what he had been doing until the police knocked on the door that morning. He pulled the wool over all our eyes, but I've told him face to face now and he'll get his order served after Christmas."

"I can't believe the cheeky beggar thinks he's going to pick up where you left off!" said George. "He's living on a different planet."

"Yes," sighed Gina. "He really is but with the order and the divorce proceeding, he'll hopefully get the message. He thinks I live and have a job in Scotland so that should keep him off the scent."

Aunty Pat looked really sad and shook her head. "You just don't know people at all, do you?"

"Anyway," said Uncle George. "Tell us more about this new job you have."

Gina told them all about Haven Hotel and how beautiful it was there.

"We'll have to book in," said Pat.

"Yes, you definitely should," said Gina. "It's a beautiful place and the beach is amazing. You would love Abby and all the staff. They have made me so welcome, made me feel part of the team right away and now it's like we are one big family."

"I hear there is another member of staff that has caught your eye," smiled Pat. "Tell me about him, Neil isn't it?"

Gina smiled; her mother had obviously had a conversation with her sister before they had arrived.

She proceeded to tell them about Neil, how he had wooed her and how quickly she had fallen for him.

"I was very guarded to start with," she said. "I think he was a bad boy in the past but Abby and the others tell me how much he's changed, especially since we got together."

"Everyone has a past, Gina," said George. "And everyone deserves second chances."

"I know, but something happened just before I came away that made me rethink." And proceeded to tell them about Annabel.

"Well," said Pat when Gina had finished. "This is how I see it; firstly, the girl sounds deranged. Her weeks seem way out and her mannerisms as you explained are definitely off, so I would doubt very much if that child is Neil's; secondly, all this happened way before he met you."

"What if it is his child though, Aunty Pat? How would that work with them being halfway across the country from each other? I don't know how I would be when he went to visit."

"There's a lot of what-ifs in there and they are no good for anyone. You need to find out what has happened since you left, so you need to make that call on Monday. Oh, and Gina, if you love him, there is always a way forward."

Pat smiled at her and Gina realised just how right she was.

"I had better shower and dress before Dad wants to watch all the Christmas programmes together," laughed Gina and she went upstairs to get herself ready.

The afternoon was spent watching TV and sipping wine. Henry always insisted on watching the royal speech on Christmas day, so programmes had to be timed around that. It was a family tradition he was never going to break. After that, they all sat and watched a Christmas movie which prompted George and Henry to doze off in their armchairs. Kathleen was in and out prepping for the Christmas dinner later and Gina and Pat were giggling at the film they were watching.

George and Henry both awoke abruptly when the doorbell went at 5:25 pm.

"Who could that be on Christmas day?" Henry said.

"It will be Sammie, Dad," Gina laughed. "Have you forgotten already we invited her for dinner?"

"No," he said. "Only for a moment."

"Sammie!" Gina squealed when she saw Sammie and threw her arms around her. "Merry Christmas."

"Merry Christmas," said Sammie. "Steady on, I saw you last night, ha."

"It's just so nice to be spending Christmas with you," said Gina. "How was your shift?"

"A tough one," said Sammie. "I need a drink."

They laughed and walked through to the lounge; Sammie hugged everyone while Gina poured her a glass of wine. Sammie was like a part of the family and knew them all.

They were all sitting chatting when Kathleen called them through for dinner. They all duly got up and headed for the kitchen.

"Wow," said Sammie. "How many are coming, Kath? There sure is a lot of food."

Gina and Sammie looked at one another and then burst out laughing. Some things never changed.

"If there's leftovers," said Kathleen. "You can take a dinner for tomorrow, Sammie."

Sammie knew for sure there would be leftovers, so she would look forward to another dinner tomorrow night.

"Are you staying over, Sammie?" Henry asked.

"If that's ok with everyone, I can have a drink and then leave mid-morning, I'm on an afternoon shift tomorrow."

"Of course, it's ok," he said. "You can share with Gina as Pat and George have the spare room."

"Great," said Sammie and started tucking into her dinner.

Gina looked round the table; everyone she really loved was there enjoying Christmas dinner together. Her family really were her safety blanket and she felt really happy at that moment.

Abby had set her alarm early on Christmas day; there was lots to do at the hotel today and she needed to prep. She got up, showered, dressed and went downstairs. She stood for a moment and admired the reception tree. It was 8ft and fully decorated, such a nice welcome for the guests.

She went into the dining room; Oliver and Peter were already there.

"Merry Christmas," she said. "You're up early I see."

"Merry Christmas, Abby," replied Oliver. "Just prepping the breakfast for the guests before we start on the dinner preparations."

Abby only had a few guests booked in for Christmas; four rooms only, otherwise, it was too much for her and Oliver to cope with. Harry had always helped when he was alive but now she had to rely on Neil, who she noticed wasn't up yet; 'typical' she thought.

Guests were served breakfast in their rooms on Christmas morning so that the dining room could be prepped for lunch. The guests had full English and a glass of Bucks Fizz delivered to their doors at 9 am. by Peter. Bless Peter for working Christmas day; he was such a loyal member of staff.

Oliver was plating the breakfasts and putting them on a trolley and Peter was pouring the Bucks Fizz before he made his way to the lift.

Abby gave the rest of the staff the day off and invited them and their families for Christmas dinner if they weren't visiting their own families.

There were a few of them this year. Sheila and Gregg were away together for a few days. Steven and Jenny were visiting Jennie's family for the day and Keith was going to his mum's for the day. So, there would be Derek and Paul the maintenance staff, Carol and her husband Derek, Tracy, Roger and the two girls, Annie and Katherine, Janice, Peter, eight guests, Oliver, Neil and herself. *Twenty-one for dinner* then, she thought, she had better start on the table preparations.

"How many for dinner today, Abby?" Oliver asked.

"Twenty-one in total," she said, "19 adults and Tracy's two girls."

"Great," said Oliver. "Love cooking for a big crowd."

"What menu did you decide on?" Abby always left the meal planning to Oliver. He was, after all, an expert in his field.

"Prawn and crab cocktail or pate for starters, beef or turkey dinner, or even both if required dinner and I have made a trifle for dessert or profiteroles," he said.

"Sound divine," said Abby. "What about Janice, is she not vegetarian?"

"Nut roast already prepped for Janice," he winked.

Abby smiled. "Of course, it is." She smiled.

Abby set about table planning, the eight guests would all have a table for two each, Tracy, Roger and the girls needed a table for four. Then, she would do a table for four and a table for five for the staff, including herself and Neil.

She set about moving the tables around and decorating them. *Where is Neil?* She thought. *I need him to start on the lounge.*

Neil woke with a start and looked at his watch.

"Bloody hell, it is 9:30," he said out loud. "Abby is going to kill me."

He hadn't slept well the night before. He couldn't get Gina out of his mind at all. He missed her so much and was terrified she wouldn't come back. He had wanted to call her so badly to wish her a Merry Christmas but she had said no contact and Abby had told him to leave her alone for a while or he would make matters worse. *Worse? How can they get worse?* He thought. *The love of my life has left and I don't know if she's coming back, how can it get worse.*

Did she miss him? Did she even think about him now? What was she doing? Had she opened her gift from him? He so wanted to know the answers to all these questions but he knew he had to wait.

He had sent her the watch with the note to show her just how much she meant to him. He had found her address on her personnel file. Abby wouldn't have been happy if she knew, but he had to do something! He was going out of his mind.

He wasn't feeling very festive at all but he knew he had better get downstairs and start helping. It was the same every year since Harry had died, Abby, Oliver and himself all worked hard in the morning so everyone could enjoy their day. He had to admit Abby did go to a lot of effort to make it special for everyone and they did have a great afternoon after lunch was over, although he suspected it wouldn't feel so great this year.

Neil made his way downstairs. Abby was busy in the dining room and Oliver and Peter were busy in the kitchen.

"Merry Christmas, Abby, Where do you want me?" He said.

"Can you start putting the presents under the tree in the lounge for after lunch?" She said. "There are two sacks in my office."

"Two sacks!" Neil said. "How many have you bought?"

"We have the kiddies here today, so there's a few for them and one for everyone else," she replied.

"Ok, I'm on it," Neil said and turned to leave.

"When you've done that, you can help out in the kitchen and when you are around our guests, you will paint a smile on that face, Neil," said Abby.

Neil went to the office. He wasn't looking forward to being in such close proximity with Oliver while he was in his kitchen. Oliver would lord it over him and pick fault with everything he did but he knew he would have to do it, it was tradition!

When Neil had finished placing the presents under the tree, he made his way back to the dining room. He had to admit Abby had certainly made a grand job of it; it all looked beautiful. He went into the kitchen where Oliver, Peter and now Abby were all busy prepping food.

"What can I do to help?" Neil asked.

"Leave?" Oliver said.

"I'm not having any of this nonsense today," shouted Abby. "You two will put aside your differences for today and work together to make this day special for everyone as we always do; you two will not ruin it."

"Sorry," said Oliver. "Neil, start on the carrots."

"Great," thought Neil, peeling carrots was not his bag at all but he got the sack and made a start.

"Oliver and Neil didn't converse much. They got on with their jobs and before long, everything was prepped and ready to be plated when the guest arrived in the dining room. Lunch was to be at 1:30 and it was 1:45 so they had made good time with everything."

"The food looks great," Neil begrudgingly said to Oliver. He couldn't deny Oliver was an excellent chef.

"Thanks," said Oliver. "Appreciate the comment."

Progress thought Neil, he hadn't snapped his head off. He so wanted to make it up to Oliver. He had been his best friend for years and he missed him a lot. He supposed he would have to just chip away until maybe one day, they could be civil to each other again.

"Right," said Abby. "I think we all deserve a drink before the rush starts, I will fetch the brandy we need and we will have it in the dining room."

Abby went off to fetch the brandy and glasses when all of a sudden there was a huge crash from the kitchen. Oliver rushed in and Neil followed him; the whole kitchen floor was covered in sprouts!

"What the hell happened?" Oliver shouted at Peter.

"I'm so sorry," cried Peter, "I was trying to lift the saucepan to add a bit more water and the whole thing dropped to the floor." He was standing there holding the handle of the saucepan.

Neil burst out laughing at the sight of Peter with the handle and the sprouts on the floor.

"This is not funny," shouted Oliver.

"Well, it kind of is." Neil laughed.

Oliver looked again at the scene and all three of them burst out laughing. When they composed themselves, Oliver said, "Right, Peter, get this mess cleared up. Neil, fetch the rest of the sprouts; we had better start peeling!"

Neil was feeling a bit happier inside. It had taken an incident to get them to laugh together but it was a good sign. Inwardly, Oliver was feeling the same.

When Abby returned with the brandy, she looked at the three of them in the kitchen and squealed.

"What on earth happened here?" She cried.

"It's all under control," Oliver laughed. "Go into the dining room and pour the brandy, we will be in shortly."

Abby poured four brandy and sat down; she took a sip while looking around the decorated room. She was pleased with the efforts and she was always pleased to see Neil and Oliver working together; it was going to be a good day.

The guests started to arrive in the dining room at 1:20 pm. "Merry Christmas," smiled Abby as she showed them to their tables. "There a glass of prosecute for each of you, lunch will be served when everyone is here."

"The room looks amazing as always," said Ruth, one of the guests. She and her husband Ralph came every Christmas; they had never had children and always enjoyed their Christmases at the Haven Hotel.

"Thank you," smiled Abby. "We aim to please."

"Oh you always do that," replied Ruth.

More guests arrived and were seated until everyone was there sipping their drinks.

"Ok," shouted Abby to get everyone's attention. "Merry Christmas to you all and welcome to the Haven's Christmas day. We all hope you have a fabulous day. Lunch will be served shortly, then you will all be invited into the hotel's lounge for drinks and present opening."

"We have presents," squealed one of Tracy's girls Annie.

"You certainly do," laughed Abby. "But only if you eat your lunch first."

Tracy mouthed a thank you towards Abby and Abby smiled back at her.

"On your table, there is a menu. You all have one each with your name on so if you could tick your choices, I will come around and collect them and we can get started."

Lunch was a great success, everyone complimented the food that Oliver had cooked and how well-presented it was. Oliver was in his element; he was a fantastic chef and he loved his job and he loved it when people enjoyed his food.

Abby was proud of Oliver, Neil and Peter for their hard work; everything had gone really smoothly and Neil had kept a smile on his face through lunch. Oliver and Neil had even exchanged a few words which pleased her immensely.

After lunch, they all went into the lounge and Abby poured them all a drink. "Oliver, Neil and I are just going to clear the dining room while you enjoy a drink then when we return we will do presents."

Oliver, Neil and Abby went to clear up and Peter followed too.

"More hands will do it quicker," he said.

"Thank you, Peter," said Oliver.

They cleared up pretty quickly and returned to the lounge.

"Oliver, Neil and Peter, what would you like to drink? You deserve a rest now for the rest of today."

She poured their drinks and then gave everyone a present with extra for the children.

Everyone was so grateful to her for her kindness. After all, she hadn't charged them for dinner so to add presents as well was truly generous. They all loved their gifts and the children played happily with their new dolls while the adults sat around chatting.

Janice got up. "Abby, we have a gift for you, we all put together so you could have one nice gift rather than lots of small ones, we hope you like it."

Abby took the present. It was heavy. She opened it and tears started to roll down her eyes at their kindness. It was a beautiful clock with a picture of the hotel on the clock face and 'the Haven Hotel' engraved on the wooden surround. "Thank you so much," she sobbed. "I absolutely love it." She was just so happy they had chosen to put the hotel on the face, she would treasure it.

The rest of the afternoon passed happily; everyone was chatting and drinking. The TV was playing in the background but no one was really watching it. Neil was talking to the guest and a couple of the older guests had nodded off. Abby looked around; *'almost perfect'* she thought happily; she missed Gina too.

By early evening, most of the guests had either left or gone to their rooms, they had all complimented them on such a wonderful day and Abby was buzzing but also tired. She had been up early and worked hard so decided she would also go to her room to watch TV.

Only Neil and Oliver were left in the dining room.

"I am genuinely sorry that that girl turned up and ruined things for you and Gina," Oliver said suddenly. "Gina was good for you, even I saw a change in you."

"Yeah, I'm sorry too. I do genuinely love her and I'm scared she won't come back after the holiday," sighed Neil.

"Have you called her?"

"She told me not to; she needed space and time to think."

"And you listened?" Oliver replied shocked.

"Yes, I did, she means too much for me to ruin it further."

"Maybe she'll call after Christmas," Oliver said. "I do genuinely hope she comes back for you."

"Thank you," replied Neil, shocked by Oliver's quick turnaround. "If Gina does come back, things will be almost perfect."

"Almost?" Oliver asked.

"I miss my best friend," said Neil sadly.

"So do I," replied Oliver. "We have been stupid, haven't we? Neither of us was to blame, we didn't know what was going on."

"No, we didn't," said Neil. "We were both hurt and took it out on each other."

"Let's put it behind us and start again," said Oliver.

They both stood up and hugged each other. "I've missed you,", they both said at the same time and laughed.

"Missed you too," said Neil. "I think I'm going to head up now; it's been a long day. So happy to have you back, bro."

"Me too," said Oliver. "Let's start afresh."

They both made their way to their rooms. Oliver was smiling; he had hated falling out with Neil and in hindsight, it wasn't his fault what Linda did any more than it was his. He was glad to have him back.

Neil entered his room and flopped onto the bed. He was happy that he and Oliver had made up. It had been a good day, now if he could just get Gina back, life would be perfect.

Edna woke up Christmas morning and immediately, a dark cloud came over her. Annabel had been evil since they returned home last week and when she was evil, she was evil. That is when she was talking to her at all. She despaired of her she really did; what she had tried to do to that lad was another level even for Annabel.

They had gotten the taxi to the train station and when they got out, Annabel had said she was going back. She wasn't prepared to leave the father of her child. *The girl was deluded*, thought Edna, *everyone knew it couldn't be Neil's but there was no telling her.*

Edna had finally persuaded her again to get the train home so Dr George and the hospital could look after her during her pregnancy and unbelievably, she had agreed again. Annabel had nipped to the toilet; Edna was scared she was going to disappear again but when she went to go with her, Annabel had shouted at her so loud that all the people on the platform had turned to see what was going on. Embarrassed, Edan stayed put but took the opportunity to call Dr George to tell him she was bringing Annabel home and she was not in a good place.

"I will see her tomorrow," he said. "And we will see if we can get an urgent scan to determine how far along she is, then we will know."

"Thank you, doctor," said Edna seeing Annabel coming back. "I have to go now, we will see you tomorrow."

Annabel never spoke another word to Edna on the journey home. It was a long journey and the train was full of people returning from Christmas shopping or going to visit relatives. Edna was on edge the entire time, scared Annabel would kick off in front of them all, so she didn't speak to Annabel at all. *What a way to have to live*, thought Edna, but they remained silent for the whole journey.

When the train pulled in, they called for a taxi home where Annabel went straight to her room without a word. Edna let her go, thankful for a bit of quiet time before tomorrow.

When she got up the next morning, Annabel was in the kitchen.

"You have an appointment with Dr George today," said Edna.

"What for?" Annabel growled.

"He's going to get you a scan, so you know how far you are gone."

"I know how far I am gone," shouted Annabel. "You are just jealous because my baby will have a good father and I will have a good husband unlike you did."

Edna ignored her daughter's vicious tongue and said, "But if you know for sure, Neil won't be able to argue, will he?"

Annabel went quiet. "I suppose," she said. "What time is the appointment?"

"2 pm," said Edna.

Edna went with her; Dr George checked her over and the scan was booked for the next day.

"Everything feels in order," he said. "your scan is booked for 10 am, so I will see you at 2 pm again tomorrow, so we can discuss the results."

"Will they be able to tell me what it is?" Annabel asked.

"You may not be far enough along for that," he said.

"I'm eight weeks," said Annabel aggressively.

"Well, if you are eight weeks, they might be able to tell you, let's see what the scan gives us."

"Thank you, doctor," said Edna and they left. Annabel did not speak to her mother again that day.

After the scan, Edna asked Annabel if she wanted to go shopping with her.

"I'm going nowhere with you," growled Annabel. "You are ruining my life."

"Annabel," said Edna exasperated. "I am not trying to ruin your life. I am trying to help you and stop you from getting hurt."

But Annabel wasn't listening; she went to the bus stop to wait for the bus home. Edna went and got her shopping, then headed to the GP surgery to wait for her.

Annabel was late for her appointment but Dr George knew her well. She would think if she was late, he wouldn't be able to see her but he made time to see her at 2:45 pm.

"I've got your results, Annabel," he said.

"I'm eight weeks, aren't I? When Neil was here."

"I'm afraid not," said Dr George. "You are only six weeks gone. You got pregnant well after Neil left."

"Liar," she shouted. "You are lying. Did he put you up to this so he hasn't got to take responsibility? He's not getting away with it. You are all lying for him."

"We're not lying," said the doctor, "here's your scan and it says clearly at the top, six weeks pregnant; it's also too early to determine the sex of the baby."

"The scan is wrong," said Annabel, crying now in anger. "The scan is wrong and you are lying."

She stormed out of the doctor's surgery and ran up the road.

"I'm sorry, doctor," sighed Edna. "I don't know how this is going to end, we know it can't be Neil's and she made such a show of herself at that hotel. I just hope she'll believe it when we do the DNA after it is born. I don't even know how she will look after it."

"Sadly, we will have to assess that situation when it comes," he said.

Edna left the surgery. There was no sign of Annabel and she wasn't at home either when she arrived. Edna shook her head; *if life wasn't bad enough before*, she thought, *it's going to get a hell of a lot worse, I can feel it.*

Annabel arrived home at about 6 pm, went to her room and came back down dressed up for a night out.

"Don't bother waiting up for me." Annabel laughed at her mother. "I may not be back." She winked.

Oh no, some other poor soul being pulled into her web, thought Edna, *will this ever end?*

Edna was prepping Christmas dinner when Annabel came downstairs.

"I'm not staying in for dinner," announced Annabel.

"What? Where are you going?" Edna said.

"Anywhere but here with you, why would I spend Christmas day with someone who lies to me and ruins my whole life!" shouted Annabel almost in Edna's face.

"Annabel," pleaded Edna but Annabel was gone.

Edna sat at the table and sobbed. Christmas were never great with Annabel but this was way worse. Edna would be on her own and it would be like any other day. She had no one else coming; she couldn't invite people around in case Annabel kicked off. She didn't know how much more of this she could take.

This was the worst she had ever seen her daughter. She had never been pregnant before and Edna thought this may trigger her mental health more than before when she was committed. She was definitely heading off the rails again and sleeping around.

What is going to happen to this baby? She thought with despair; *Annabel is no mother and I'm too old to bring up another baby. Annabel is convinced it is Neil's and they are going to live happily ever after which is never going to happen even if the baby could have been his. It was clear to see he loved that other girl at the hotel and he would never want to be with Annabel when he saw who she really was. He told her straight he wasn't leaving with her even if the baby was his. When her plan doesn't work, it's going to push her over the edge again she knew it. It wasn't going to end well at all, definitely not for Annabel and herself anyway.*

Chapter 20

Back to Haven Hotel

Monday morning arrived and Gina was nervous about calling Abby. She desperately wanted to know what had happened since she left but she was anxious about what she may hear.

What if Neil had decided to go to the Sunny Cottage with Annabel? After all, Gina had simply packed and left him there so he may have decided to go with her. *No*, she thought, *he was really mean to her, he wouldn't do that if he wanted to be with her and everyone at the hotel had told Gina how he felt about her and how good she was for him.*

"You are torturing yourself," said her mum. "Just make the call and put yourself out of your misery. At least then you will know and you can plan your next steps."

"You're right," Gina sighed. "Do or die time," and she picked up her phone and called Abby.

"Gina!" Abby screamed when she answered. "Oh, I am so glad you called. I have so much to tell you but we left you alone as you requested. I really wanted to call you last week to fill you in though."

"Hi, Abby," replied Gina nervously. "I've been afraid to call for fear of what I might hear."

"I get that," said Abby "but you are going to have a surprise, a good one I hope, that's why I was desperate to call."

"What happened?" Gina questioned.

"What happened?" Abby laughed. "Talk about a turn-up for the books."

She proceeded to tell her about Annabel failing to go to the doctor's appointment Abby had arranged and the mouthful she got off her when she said she would make another. Then she told her about Edna arriving at the hotel.

"That went down like a lead balloon," said Abby. "Annabel was not pleased to see her mother at all. Edna told her she had seen their own GP and he had told her that Annabel was about three to four weeks pregnant when he saw her, so it couldn't possibly be Neil's as he was back at the hotel then. Edna told us all about her; said she has mental health problems and apparently, sleeps with most of the men that pass through. Some other poor bugger is going to get it when she finally realises it's nothing to do with Neil."

"How did she take that news?" Gina asked.

"Not well," replied Abby. "Kept saying everyone was wrong and it was Neil's. We all finally persuaded her to go home so her own GP could monitor her and we promised to send Neil's DNA when the baby is born; of course, we won't need to do that but we couldn't get rid of her without that promise. Oh, Gina, it's been a right rigmarole."

"So it's definitely not Neil's," Gina said, her spirits lifting considerably.

"No, it's definitely not Neil's, Gina."

"What about the way he left her though, with a note? He could do that to me one day."

"My dear Gina. Neil has a reason for that and I do believe him but it's up to him to explain to you. He is dying to see or hear from you; he's been like a wet lettuce since you've gone. He would never leave you like that, Gina; he is actually a changed man and he loves you, did you not receive the gift he sent?"

"I did," said Gina. "I was a surprise but it was lovely of him and I do love him too, Abby. This all just came as a shock and so early on in our relationship."

"I know," sighed Abby. "The timing was crap, I'll agree, but will you at least talk to him, Gina?"

"Yes, I will," Gina replied. "But not on the phone, I will talk to him when I come back. Is it ok to start back to work next Monday?"

"Yes," Abby squealed. "Thank god, of course, you can start back and have your old room back. Neil will be so happy that you are coming back. I'm so excited, I can see a great future for you two."

"Steady on." Gina laughed. "It's early days."

"I know," giggled Abby. "I'm just so happy you're coming back. Please come back for New Year, Gina. We are having a party at the hotel on New Year's Eve and it would mean so much to Neil for you to be here, and me, of course."

"New Year's Eve is Friday. What if I come back on Thursday to settle in first and catch up with Neil?" Gina said.

"Perfect," said Abby. "Oh, one more thing, Neil and Oliver have made up."

"Really!" said Gina. "That is good news after how close they were years ago."

"It's very good news," replied Abby. "I'm not sure how it came about and I've not asked. I'm just happy to see them getting on now."

"Do me one favour," Gina asked. "Ask Neil to let me settle in first on Thursday and I will see him in the evening. I don't want him to pounce on me the minute I get there."

"Consider it done," said Abby happily. "I can't wait to see you."

"Me too," said Gina. "Bye, Abby."

Gina ended the call and smiled.

"Everything ok?" Her mum smiled.

"I think everything is going to be perfect," Gina smiled back at her. "You don't mind me not being here for New Year. Do you, Mum."

"Gina," laughed Kathleen. "Me and your dad will just sit in and watch the television with a glass of sherry; your dad will be asleep before the New Year chimes in. You go to where you belong now; you have a new future to build."

Gina got up and hugged her mum with happy tears stinging her eyes.

"Thanks, Mum, I love you."

"And I love you right back," smiled Kathleen.

Monday morning, Henry took Gina to the train station. She couldn't believe how happy she felt to be going back. She wasn't sure what she was going to say to Neil. She actually felt a bit guilty about leaving like she did. She almost felt like she'd abandoned him when he needed her. She had panicked that she was sure of, and probably because of how she'd been hurt in the past but she knew she had to start trusting again one day and she hoped with all her heart that Neil was the one she could do that with.

She had really missed him; Christmas day had gone better than she thought it would but she had still missed him and couldn't wait to see him. She was doubting she'd done the right thing by asking Abby to tell him to leave her alone for a few hours when she got there as she really couldn't wait to see him.

No, she thought, she would need to get herself sorted before she saw him; there was plenty of time especially since they were going to have a future together. A smile spread across her face at the thought.

Her phone ringing disturbed her thoughts; she didn't recognise the number but answered it anyway.

"Hello," she said.

"Gina, it is Mike Johnson," said the caller.

"Oh hello, Mike, is everything ok?" She asked.

"Yes, all good," he said. "I just wanted to let you know that a bailiff went to the prison this morning and served the order on David and also handed him his divorce papers."

"Oh, that was quick," said Gina surprised. "What happens now?"

"We have to wait to see if he contests it or not. He won't get anywhere if he does after what he's done but it could delay things just a little. If he doesn't contest, you could be divorced in six to eight weeks."

"And if he contests it?" Gina asked.

"Well, it will go to a judge and he will say whether he upholds the contentment or not, that can take three to four weeks. No judge will uphold it though, Gina, with the crimes he's committed but I'll keep you up with any changes as they happen."

"Thank you, Mike, I appreciate it," she said.

"No problem, Gina, bye for now," and he was gone.

That was quick and sounded promising, she thought as she put her phone away. "Goodbye, David, hello new life."

As the taxi pulled up at the hotel, Gina was still in awe at how large the place was with the land surrounding the hotel and the gardens that were truly beautiful. She could hear the waves of the sea and that warm glow that had engulfed her on her first day. It really was good to be back.

She started making her way up the path and was met by a man in a uniform that she didn't recognise.

"Hello, Miss Gina," he said, "I am Troy, the new day porter."

"Oh," said Gina. "We never had a day porter before."

"I know," he said. "Mrs Adams said it was a new post. I only started this morning. Please, let me take your things, ma'am."

"Please call me Gina, we will be working together after all."

Troy smiled. "Let me take your things, Gina."

"Thank you," she smiled back; he seemed really nice for a young lad, "and welcome to the team."

Troy smiled and started walking up the path with her to the hotel.

They went inside and she could see Abby at the reception.

"Gina," she squealed and ran around to give her a big hug. "I am so happy to see you."

"Me too," said Gina. "But I'm struggling to breathe."

Abby let her go, and they laughed. Gina looked around.

"I've sent Neil into town to run a few errands, it'll give you a chance to settle back in."

Gina was slightly disappointed and then told herself she had asked Abby to tell him not to bother her as soon as she arrived.

"Do you want a drink or something to eat before you go to unpack?" Abby asked.

"No, thank you," replied Gina. "I think I'll go to my room and shower first before anyone sees me, otherwise it may take some time to get there."

"Good idea," said Abby. "Troy, could you take Gina's things to her room, please?"

"Of course, Mrs Adams," replied Troy, picking up Gina's bags and headed for the lift.

"New job role?" Gina questioned.

"Yes," said Abby. "I want to alleviate some of Neil's duties. I need him more for the garden and maintenance. Troy only started this morning but has settled well and seems to be doing a good job."

"Oh, I see," said Gina. "Yes he is a nice lad, I think the guests will like him very much."

Both of them suddenly heard Sheila and Tracy talking in the corridor.

"I'm going to make a quick getaway before they see me," said Gina, "otherwise, I'll be here ages and I really need a shower after that journey. I'll catch up with everyone later."

"Go," said Abby. "I won't tell them you've arrived yet; they are all excited to see you."

Gina walked into her old room; it felt so good. She had missed this too and her job. She loved her job and meeting all the guests that arrived and she loved her room.

Gina let the shower water run over her; it was heaven after the long train journey. She was so happy at this moment; she stayed in there for ages.

When she got out, she dressed, applied makeup and styled her hair. Yes, she was making an effort when she saw Neil but so what, she wanted to feel good about herself. She was nervous inside but would feel more confident if she knew she looked good. She felt like she was going on a first date, like a teenager getting ready for their first big romance. It was a bit daft really because she had been seeing Neil for a while before she left and they hadn't really split up as such; just took a break, but even so, she was excited again to see him.

When she was happy with her efforts, she made her way downstairs, Abby was still at the reception.

"How was your Christmas, by the way?" Abby asked,

"It was lovely," Gina replied and told her all about her aunt and uncle and her best friend Sammie.

"Sammie must come and visit one day; in fact, all your family should," said Abby. "They will be my guests, so no payments are required. I'm surprised they haven't been before Christmas."

"That would be lovely," smiled Gina. "One day, they will." She couldn't really tell her they hadn't been because they were scared of being trailed and David finding out where she was so she just added, "They are not good at travelling but one day, they will come and stay. How was Christmas here?" Gina asked.

"Oh, it all went well, everyone seemed to enjoy it, even our Neil painted a smile on his face when I told him." She laughed. "It was Christmas day that he and Oliver made up, so although he was missing you very much, he had one positive from it and now you're back to make him whole again." She smiled.

"Let's hope so," said Gina.

"Everyone is in the staff dining room if you're hungry, they will love to see you, go and surprise them."

"I will," said Gina happily and started walking down the corridor.

"Was that Gina I heard?" Neil said, entering the reception.

"Yes, it was, she's gone to catch up with everyone and have a snack after her long journey. Leave her be for now; she will catch up with you later. Did you make that dinner reservation?"

"Yes, of course," he said. "Do you think she'll be up for it?"

"Oh, I think she'll definitely be up for it," replied Abby. "Why don't you go and shower and get ready then when Gina is finished, you can be waiting for her here in the reception."

"Good idea," he said. "It'll keep me occupied until I can see her. I can't wait. I have missed her so much."

"Gina!" shouted Sheila as Gina walked into the dining room. "It's so good to see you back. We all wondered if you would come back after what happened."

"Yes, I'm back and it's good to see you all," Gina said.

Everyone came to give her a hug and they were chatting about their Christmases.

"Abby did us proud again," said Tracy, "the girls had the best day."

"Oh, that's lovely, I'm glad they enjoyed themselves," Gina smiled.

"Would you like a sandwich, Gina?" Oliver asked.

"Oh yes, please," she said. "I'm starving after the journey."

"Ham salad, do you?" He asked.

"Perfect," she replied.

Oliver made her sandwich and sat next to her. "Have you seen Neil yet?" He asked.

"Not yet," replied Gina, "he was in town when I arrived and I thought I would catch up with all of you first. What are your thoughts on what happened, Oliver?"

"The girl is twisted, Gina. There was no way the baby could be Neil's if what her mother said was right about her dates. What she did to Neil was unfair."

"I heard you two have made up, I am happy about that."

"I should think so," said Carol. "Falling out over something where none of you did wrong."

"Water under the bridge now, Carol, let's just leave it there," said Oliver.

"Yes," said Carol. "Best place for it."

Oliver turned back to Gina. "Yes, we have started to rebuild our friendship, it will take time but we will get there. Neil has changed a lot since you came along, even I can see it, and I really hope you two can sort things out."

"Me too," said Gina. "I really like him and I really missed him when I was away."

"Well, get that sandwich, missy and go find him. I'm sure he wants to see you as much as you want to see him."

Gina ate her sandwich and gave everyone another hug, then left the dining room. Walking up the corridor, she could hear Neil's voice; he was talking to Abby at the reception. When she saw him, he didn't see her straight away so she took a moment to drink him in. He was so handsome, with his dark hair and chiselled features. She wondered how she had got so lucky. If they could make up tonight, she was going to do anything rather than lose him.

Neil looked up and saw Gina. He almost ran to her and scooped her up off the floor. "Oh, Gina, I have missed you so much. I am so happy you came back. I thought I had lost you and I couldn't bear that," he said putting her down.

"I missed you too, Neil," she said, "more than I thought I actually could. Can we go somewhere a bit more private to chat?"

"Use my private lounge," Abby said. "You won't be disturbed in there."

Neil took her hand and started leading the way. Abby smiled to herself. She was happy to see them back together and she was pretty sure, Gina was going to be in her life for a good time to come which pleased her immensely.

Gina sat down on the sofa while Neil poured them each a glass of champagne.

"Champagne," laughed Gina. "This goes straight to my head."

"I am celebrating you being back here," said Neil. "I really have missed you so much. Did you get my gift?"

"I did," said Gina. "It is beautiful." She lifted her wrist to show him she was wearing it.

"And the note—too much?" He asked.

"No," said Gina. "It did surprise me but also made me very happy."

"Good," said Neil. "I was scared it may frighten you off but I really needed to let you know how I felt about you, Gina. You changed me for the better and I really do love you. I have been thinking about our future together and it looks pretty goddamn good."

Future, Gina thought, *presumptuous of him but it did make her happy to think of having a future with him.*

"What about Annabel? What if the baby is yours? How will we work it?" She asked.

"Gina, did Abby not tell you that it can't be mine based on her weeks? I only agreed to get DNA after it is born to get rid of her," he sighed.

"Yes, Abby did tell me about Edna coming here and what her own GP had said. She also told me she suffered from mental health problems," said Gina.

"Yes, and according to her mother, she sleeps with almost all the guys that pass through Sunny Cottage, so it could be anyone's," he said.

"So, why did she fixate on you? Did you promise her anything when you were staying there and then just left her?" She asked.

"No, Gina, it wasn't like that. I stayed at the cottage she and her mother ran, a lovely little place actually and she used to show me the local area. We would have a few drinks together and she introduced me to Alf who gave me a temporary job. I needed to earn some money to pay my board," he explained.

"And the way you left?" Gina questioned.

"One night, we went for some food and she insisted we go to a club afterwards. We had a few drinks; a few too many drinks actually, and I'm ashamed to admit, we slept together that night. I was single at the time, so I wasn't hurting anyone, but when I woke up in the morning, I realised my mistake. I knew I would never commit to a relationship with Annabel at that time. In fact, I wouldn't have committed to a relationship with anyone back then. I didn't want her to become attached to me, so I thought the easiest thing would be to slip away quietly before she woke. I left a note, yes, but I fully explained my reasons; I didn't know she had issues or I would never have got involved with her at all."

"Well, hopefully, when the baby is born and you send DNA, she will understand it is not yours," Gina said.

"It's definitely not mine Gina," he said.

She looked into his eyes; he was telling the truth she could tell and she had a sudden urge to kiss him. She leaned over and kissed him hard and he took no persuading to respond back to her.

"Just one more question," she said. "Why did you go away in the first place?"

"There's nothing sinister there and I will tell you everything, Gina, but can we leave it for another time as I have booked your favourite Italian for 8 pm."

"Ok," said Gina, "you've won me over with the Italian. Let's go and enjoy the meal and look forward to the party tomorrow."

"You will be coming with me, won't you?" Neil asked.

"Of course, why wouldn't I be going with the love of my life." She winked at him and he smiled.

"That's so good to hear. I love you, Gina Taylor."

"I love you too, Neil Adams," she smiled. "Let's get out of here."

On the morning of New Year's Eve, everyone was busy getting things ready for the party. The Christmas guests were still there; they would be leaving on the 2nd and having breakfast in the dining room. When breakfast was done, Oliver, Janice and Peter would be preparing the buffet for the evening.

Gina came downstairs and asked Abby what she could do to help.

"We've pretty much got it covered, everyone has their jobs and it's all going to plan," said Abby. "We have 40 people coming in total, so it should be a good party."

"40!" Gina laughed. "Will they all fit in?"

"Easy," smiled Abby. "All the staff will be here with their partners and children, the guests who are staying and a few friends."

"Sounds great," said Gina. "Are you sure there is nothing I can do to help?"

"No, we are all good," said Abby. "I haven't seen my brother this morning, I take it last night went well." She smiled at Gina. "Are you two back on?"

"Yes, we are back on but we didn't spend the night together!" replied Gina. "I haven't seen him this morning either."

Abby laughed. "Just pulling your leg," she said. "He's gone into town to get extra booze for tonight. He looked very happy this morning."

"We had a lovely evening," said Gina. "We straightened a few things out and things are good now," she smiled.

"I'm so happy to hear that," said Abby. "He's changed since he met you and for the better."

With that, Neil came through the front door with a trolley full of boxes.

"Morning," he said, smiling at Gina.

"Morning," she smiled back.

"I'll get this into the lounge and lay it out, then how about we grab some lunch in town later?" He said.

"Sounds great," Gina said. "As long as everything is done here ready for tonight."

"Don't worry about that," said Abby. "I told you we have it covered."

"See you about 12:30 here," said Neil and pushed the trolley into the lounge.

Edna was having a cup of tea at the dining table in Sunny Cottage when Annabel came through and went straight out without so much as a good morning.

New Year's Eve, she thought, *and I'm probably going to be alone again. Where had she gone so early again*? Life had been hell since they had returned from the Haven Hotel. If Annabel had spoken to her at all, it was to shout at her. Annabel was still really angry that she had turned up for her and resented her more than ever it seemed.

It had been a bleak Christmas for Edna; Christmases had never been great since Annabel had grown up with her issues but this one was the worst ever. She had hardly seen a soul all week; her friends were busy with their own families over the festive period, so Edna had pretty much spent the week alone. *Where did Annabel keep going and how was she affording to stay out all the time? Was this her life now*, she thought, she really hoped it would improve but at the moment she couldn't see a way through it all.

Edna decided she would go for a walk; it was cold out but the fresh air would do her good and if she went to town she could do a bit of shopping while she was out. She took her cup to the sink and headed off to get her coat.

Meanwhile, Annabel was heading into town; she needed to get some money so she could go out that evening. She had found the perfect way to make a few pounds each day and it took little effort as long as she wrapped up warm.

I hate my mother, she thought, *I could have made a life with Neil and the baby; his family had money, so she would never have to work, but no, her stupid mother had to turn up before she had a chance to win him over*. She was so angry with Edna that she had purposely set out to ruin her Christmas and New Year by leaving her on her own. She knew that Edna's friends would be busy over the festive period doing things with their families, so the stupid bitch had spent all week in Sunny Cottage alone, ha.

They didn't take guests in over Christmas as Edna had always said that week should be for them to be together. *Sod that*, thought Annabel, *she wasn't spending time with the scheming bitch.*

There was still time to get to Neil, she smiled to herself, when this kid is born, he will have to take his responsibilities seriously. That whore he was with needed destroying. Gina was her name but she didn't know her surname—yet, she would find out and do some digging on her. There had to be some way to bring her down.

Ok, it wasn't Neil's child she was carrying, going on the number of weeks she was pregnant. It was probably that Alan or Wayne that had passed through but what the hell, Neil didn't know that and she would convince him to come to her and they could be a proper family or even better, she could move into the hotel and be waited on hand and foot. Yes, she liked the idea of that but in the meantime, she had to make her own money.

Edna was just walking up the high street just as she spotted Annabel putting a board in front of her. She was sitting on a bench and it was freezing. *What on earth is she doing?* Edna thought as she made her way towards her. As she approached, she could see a bowl on the floor; she looked at the board Annabel had placed there. It read:

Homeless, please spare a pound to help me get food.

"Annabel! What on earth are you doing, you are not homeless and people from around here know that."

"Get lost," said Annabel angrily. "It's none of your business."

"But why on earth are you doing this?" Edna cried. "It's not true and you will catch your death of cold out here. Is this where you have been coming all week?"

Annabel repeated, "It is none of your business."

"Please, come home, Annabel," begged Edna. "There is no need for this."

"I need to make some money to go out tonight, now get lost." Annabel was getting angrier each second.

"I can give you money to go out," Edna said.

"I don't want anything from you and I'm not walking anywhere with you, now get lost!" said Annabel gritting her teeth.

Edna knew when to quit; she started to walk away. This was a new low for her daughter; things were steadily getting worse and worse.

It was 6:30 pm and the guests had started to arrive at the hotel for the party. The paying guests were already in the lounge, chatting and drinking. Gina was directing the arriving guests to the lounge and getting them a drink, Neil was in charge of the music; Oliver, Janice and Peter were laying out the buffet in the dining room and the other staff had left earlier to get ready to return with their families.

The atmosphere was already lovely thought Gina; it was going to be a great night. Neil kept glancing over at her and winking; she smiled back at him and kept serving the drinks. Abby was chatting to all the guests as they arrived and welcoming them to the hotel to see the New Year with them.

By 7:30 pm, everyone had arrived and they were all in good spirits. The children were dancing with each other to the music Neil was playing and Gina was mingling. Some of Abby's friends hadn't met her before so she went over to introduce herself.

"Oh, Abby has told me all about you," said her friend Jenny.

"All good, I hope," Gina laughed.

"All good," replied Jenny. "She told me how much Neil has changed since he met you; she's not had an easy ride with him, so it's good to hear he is settling down."

Gina decided not to pursue 'She's not had an easy ride with him.' But she had already decided that if they were to have a future together, he needed to be straight with her about his past and she had to be honest about hers. She wasn't looking forward to reliving that but she didn't want any skeletons in either of their cupboards.

She mingled a bit more then she went over to Neil. "Hi, gorgeous," he said and gave her a kiss.

"Hi yourself," she smiled. "It's all going well, isn't it?"

"Always does," he said. "Our Abby knows how to throw a party, that's for sure; I can't wait to see the new year in with you later, new year, new start for both of us."

"Sounds good to me," smiled Gina.

"Gina! Come and have a dance." It was Sheila calling her. She and racy were on the makeshift dance floor that Abby had instructed the maintenance guys to construct. She really had thought of everything.

She smiled at Neil. "Guess, I'll see you later," she said.

"Go and enjoy yourself, I'll be watching," he winked.

Gina went over to the girls and danced for hours on and off until it was nearly midnight.

"Everyone, make sure you have a drink," shouted Abby. "Only five minutes to go."

Gina and Sheila made sure everyone's drinks were topped up, then went over to Neil.

Abby had put the TV on for the Big Ben chimes. "30 seconds to go," shouted Abby then.

Ten, nine, eight, seven, six, five, four, three, two, one

"Happy New Year," everyone shouted and proceeded to do *Old Lang Syne*. Gina and Neil joined them all and then turned to each other for their New Year's kiss.

"Gina," said Neil seriously. "I need to ask you something."

"Sounds ominous," laughed Gina.

"Depends on what you say," said Neil. "I know we've only just got together but I love you so much and I know I want to spend the rest of our lives together."

Oh, God thought Gina, *is he going to propose*? She had said she would never rush into another marriage after David; she rushed to say yes to him and look how that turned out. She did love her life now and she did love Neil, more than she realised. When they were apart over Christmas, it almost tore her apart so she knew she didn't want to lose him.

"Marry me, Gina," Neil said interrupting her thoughts and producing a beautiful diamond and sapphire engagement ring. "This can be altered if you need it to be."

He has proposed, she thought. Oh god, she was torn; she didn't want to rush things, but she also knew she wanted to be with him forever.

She started to cry. "Oh god," said Neil. "I've upset you, I'm so sorry."

"You haven't upset me, I've just realised that I'm just so happy."

"Is that a yes?" Neil questioned.

"Yes, yes, yes," she said.

"Omg," said Neil slipping the ring on the fourth finger of her left. "You've made me the happiest man on earth."

"It's so beautiful," she said. "And it fits perfectly."

"Just like you and me," he smiled.

"Let's not tell people tonight," said Gina, "it's their night, so let's wait."

"I'd wait for you forever," said Neil wrapping his arms around her.

She snuggled her head into his toned chest; she didn't think she could be any happier.

Gina woke up on New Year's Day and looked at her ring. She was so unbelievably happy; she was getting married—again! *I hope I'm doing the right thing* she thought but she knew she had never been this happy before, not even with David in the early days, she knew it was meant to be.

She thought about her journey to today. She had been married to David when he committed his awful crimes; she had 'run away' miles from home and found a job she absolutely loved and met Neil who she also absolutely loved. It was destiny, she knew it.

When Neil awoke on New Year's Day, he knew he was the luckiest man on earth. His journey today had consisted of lots of mistakes in his life but Gina had arrived at the hotel and turned that messy world on its head. He loved her so much and knew life was going to be great from now on. If she hadn't arrived at the hotel when she did, god knows where he would be now. It was destiny, he knew it.

Gina's phone pinged with a message. "Morning, beautiful," it read.

"Morning, handsome," she replied.

"Fancy breakfast?" The next message read.

"You bet," she answered.

"See you downstairs in 30 minutes," he replied.

Gina showered, got ready and went down to meet Neil; he was already in the staff dining room, and she sat down and joined him.

Janice came over to their table. "Shall I serve you this morning?" She said. "You two did enough last night."

They smiled at each other; they certainly did do enough last night.

"There's no need to wait on us, Janice, I very much enjoyed last night," said Gina grinning. "But thank you for the offer."

"No, it is fine," said Janice. "I've eaten and there are no guests down yet to see too, full English?" She asked.

"That would be great," said Neil. "Thank you, Janice."

"Two full English's coming up," she said as she headed to the kitchen.

"I can't keep having full English's with a wedding dress to fit into," Gina laughed.

"You have a beautiful figure and anyway, we are celebrating today, even if it is our secret," said Neil.

"About that," said Gina. "I think we should tell Abby today before anyone else, after all, I'm wearing an engagement ring. I put my hand under the table when Janice came over, but I don't want to keep hiding it."

"We'll go and see her straight after breakfast," he said. "Once we've told her then we can tell the others know."

Oliver came out with the breakfasts; Gina put her hand under the table. "Morning," said Oliver brightly. "How are we this morning?"

Gina thought how lovely it was that Neil and Oliver had made up, no more unpleasant atmosphere when they were together.

"Top of the world, mate," Said Neil. "How about yourself?"

"Feeling good," replied Oliver. "Got a few days off after today. The guests are going in the morning and Abby's told me I can have a few days to go and see Mum and Dad."

"Oh, how lovely," said Gina. "Do they live far?"

"They live in Stone, Staffordshire, it's a good way, about 4½ hours' drive but if I set off early, I should miss the traffic," he said.

"When will you be back?" Neil asked.

"Friday evening," said Oliver. "Ready for the new arrivals on Saturday."

"Have a great time," said Gina. "Enjoy your time with your family."

"Thanks," said Oliver, "there's a few family members to catch up with, I'm looking forward to it."

"Yeah, have a good time, mate, and thanks for breakfast," said Neil.

"You're welcome, see you later," said Oliver as he headed back to the kitchen.

Neil and Gina ate their breakfast and then headed to the reception. Abby wasn't there and Troy was sitting behind the reception.

"Morning," said Troy. "Mrs Adams has just gone back to her office, she said she'll be about 15 minutes."

"Morning," replied Neil. "No problem, I'll catch up with her there."

When they arrived, Abby wasn't in the office, so Neil went through to her lounge. He knocked and opened the door, what he saw gave him the shock of his life.

"Abby!" said Neil. "What on earth happened?"

Abby quickly put her cardigan back. "It's nothing," she said.

"It doesn't look like nothing, where did that scar come from?"

Gina came through. "What's wrong?" She asked.

"When I walked in, Abby was applying cream to a big angry scar on the top of her right arm. Well, Abby?" He questioned her again.

"You shouldn't have just walked in, Neil." She started to cry. "You were never meant to see it."

"No wonder, you always wear long sleeves even in the summer," said Neil still shocked.

"What happened, Abby?" Gina asked. "Did you have an accident?"

"Sort of," said Abby, tears still streaming down her face.

"I don't remember no accident," said Neil. "I don't remember you going to the hospital either and I'm sure with a big scar like that, you would have needed the hospital."

"I have tried to keep it away from you," said Abby.

"Keep what away from me?" He asked, "Why would you need to keep an accident away from me?"

"It wasn't so much of an accident, more inflicted and I didn't go to hospital as I didn't want you to find out."

Neil was so confused, Inflicted, what did she mean inflicted? And then it clicked—someone had done this to her.

"Who hurt you, Abby?" He asked.

"It doesn't matter," she said. "It happened a few years ago; you don't need to know."

"Omg," he said suddenly realising why he hadn't told him. "It was Harry, wasn't it?"

"Yes," she replied. "He wasn't the saint he made himself out to be, not with me anyway, but you loved him so much, Neil. I didn't want to tarnish your memories of him. Then you barged in and saw it. I've tried so hard to keep it from you," she started to sob again.

"Oh, Abby. Harry has been gone for five years now, you could've told me before now."

"I didn't think you would believe me," she cried.

Gina was standing in shock; more secrets were being kept; it wasn't good for anyone she thought.

"Of course, I would have believed you," said Neil.

"No, Neil, you wouldn't have back then. You idolised him and it hit you hard enough when he went," she said.

"I'll believe you," he said. "I want to know everything."

Gina had been listening in shock but all of a sudden she spoke, "Keeping secrets is no good for anyone, I should know. I think it's time for all of us to tell the truth…"

HMP, The Verne was the same on New Year's Eve as any other day. The daily routine was still in place, however, they would be getting another Christmas dinner tomorrow. If it was anything like the actual Christmas dinner, they had Christmas day they could shove it, David thought, it had all the elements, turkey, pig in a blanket, Yorkshire pudding, roasts and sprouts but it was the tiniest portion and everything was burnt to a crisp.

No, the only privilege they were getting today was an early lock up with their televisions, so the guards could go home and party; those that were on shift would be having their own party in the staff room.

David was sitting in his cell and he was still fuming. How could Gina do this to him? He had been served with divorce papers yesterday and an order that prevented him from contacting her in any way! She is my wife and she will not divorce me, he raged inside, he needed to speak to her; stuff the order, but how? She said she had moved to Scotland; he had no idea where and she had given up their home. He was still appalled by that too, why would she do that? Where would they live when he got out? Ok, he knew it was a few years away but he thought she would wait for him; he hadn't hurt her in any way. He had only treated her with love.

In court, the prosecution did actually acknowledge that but followed up with *serial offenders, especially psychopaths, who often separate their lives, they put their family on a pedestal which is why he never hurt his wife but committed these awful crimes against other women to gratify his own needs.*

"Bullshit," said David out loud. How could this be happening to him? When she agreed to a visit last week, he thought it was to enable him to explain but Gina had told him not to contact her at all ever again and left! Then he was served with this crap. *It's not happening,* he thought, *I need to speak to her.*

Suddenly he had an idea. Kathleen and Henry; he would get them added to his call list and he would call them to see what he could find out. He'd always got on really well with them so he knew they would accept when the prison rang to ask them if they would go on the list.

He smiled, he would find Gina and put a stop to all this nonsense…

Chapter 21

No More Secrets

Neil, Abby and Gina were all sitting in the private lounge; all deep in thought and all wondering how they were going to explain their pasts. Gina felt sure hers was the worst and she was scared it would put Neil off. Neil felt sure his past history with women would definitely give Gina doubts and he wasn't looking forward to telling her everything. Abby was dreading telling Neil about Harry; she was going to burst his memories of him for sure, where would she start?

They all knew that if they were going to move forward, the truth had to be told. All skeletons needed to be released; honesty was the only way to build the foundations of a good relationship. They had to tell their stories whatever the consequences, otherwise, they would all be living scared the others would find out another way. No, this was the best way. They knew that if they could all move on from it then life would be so much better, with none of them scared of being ousted.

Neil broke the silence. "What did Harry do to you, Abby?" He said.

Abby sighed. "I'll tell you everything, but it's not easy, so please let me just get it out and ask me anything after."

"Ok," said Neil, a bit apprehensive of what he was going to hear. Harry had been his hero; his father figure; they had done everything together. He couldn't comprehend that he could hurt his sister but she had the scar to prove it. "I'll keep quiet until you've finished."

Abby took a deep breath…

"When we met, Harry was such a gentleman and he readily took you on as part of the deal, so to speak. He was caring, attentive and loving. He couldn't do enough for either you or me. I loved him very dearly and we had a wonderful wedding."

"I remember," said Neil, but said no more.

"When we bought the hotel, we thought all our dreams had come true and we worked together so well. He'd take you out to look after the gardens, the animals and the maintenance of the hotel. I would make sure everything was running smoothly inside, everything was perfect and the hotel got busier and busier."

"As time went on, Harry got complacent and instead of pulling his weight the way he used to, he'd spend more time in the lounge watching television and drinking. It got more and more and led to lots of arguments. I realised he had a nasty temper but his true colours were really starting to shine though. I never really thought he was the violent kind even though he'd given me the odd slap here and there; I put it down to the drink."

"This went on for years, but we always hid it when you were around. In fact, you were the only one that he got out of the hotel to do the gardens. He lost interest in the inside and things started to look worn; it's an old building and without the constant upkeep, it didn't take long for it to start to look tired. Consequently, we started losing some of our returning guests which was a great shame. I missed them greatly."

"As time went on, I realised that we couldn't keep up with the running costs and suggested to Harry that we should sell up and get a nice little cottage. He would hear none of it. 'We had bought this hotel together and we would be there forever,' he said."

"After some time, he realised that we couldn't keep going, all the time getting nastier and nastier with me, blaming me for the downfall of Haven. I kept my mouth shut because he had begrudgingly agreed to sell."

"I found a cottage just outside of town, he liked it actually, but that was for him. Secretly, I had arranged to rent a flat on the other side of town. I felt this was my opportunity to get away from him and obviously, I was going to take you with me, but I kept it secret from him. I knew if I told him he would pull the sale of the hotel."

Abby started to cry and Gina went over to console her.

"Take your time, Abby," she said. Abby composed herself and continued.

"The night before the completion, Harry found my paperwork for the flat and asked me what it was for. I told him it was your paperwork, Neil, but he didn't believe me as my name was on them. I think he had seen it coming, to be honest and he pushed and pushed me, shouting and hurling abuse."

"In the end, I caved and told him I couldn't take no more and I was leaving him to make a fresh start with you, he took it very badly."

"He said there was no way I was leaving him; he would kill me first. I couldn't believe what I was hearing. Kill me? Was he serious? But he was definitely serious; he went into the kitchen and came back with a knife. He ran at me and started to attack me. I managed to get free and move out of his way. When I looked at him, he was red in the face with rage. I'd never seen him like this before and when I looked down, my arm was red with blood; he'd stabbed me three times in my arm. He came running towards me again but stopped midway, started clutching his chest and then fell to the floor. I was scared to move, in case he got back up again but he was there for ages."

"I eventually went over to him and his lips were starting to go blue. I immediately called an ambulance but I have to admit, Neil, and I'm sure you will hate me for this, I was secretly relieved, and I thought I was going to die that night."

"I don't hate you, Abby. If anything, I hate him now for what he did to you, I had no idea."

Abby continued, "The ambulance came and pronounced him dead; he'd had a massive heart attack. They said it was a mixture of the booze he'd drank and the intense rage he had got himself in. I had told them about the argument you see, I didn't hide it from them."

"I think your arm would have backed you up, anyway," said Gina softly.

"Yes, they wanted me to go to the hospital for stitches but I refused, if you'd have seen it then I would have had to lie to you and I couldn't, so I just didn't let you ever see it. They agreed to clean it and stitch it here for me when I explained."

"And that's why you always were long sleeves," said Neil.

"Yes," she replied.

"So, what did you do next?" Neil asked.

"Well, after a good think about what I should do, I explained to the staff that Harry had died from a massive heart attack and that I wouldn't be selling up after all. I told them I couldn't face moving without my beloved husband and needed to stay on familiar ground."

"Well covered," said Neil. "But you should've told them the truth, this is not your shame to have," he said.

"I just couldn't," said Abby. "I didn't want to admit I'd been that victim. Anyway, I took the hotel off the market, cancelled the agreement on the flat and pulled out of the cottage."

"How did you manage?" Gina asked.

"Well," said Abby. "It was a struggle to start with until the insurance money came through but it was a hefty sum, so it enabled me to do up the hotel to my taste and continue taking guests. I wrote to all my old guests and explained we had modernised and they would receive a hefty discount if they would return and review the place. They have been coming back every year since; the hotel is busy again and we have a great team of staff, you, Gina, my dear, have completed that."

"I love this place and never wanted to leave in the first place. It was my dream and Harry was ruining it but now, I get to make all the decisions and I'm proud of it."

"And so you should be," Neil said.

"I'm so sorry, Neil," she said. "I so wanted to shield you from this. It hit you really hard when he died."

"If I had known what he did, Abby, I wouldn't have been so unhappy about it. I just can't believe he could do that to you. What a bastard."

"Don't say that," said Abby. "These are my bad memories, you keep your good ones."

"I'm glad you've told me," Neil said. "It must have been a hell of a burden trying to keep it quiet."

"It was but at least now I can wear a t-shirt; summers have been a bummer!" she laughed and Neil and Gina laughed too.

"Always a bright," said laughed Neil.

"Always," smiled Abby. "Now, what did you come to tell me?"

"We came to tell you that Neil proposed last night," said Gina smiling from ear to ear.

Abby squealed. "Now, that is the best news I've heard in a long time. Oh my god, I am so happy," she said giving Gina a big hug. "Welcome to the family."

She went over and gave Neil a hug. "Well done, the boy finally sees sense. I'm so happy for you both."

"So are we," said Neil giving Gina a wink. "We just have to sort out a date now."

"Yes," said Gina. "We do but first we need to tell our stories because, Neil, I know you definitely have one and so do I."

Oh god, thought Neil, here goes...

They all sat back down. "I'll go next," Neil said dreading what was to come.

"Everything remember," said Gina. "We are going into this marriage will a clean slate and no skeletons."

"I know," replied Neil. "Everything. Here goes."

Gina was a bit anxious about what Neil was going to say, would it be awful, something that she would feel she could live with? Everyone had said he had been a bad boy but how bad had he been? She sat quietly while he began to talk.

"My parents died in a hit-and-run when I was 14 and Abby was 19; their deaths hit me very hard and Abby looked after me as well as any mother could. But I resented the fact that they had gone. I know I gave Abby a hard time but she still wouldn't give up on me. I wanted to push her away and started staying out late, drinking and basically, sleeping my way through anyone I came across."

Gina winced "I know," said Neil. "I am so ashamed of myself for it but I was off my head most of the time."

"I didn't know your parents had died so tragically!" Gina asked shocked. "Did you take drugs?"

"Never!" exclaimed Neil. "That is one road I didn't go down; however, I did some pretty stupid things back then, petty thefts, fights, fights with anyone who even looked at me the wrong way. I never went to prison though which I'm grateful for, but I carried on like that for about five years. Abby, I'm so sorry for what I put you through."

"It's history," said Abby. "We've all done things that we are ashamed of but we have to leave them in the past if we want a future."

"What changed?" Gina asked.

"Linda Green," he said. "I was besotted with her. I had never felt like that with anyone before and I knew I needed to clean my act up. I couldn't believe my luck when she agreed to go out with me although I thought it a bit strange that she wanted to keep it a secret, but I would have done anything for her."

"Oliver did mention her," said Gina.

"Yes, she was also dating him; neither of us knew until we met in town that day. I think we both felt equally as stupid. We had both been telling each other about a great girl we had met but we were keeping it on the down low for a while. We felt lucky we had both met someone who we thought was special; we were best friends and it would be good for both of us. That day in town, we both felt like we'd had a massive kick in the stomach, she had been dating us both! And we then realised why she wanted to keep it a secret."

"What happened?" Gina asked.

"Oliver told her she had to choose, and boy, did she take her time, weeks in fact. That is when Oliver and I drifted apart and became hostile to each other; another thing I am really sorry about, on reflection, she really wasn't worth it."

"Do you still love her?" Gina asked.

"God, no!" said Neil. "I can see now it was an infatuation; you have taught me the true meaning of love, Gina."

Gina blushed. "I mean it, Gina," he said. "I never knew what love really was until you came into my life."

"So, what happened next, did she give you both an answer?" Gina asked already knowing the answer.

"Oh, Linda gave us an answer alright," he said. "She left with the waiter from the town's café. Oliver and I both blamed each other at the time and we stopped speaking completely, which was a great shame as we were best mates once and I missed the laughs we used to have."

"How did you move on from it?" Gina asked.

"Well, I wasn't really in a great place, to be honest; I'd lost my girlfriend and my best friend in one hit and Abby had told me they were selling the hotel. I tried to pull myself together by throwing myself into helping with the hotel, trying to get it improved for the sale but it was hard trying to avoid Oliver all the time, so I started working outside just to keep a distance," said Neil. "I was just getting my head a bit straighter," he continued.

"Uncle Harry died suddenly which completely knocked me off my feet again. I adored him, and had done since I was younger; he was like the father I never had. I tried to be strong for Abby, but the strain of everything just got too much, so I decided to go away for a while and take a break from the people and surroundings that held so many bad memories for him."

"That's understandable," said Gina, knowing full well that is what she had done by coming here in the first place. "Where did you go?"

"When I left, I really wasn't sure where I was heading, so I just bought a train ticket and took it from there. I had a bit of money that I had saved and Abby had given me some to help me out too. I visited a few places and generally took a complete break. However, after a few months when I started to run low on cash, I knew I would need to look for a job. I reached Scotland and found a lovely little guesthouse called Sunny Cottage."

"Scotland?" Gina said. She thought how ironic it was that she had told David that was where she was living now.

"Yeah, I went some distance," Neil replied. "But the landlady at Sunny Cottage was so nice and the room was lovely, overlooking acres and acres of greenery, but it all went horribly wrong after a while."

"How so?" Gina asked.

"In a word, Annabel," he said.

"Oh," said Gina. "The girl who turned up here?"

"Yes," he said. "She was great at first, showing me the local places to go and she even introduced me to Alf who gave me a job. Everything was going great; she seemed perfectly normal then."

"What happened, Neil?" Abby asked, "You've never really said other than how you left her that day."

Neil sighed. "We went out for a meal and I wanted to return to the cottage when we had finished, but she insisted she wanted to go dancing at a club in town. One drink turned into two and two turned into three, you know how it goes."

"Easily done," said Gina. "If you're enjoying yourself."

"That's just it," he said. "I don't really like clubbing but I was drunk, unfortunately, and when we got back, one thing led to another."

"How?" Abby said.

"I don't need to spell it out, do I?" Neil said. "We somehow ended up in bed together. When I woke up the next morning, I couldn't believe what I had done. I was in no headspace for a relationship and if I had, I wouldn't have chosen Annabel, she was a nice girl but a friend. I knew if I was there when she woke up, she would want more and I didn't want to hurt her feelings or string her along, so I left a note explaining that to her. Obviously, that was the wrong thing to do."

"Did you not notice she had issues?" Abby asked.

"Honestly," said Neil. "No, there was no sign of it when we were out."

"And then you came back here," Abby said.

"Yes," said Neil. "I felt it was time to return and try and move on with my life as a single person."

"I thought you had a girlfriend when I arrived here," said Gina.

"Yes," Neil said. "Yet another mistake. I still wasn't ready for a relationship, so I just went into the bars in town with friends. It was there I bumped into an old friend, Gemma, a few weeks later. We got on well and had a bit of a casual relationship; no commitments, just someone to go out with, share dinner with now and then and I'd stayed over at her place a couple of times."

"So, why did you finish with her?" Gina asked.

"She started to get heavy," he said, "wanted me to move in and for us to get engaged. I knew I didn't want that and when you arrived here, you bowled me over, to be honest."

"You did," laughed Abby. "He was a changed man."

Gina smiled. "What happened with Gemma?"

"After you'd been here a couple of weeks, I could think of no one else," he said smiling at her. "I knew it wasn't fair on Gemma to keep going with whatever it was we had. She was going to get hurt. Gemma wasn't happy when I told her at the arcade, even saying she thought we would marry one day! I couldn't see where that was coming from. I knew then I was doing the right thing."

"So, who was the man I saw you arguing with at the arcade, was he something to do with it?" Gina asked.

"That was her dad, Bill," he said. "I was trying to explain to him that whatever Gemma had told him I had never intended on a relationship or marriage and Gemma had agreed to that at the start. Bill exploded and told me never to set foot on his arcade again or he would have me escorted off. It wasn't a pleasant situation but one that had to be done."

"Have you heard of her since?" Gina asked.

"No," he said. "Gina, I'm not proud of my track record. I seem to have picked the wrong woman but with you, it is different. I have never felt this way about anyone. My playing around days are over. I love you so much and I want us to be together for the rest of our lives if you'll still have me."

"Yes," Gina said. "We have all made mistakes and we all have a past but that is where it should stay."

"Hallelujah to that," said Abby.

"Thank god," said Neil. "Things are finally going right in my life and now I know what Harry was like with you, Abby, I don't think I will miss him half as much."

"I should have told you sooner," Abby said. "It may have helped you, but I thought I was protecting you and I'm sorry."

"Abby," he said. "You do not need to apologise to anyone, what he put you through would have driven anyone to the brink. At least the hotel is all yours now. I have regained Oliver as my best friend and I have met the woman I was destined to be with."

"Gina has been really good for you, Neil, there is no arguing that," she smiled at Gina.

Gina looked at Neil and said, "Let's hope you still want to marry me when I explain my past and recent events."

"I really don't think there is anything you could tell me that would make me not want to marry you, Gina," he said.

Gina took a deep breath and started to talk…

"Seven years ago, I was in a nasty car accident and although I am fine now, the road to recovery was a long one," she said.

"Omg," said Neil. "Thank god, you survived it."

"I did, and I'm here to tell the tale, but like I said, it was a long healing process and after a few months, I was pretty much climbing the walls. So, I went to stay with Aunty Pat and Uncle George at their cottage in Norfolk for a few months. The country air and the peace and quiet were perfect for recuperation."

"One day, they took, me to a large garden centre; we were going to have a walk and then have some lunch. It is such a lovely place to go," she said.

"I'll have to take you back," said Neil.

"Well, we'll see," she sighed. "It was there I met David and where the story begins."

"David?" Abby asked.

"My husband," said Gina.

"Husband," Neil said shocked, "I had no idea that you were married."

"I'm separated and soon to be divorced," she said. "Please, let me just tell you, this is as hard for me as it was for you two."

"I'm sorry," he said. "I'll stop interrupting."

"We hit it off immediately and he used to take me out now and then while I was staying there; like you Neil, I became besotted with him. When I returned home, we wrote to one another almost daily. I really missed not seeing him regularly as he could only visit every other weekend due to work commitments. I did offer to go to his place when I was driving again but he said his mother would give him the third degree and he wasn't sure that I would want that so early in the relationship. I should have heard the alarm bells then but like I said, I was besotted with him."

"I would have done anything for him but I didn't push the issue and we continued with his fortnightly visits. After only eight months, David had proposed and to be honest, I hadn't thought twice about accepting as I thought then I wanted to be with him forever."

"Mum thought it was way too quick and that I was too young but I reassured her that there was nothing she didn't know about David now and why wait any longer, if only I knew then what I know now!" Gina sighed.

"Hindsight is a wonderful thing," said Abby. "What happened, Gina? It must have been bad for you to run away."

"Oh, it was more than bad, Abby," Gina said, her eyes welling up. "I couldn't have ever imagined what was to come. We were married for five years in total and the first two were blissful; we set up a home together and David got a good job almost as soon as he had moved down. At first, I had ignored the warning signs that our love life was dwindling. I just kept telling myself that the novelty would wear off after a while, but soon, it became non-existence and our rows became more frequent. When I asked him about it, he refused to face up to the fact that there was any problem at all but then he finally admitted that he was infertile."

"This didn't matter to me, and I told him so. I loved him and told him we could get help for him but he refused; said he didn't want doctors messing with him, so I stopped speaking about it to him."

"I thought now it was out in the open things might improve, but they didn't. Life carried on and the subject wasn't brought up again. Things seemed to settle back down and life resumed to how it was in the beginning until that awful knock on the door one morning changed my life forever."

"Who was it?" Neil asked now intrigued by this story; he hadn't been expecting to hear she was married but he really needed to know how this had ended up here.

"I opened the door expecting to see a delivery man but instead, there were two policemen standing there. They had asked if I knew where David was and I told them he was watching TV in the lounge. I was really confused as to why they wanted him, so I followed them into the lounge to where he was."

"I listened in complete disbelief as explained to David that he was being arrested on the charge of rape!" She said, tears still stinging her eyes.

"Oh my goodness," said Abby. "That must have been awful for you."

"It got worse. I can tell you," said Gina. "They led him away in handcuffs; he didn't say a word. He seemed resigned to it, as though he had been expecting them. They didn't release him on bail and over the next few months, he was accused of several more rapes. I just couldn't believe the man I had married and shared a bed with was capable of something so heinous. He did nothing out of the ordinary at home, he went to work and was never late back, and I just kept thinking when was he doing all these terrible things!"

"Was he guilty?" Neil asked sympathetically.

"Yes, very much so," Gina said sadly. "There was a trial and a guilty verdict was returned, although he offered no defence at all. I couldn't believe that he was the man I knew and loved; all I could see was a monster standing in the dock. I would never come to terms with the fact that man and the man I once knew were the same person; he was handed a life sentence which is exactly what he deserved."

"Wow," said Neil. "He must have committed a few rapes to get life."

"He did," said Gina. "But I didn't feel sorry for him. I felt sorry for his victims and I would have felt sorry for myself if I had known what was to come."

"How do you mean?" Abby asked.

"The media," Gina said. "It was awful. Newspaper reports about the poor wife who knew nothing about it. Everyone was so sympathetic although I was always sceptical about whether they really believed that I didn't know, which of course, I didn't. Every time the news came on the television, my face was there, me leaving court, me arriving home. For about three weeks, the press was camped out in my front garden! I wouldn't leave the house for weeks and my mother had a nervous breakdown with the pressure; it just seemed to go on and on."

"It must have been awful," Neil said starting to stand up to go over to her.

"No," she said. "Not yet, I haven't finished and I need to get this out in the open, if you come and hug me, I'll just break down."

"Ok," he said sitting back down.

"Eventually, it did calm down and I realised that I needed to start somewhere fresh, where no one would recognise me," she said.

"But you did nothing wrong," said Abby.

"I know," said Gina. "But my life in Penrith had been tarnished and I knew if I was ever going to move on, I needed to move where I lived. That is what brought me here. I couldn't afford a divorce and I was struggling with the rent on the house, so I knew it was best to give it up and start again."

"Well, we are both so happy you chose here," said Abby. "You have been through what most people never experience, yet you still have a lovely nature and you are so good with the guests."

"Thank you," she replied, looking at Neil. He had tears in his eyes.

"Gina, you poor thing, no wonder you wouldn't go out with me right away. I'm surprised you'll ever trust me again. I will never do anything to hurt you; you know that, don't you?"

Gina was relieved; he hadn't walked out in disgust and was still talking about them as a couple, thank god, she thought.

"I know," she replied. "But there is more."

"More," said Neil. "How could you go through anymore?"

"When I went home for Christmas, there were a pile of letters he had written to me. I had left a forwarding address on my old place to my mum and dad's which has run out now, but when I read them, he was still talking about us being together, me waiting for him and us living our life again! I couldn't believe it, how could he even think I would want anything to do with him after what he put those women through? So, I decided to pay him a visit and tell him it was well and truly over."

"In prison?" Neil asked horrified.

"Yes, in prison," she said.

"What happened?" He asked. "That must have been a daunting experience for you."

"It was," replied Gina. "But I did see him and explained it was over."

"What did he say?" Abby asked.

"Believe it or not, he was really shocked, he thought I had visited him to discuss our future!" she said. "When I saw him, I got angry, which was a good thing really as it made me realise one hundred per cent that he was a nasty person who had hurt a lot of people. I think I actual hated him in that moment," she said.

"How did he take it when you told him?" Neil asked.

"I told him I had left the house and got a job in Scotland, which is why I smiled when you said you went to Scotland," she laughed.

"Ironic," laughed Neil.

"Very," she said. "He wasn't happy but like I told him, I had moved on, there would never be us ever again and he needed to accept it because I was really happy and would be staying there for good."

"Did you mention me?", Neil asked.

"No, I didn't," she said. "Because he would have thought that was the reason I didn't want him; I needed him to see I just didn't want him full stop."

"Good idea," he said.

"I told him to stop writing as they wouldn't get anywhere but he just kept on he was giving up, so I got up to leave. I had said what I went to say and I didn't want to be in his company a minute longer," she said.

"Have you heard from him since?" Abby asked.

"No," said Gina. "Even if he writes, he only has our old address, so his letter will be returned to sender. But I have spoken to a solicitor and set things in motion now."

"How so?" Neil asked.

"When I was on the train back here on Thursday, my solicitor called me to tell me that David had been served a non-molestation order and divorce papers that morning," she said smiling.

"Oh, wow, you don't do things by halves, do you?" Neil said.

"What is a non-molestation order?" Abby asked.

"It means he can't come anywhere near me or contact me in any way, not by letter or telephone," answered Gina.

"Oh, I should have had one of those on Harry," Abby laughed.

"Yes," Neil laughed. "You should have and Gina, none of that affects how I feel about you, I'm just sorry you had to go through that."

"Thank you," said Gina. "I am glad it's out in the open now; trying to live with a secret is hard work."

"Well, we've all had them," said Abby. "And I'm sure, we all feel better for being honest."

"Absolutely," said Gina. "I don't want to go into a marriage with either of us having skeletons."

"Well, I've told you everything," said Neil. "No more skeletons here."

"Nor here," said Abby.

"Ok," said Neil. "Let's set a date for our wedding."

"Well, I'd like a summer wedding but obviously, I have to wait for the divorce to be finalised. Hopefully, it won't take too long."

"Did your solicitor say how long?" Neil asked.

"We have to wait to see if he contests it or not," Gina said, "but Mike said he won't get anywhere if he does after what he's done but it could delay things just a little. If he doesn't contest, it should be six to eight weeks; if he does, it could delay it by three to four weeks."

"So, we should be good for a June or July wedding then," smiled Neil. "Shall we go for 30 June?"

"Perfect," said Gina. "30 June it is."

"Oh, this is so exciting," said Abby. "I couldn't be happier."

"Can I just ask that we don't tell anyone until I have phoned my mum and Aunty Pat," Gina said. "Then we can tell everyone else, I will call them later."

"Of course," said Abby. "Shall we go and grab some lunch? It's been a heavy morning."

"Yes, I am actually starving," said Neil.

"Me too," said Gina.

They all walked towards the staff dining room; all happy that they had gotten the burden of their own secrets out. They knew things would be a lot easier now. Secrets are never a good thing; they cause stress because you are always watching what you say. They all had a clean slate now and a wedding to plan, the future was looking very bright…

"Hi, Mum," Gina said when she picked up. "Happy New Year."

"Oh, Gina," said her mum. "How lovely to hear from you, how was your New Year?"

"It was lovely," said Gina. "Abby put on a lovely party for everyone."

"Oh, that's nice to hear," she said. "How did it go with Neil?"

"We are good," said Gina. "We all sat down this morning and all told each other the things we have been hiding; it feels good to have it in the open. The situation with Annabel was a misunderstanding." Gina went on to explain what Neil had told her about Annabel.

"I knew there would be a good explanation for it," said Kathleen. "You said he was adamant he wasn't the father. Have you told him about David?"

"Yes," said Gina.

"Everything?" Kathleen asked.

"Everything," said Gina. "Everything is fine between us and I'm glad he knows."

"Oh, I'm so relieved," said her mum. "That makes me so happy, I can't wait to meet him."

"You'll be meeting him soon," said Gina. "He proposed on New Year's Eve."

"Oh my god," shouted Kathleen. "And did you say yes?"

"I did," laughed Gina. "And before you say, I'm rushing in, everyone has told me how he's changed since meeting me and how much he loves me. I love him, Mum and we've set the date for 30 June."

"I wasn't going to say that," laughed Kathleen. "I'm happy for you, I really am. I was just going to say you are actually still married."

"I know that, Mum," said Gina, "but when I was on the train back, Mike called me to say that he has now been served with divorce papers and a non-molestation order. It should all be through before the wedding. Mike said 12 weeks tops even if he contests it."

"Do you think he will?" Her mum asked.

"Without a doubt," said Gina. "I told you how he was when I went to visit but Mike said the judge will rule in my favour because of what he's done."

"That's good news then," said Kathleen. "And it makes a nice change to have some of that. I'm so happy for you, Gina, I really am. Do you want me to tell your father or do you want to do it, he has something to tell you too?"

"Is he there?" Gina asked.

"Yes, he's in the garden, I'll go and fetch him."

Gina waited for her dad to come to the phone wondering what he had to tell her when he came on the other end.

"Gina," he said. "How lovely to hear from you, Happy New Year."

"Happy New Year, Dad, how was it?" She replied.

"Oh, same old same old, nice and quiet, glass of sherry and watching the TV," he laughed. "What about yours?"

"Mine was pretty special," said Gina. "The party was great and Neil proposed at the end of the night."

"Proposed," said Henry. "Have you told him about David, you're still married."

"I've told him everything," said Gina. "I've started divorce proceedings and took out an order on David to stop him contacting me."

"Oh, that's brilliant," said Henry. "I am really happy for you, I'm sure a clean break from around here is just what the doctor ordered."

"It is," said Gina. "You and Mum must come and stay soon, so you can meet everyone and Aunty Pat and Uncle George, the rooms are lovely here."

"That would be great," said her dad. "Arrange it with your mum, you know I just do what she tells me."

They both laughed. "I will do," said Gina. "Mum said you had something to tell me."

"Yes," he said. "It's about David."

Gina's heart sank; she thought she had sorted that problem out.

"What about him?" She asked.

"The prison rang," he said. "David had requested we go onto his phone call list."

"What!" exclaimed Gina. "Why would he do that?"

"Well, I'm guessing now it's because he can't contact you after receiving that order, he probably thinks he found things out through us. We always got on well before he turned bad," said Henry.

"What did you say?" Gina asked.

"I said no way, of course," he said. "I don't want to speak to that piece of scum and he's not using us to pass messages to you either."

"He's not going to give up, is he?" Gina said.

She was gutted; she'd been to the prison and told him, she had had the order and divorce papers served and he was still trying to get to her, when would this end? She had been so happy when she called and this had knocked her for a six.

"Don't worry," said her dad. "I've told the prison to intercept his post so anything addressed to us doesn't get through. He can't ring us and he can't contact us, he'll give up soon enough."

"I hope so," said Gina.

"He will," said Henry. "Now you concentrate on your future, not your past and make sure you make those arrangements with your mum."

"I will," she said. "You'll definitely be booked in around the wedding anyway, but I'll try and arrange something around Easter."

"Brilliant," said her dad. "Do you want your mum back?"

"Yes, please," said Gina. "Bye, Dad."

"Bye, my sweet girl," he said and went to fetch Kathleen.

"Hello," Kathleen said. "Now, don't get worrying about what your dad's told you; it's all sorted now but we thought we should tell you."

"I'm glad you did," said Gina. "I just want him to go away, he's caused us enough problems."

"He will," said her mum. "Just give it time."

"I know," said Gina. "I would like you and Dad, Aunty Pat and Uncle George to come and stay at the hotel over Easter and meet everyone."

"Do you need to run it past the lady who owns it—is it Abby?" Kathleen said.

"Abby will be fine with it, she can't wait to meet you all," she said.

"Well, that would be so lovely. We will come on the Thursday before Easter weekend if that's ok?" Kathleen said.

"That would be lovely," said Gina. "I can't wait."

"Just send your dad the address and we will see you then."

"I will and would you tell Aunty Pat for me, I know you speak every day."

"Of course, she will be thrilled," said her mum.

Gina smiled. "Bye, Mum, speak to you soon," said Gina.

"Bye, my darling," said Kathleen and they both hung up.

Gina went to find Neil and Abby.

"My parents are thrilled," she said to them both. "Is it ok if my mum and dad and aunty and uncle come and stay over Easter?" She asked.

"That would be delightful," said Abby. "What day will they be coming? I'll make sure we have our best two rooms free."

"The Thursday before the Easter weekend, if that's ok," replied Gina.

"It is more than ok," said Abby. "I'll go and reserve the rooms in the diary now."

"Thank you," said Gina.

"It will be great to meet them," said Neil. "If they are half as lovely as you are, everything will be fine."

"You'll love them," she said reaching her face up to his to kiss him.

She decided not to mention what they had said about David; she didn't want to spoil the moment and she was rather hoping he would just fade away from her life—and the sooner, the better…

David was in his cell alone; his cellmate Phil was still on work duties; they had to take the work duties to alleviate the boredom of this vile place, especially being on the vulnerable prisoners' wing. He had been placed there because of his crimes but it meant he spent most of each day in his cell. He slept, ate, used the toilet and watched television in there; it was either too bloody hot or freezing so the odd work duty was welcome to just get out of there and do something. Sometimes, he would read a book, but they never held his interest for long and he found the crossword puzzles just too easy. Playing cards with Phil was perhaps his highlight of the day. Phil had committed sexual offences too, which he said he deeply regretted. He had been here a few years and had helped understand the prison life and routine, which was as rigid as fuck. Phil offered good conversation and he felt sure he would have gone out of his mind had it not been for him.

The jobs they were given were not pleasant, that's for sure. David had just returned from cleaning the toilets on the wing, and he definitely wasn't happy with that task. He had a really good job before he came here; he was sure he could be put to better use here but no, deny duty it was.

David was angry, very angry; things were going from bad to worse. First, he got served with divorce papers and now Kathleen and Henry had refused his request for them to go on his call list.

"How the hell am I supposed to get things sorted stuck in this dump and no communication with the outside world?" He said out loud, smashing his hand down on the small table by the bed.

"Hey man, what's up?" Phil said, returning to the cell.

"Gina's mum and dad have refused to go on my call list," he said.

"What did you expect?" Phil said. "You were married to their daughter when you raped those women."

"We always got on well," said David. "I can't understand why they won't talk to me; I didn't do anything to them."

Phil laughed. "Man you are deluded; their daughter probably went through hell after you were convicted."

"She went through hell!" shouted David. "What does she think I am going through?"

"Whoa," shouted Phil. "You committed those crimes, not her."

"I know that," said David. "But she won't talk to me, she's served me with an order to stop all communication and issued divorce papers. How the hell can I sort anything out stuck in this shithole?"

"What exactly do you want to sort out?" Phil asked.

"When she came to visit me, I thought we were going to work out a plan for when I got out."

"When you got out!" Phil said. "David, you got life! Do you really expect her to put her life on hold for so long after what you did?"

"We were very close," said David. "I didn't think she would just bail."

"For Christ's sake," said Phil. "You raped multiple women when you were married to her; you put the nail in your marriage, not her. She'll never want anything to do with you again."

"I just need to talk to her one last time," said David calming down a little.

"How do you propose to do that?" Phil asked. "You should just leave her alone to get on with her life. At least I had no partner when I did those terrible things; you were married."

"You judging me as well now?" David said.

"Nope," said Phil. "Just saying it as I see it, you do what you need to do but I don't think you will get very far."

"I know what I did was wrong, very wrong, but everyone deserves a second chance, I don't deserve to be cut off like this."

Phil lay on his bed shaking his head. *The bloke is nuts*, he thought, *she'll never come back to him, she issued divorce papers for god's sake.*

"There's got to be a way," said David and he lay down on his bed to think.

"Give it up, pal," said Phil. "It's never going to happen, all my family disowned me and I had to accept it. You're going to be inside a very long time, time to make new acquaintances."

"I'm never giving up. There is a way, I just need to think about it," said David.

Phil closed his eyes, *bloody idiot,* he thought and fell to sleep.

David lay there thinking; he just needed to get to speak to Gina. He wasn't signing any divorce papers and he wanted to know why she had done it. What grounds did she have? He hadn't actually had affairs with those women and he had never harmed Gina in any way. She couldn't do this; she simply couldn't, knowing she was waiting for him had been the only thing keeping him going in this dump.

He just needed a contact on the outside to help get word to her but who? Kathleen and Henry were out of the question now; they had refused to even speak to him on the phone, so they weren't going to help him. His cow of a mother had written to him when he was convicted to say she had disowned him. How dare she? He hadn't hurt her and he was her flesh and blood! She wasn't going to help him, was she?

The only person he had on his call list was an old friend John. Would he be able to help? Maybe, yes he was sure he would. They had been long-term friends and although he was a bit frosty with him on the last call, at least he had spoken to him.

"Got it," shouted David.

"Fuck sake, man," said Phil sitting up quickly. "You nearly gave me a heart attack, what have you got."

"A communication on the outside who I know will help me track Gina."

"Not this again," said Phil. "Give it up, she's never going to have you back."

"Maybe but I need to talk to her so I'm not giving up," said David banging on his cell door for a guard to come.

"What is it, Taylor?" The guard said.

"I want a phone call," he said.

"To your one and only contact," laughed the guard. "I'll sort it."

A few hours later, the guard came to collect him from his cell. "Time for your phone call," said the guard.

He led him to the corridor with the phones and stood back while David made the call. David didn't think John was going to answer to start with but all of a sudden he picked up.

"Hello," said John.

"Hi, John, it's me, David."

"Oh," said John sounding slightly taken aback. "How you doing?"

"Not great," said David. "I need your help."

"To do what?" John asked.

"I really need to speak to Gina; she came to see me and told me to leave her alone, but I need one last conversation with her. She's issued divorce papers and I need to discuss it," he left out the non-molestation order because he knew John wouldn't get involved in anything with that in place.

"Can't you call her mum or dad?" John asked not really wanting to be involved at all.

"They refused to go on my call list," said David.

"Go figure," said John with mock surprise.

"I really need your help, John," said David. "Will you visit them and ask them to contact Gina and tell her to visit me again?"

"Sorry," said John. "I am not turning up on their doorstep after what you put them through. That's not fair. If they've refused to talk to you, they are hardly going to speak to me, are they?"

"I need to do something. She said she's moved to Scotland and got a job," David said. "And I have no idea where."

"I have a mate in Scotland," said John. "I could ask him to listen out but Scotland is a big place."

John was feeling really uneasy with this situation; he was really against what David had done and had only agreed to go on his call list as no one else would. He thought if he had at least one person to call, it might help but he wasn't feeling getting involved in tracking Gina; the girl had been through enough. He felt he was stuck between a rock and a hard place now because if he told David he wouldn't help and it caused him to harm himself, he would have that on his conscience.

"Where is your mate in Scotland?" David asked.

"St Andrews," replied John. "I'm actually visiting him next week so could have a word."

"Taylor, time is up," shouted the guard.

"Look, John, I have got to go, can I call you tomorrow? I'll have a think overnight."

"Fine," said John and he hung up.

"I want to book a phone call for tomorrow," said David to the guard.

"I'll sort it," replied the guard. "Now get back to your cell."

"How did you get on?" Phil said.

"Finally, getting somewhere," said David. "I just need to think."

Phil turned over and went back to sleep and David lay on his bed.

The next morning, David got up brighter, he had an idea; he just needed to get back onto John. This would work he was sure of it.

The cell door opened and the guard came in. "Taylor, pack up your stuff, you are being transferred."

"What?" David shouted. "Why? Where am I going? I had booked a call today and I really need to make it."

"You can make it when you get to HMP Littliehey," said the guard.

"Where is that?" David said.

"Well, not that it matters as you have no visitors and you will not be viewing the local attractions," the guard smirked at him which only added to David's anger, "but it's in Cambridgeshire, it's for your kind and you are being shipped out at 11 am, so get you stuff ready."

"Fuck, fuck, fuck," shouted David. "I have just thought of a plan and now they are moving me. I really need that phone call."

"It'll probably be tomorrow when you get that now," said Phil. "They'll need to induct you over there first before they'll allow privileges. Looks like I'll be getting a new cellmate. Look on the bright side; Littlehey is full of sex offenders, so you'll have a bit more freedom around the prison."

"Fucking, great," said David and started to pack his stuff into a plastic bag.

He arrived at the reception at HMP Littlehey; he was still fuming. How would Gina know where he was now? How would anyone know? Was anyone actually interested?

The reception guard went through all the paperwork and he was strip searched and given a different prison uniform to wear.

He was given his personal belongings back and took to a cell on B wing. He was in a single cell which he wasn't sure was a good or bad thing. Sharing offered company but if he was allowed out of the cell more that may compensate a little and at least he wouldn't have to listen to someone snoring all night.

"I had booked a phone call for today," David said to the guard.

"How you manage that, lad, you've only just arrived." The guard laughed.

"I requested it yesterday at The Verne and they said I would be able to make it here," David said.

"We have to get your call list over first, it should be here by morning," said the guard, "now get settled in and I'll get our offender supervisor to come over and explain the routine."

"Tomorrow," said David. "I told my friend I would call today."

"Well, we don't always get what we want, do we, lad? Ask those young ladies you hurt." The guard was getting a bit pissed off with him; he'd only just arrived and his demands had started.

David didn't answer, just did as he was told. The offender supervisor came over and gave him the rundown on how things worked here.

"If you play by the rules, the guards will look after you," he said. "Piss them off and you get nothing and they'll make your life hell. They don't like what any of us have done, so just keep your head down and do as you are told. My name's Derek but everyone calls me Decca in here."

"I'm David," he said.

"I know," said Decca and he walked out of the cell.

David lay on his bed. He would just have to wait until tomorrow now to call John and hope that he was in; it was a bummer but there wasn't much he could do about it.

The next morning when the guards came round to unlock the cells, David asked, "Do you think I could get my phone call today, please? I was supposed to call my friend yesterday but I was transferred."

It was a different guard than yesterday; he seemed a bit friendlier. "I'll check if your list has come over from The Verne, if it has, I'll put the request in for you."

"Thank you," said David and headed to the showers.

After David had showered and had breakfast, which was disgusting slop, he went back to his cell. The guard came in to tell him he could have his phone call and as soon as everyone had finished breakfast, he would take him to the phone.

David was buzzing; he could put his plan forward to John. He only hoped he was in.

"Hello," said John.

"John, it's David."

"What happened to yesterday?" John asked.

"Last minute transfer," replied David. "I wasn't able to get my call until now."

"Oh, where are you now?" John asked.

"Littlehey in Cambridgeshire," said David. "Listen, I've thought of a plan for when you go to Scotland."

"Go on," said John sounding a little dubious.

"Get some posters printed with Gina's face on it and ask for anyone who knows her whereabouts to get in touch."

"In touch with who?" John asked.

"You," said David. "Then if they get in touch, you take their details and pass them on to me. You can write to me with the details or tell me when I ring."

"I don't know," said John. "Who's paying for them and is it even legal?"

"It can't be illegal; Gina is a missing person to me," David said, "and I can hardly put my contact details on, can I?"

"I'm not sure," said John. "It doesn't sound right."

"Please, John," David pleaded. "I just need to speak to her and I can't exactly hurt her from in here, can I?"

"I suppose," said John, not feeling at all happy but scared David would do something stupid if he didn't help.

"I'll go on the prison computer and create the poster, then email it to you and I'll transfer money to you to pay for them," said David.

John still wasn't sure. He could have the posters done he supposed. He didn't have to hand them out. David wouldn't know, would he? He could take them to Scotland and dump them, then that way when he told David he took them up north, he wouldn't actually be lying. He didn't like this at all, he really didn't.

"Ok," he said. "I'll do it."

"Thank you so much," said David. "You don't know how much this means to me. I'll get onto make them as soon as I am allowed and email them to you. I have your bank details from before so I can send money from here."

"Did they not freeze your assets when you were arrested?" John asked.

"Only the ones they knew about." David laughed.

He's playing a dangerous game, thought John, *and I really wish he wasn't involving me.* He would have the posters printed so he could send a picture by email to David, that would pacify him but then he would definitely dump them as soon as he got to Scotland. He wanted no part in finding Gina for David. She deserved some peace after what he put her through but he also didn't want David on his conscience either. He would just tell him no one had come forward. Oh god, why had he agreed to go on his call list!

David put the phone down and smiled to himself; he went off to find a guard to see when he could use the prisoner's computers.

Annabel was sitting at her laptop searching for 'Gina-Weymouth' but nothing was coming up at all.

Damn, she thought, *I need more information about her for me to find anything about her. I need to dig up some dirt on her somehow that will make Neil not want her, and then he will be free to come to me and our baby.* If she couldn't find anything on the internet, she would make something up just to lay some doubts in his mind.

She had a think about how she could get this extra information when she had an idea. She would ring the hotel and ask a few questions but how was she to do that without raising suspicion?

When she was there before Christmas, she remembered Abby saying good morning to a Mr & Mrs White when they came down for breakfast. *That's it*, she thought, *I'll be Mrs White and I'll change my voice.*

She smiled as she made her way downstairs to the telephone. Edna was shopping in town, so she wouldn't be disturbed. She looked up the number in the directory and dialled it.

"Good morning, Haven Hotel, how can I help?" The voice said. She recognised it as that witch Abby. She immediately began to feel angry with her at the way she had treated her but knew she had to stay calm.

"Good morning," replied Annabel. "I just wanted to enquire about your receptionist."

"What about her?" Abby replied a bit sharply.

What was it with this woman; she was only a damn receptionist at a hotel and everyone seemed to want to protect the bitch.

"Oh, nothing bad," said Annabel more patiently than she felt. "My name is Mrs White. I stayed with you before Christmas and your receptionist, Gina, I think her name was, was so lovely and helpful."

"Thank you," said Abby. "Yes, it is Gina and she is an asset to our hotel that's for sure."

Annabel felt her rage rising again and desperately tried to suppress it so she could continue with Abby getting suspicious. "I wanted to write a review on TripAdvisor about your lovely hotel and especially wanted to give a shout-out to Gina but I would like to recognise her fully with her surname."

"Oh," said Abby, "Gina will be fine, there's only one Gina here."

"I really would like to put her name in full," replied Annabel, getting agitated. *Just give me the bloody name*, she raged inside.

"Ok," said Abby, "it is Gina Taylor."

"Oh, thank you," said Annabel, smirking to herself. *Bingo*, she thought, *I have her full name but I need a bit more.*

"She had a lovely accent," she said. "Not a Weymouth accent, is it?"

"No," said Abby. "Gina came down from Cumbria to work for us and like I say, she is an asset so we are really happy that she is staying with us."

Annabel did a little happy dance, she had got what she needed. "Oh, yes," she said, "I bet you are. Anyway, I'll leave that review for you, thank you for your help. Bye."

"Bye, Mrs White," said Abby and hung up thinking that felt like a very strange phone call but couldn't put her finger on why. She thought no more about it and went about her daily chores as usual.

Annabel was delighted as she returned to her laptop and loaded Google.

Gina Taylor-Cumbria.

"Oh my fucking god," she said out loud when the results loaded. There was so much information about her and her rapist husband. *I bet Neil doesn't know about this, no wonder she ran away to Weymouth.* Her husband had raped several women and she had been splashed all over the papers. Neil had to find out about this, he definitely wouldn't want her when he knew. She just knew it. *Happy family, here we come*, she thought, putting her hand on her tummy.

Now, what to do? She would write to Neil but she would need a little time to think about how to write it. If she was too nasty, he may think she was just being vindictive. She needed to word it so that he would have a look for himself, then he would kick Gina out and leave room at the hotel for her and their baby. Today was a good day and she was going to go into town and watch the trains come in for a while, something she often did when she needed time alone. It would allow her some thinking time without her stupid mother wittering on in her ear all the time. That woman was seriously getting on her nerves; she needed to do something about her but she would have to wait. She had more important things to sort out.

John had had the posters printed and emailed David a picture as proof to his prison email. He was surprised the prison hadn't picked up on it; he felt sure they vetted all correspondence, be it post or email. He wasn't happy about doing any of this and he had no intention of distributing them anywhere.

He told David he would take them to St Andrew's when he went up, and he would. At least then he had fulfilled his part of the deal and he wouldn't have David on his conscience if he did anything to harm himself. He certainly was sounding a bit manic on the phone, so he knew if he let him down, he could be capable of anything. However, he would just dump them in the first trash bin he came across. His job would be done then; he would just tell David no one had been in touch.

David was happy with the posters; they had a picture of Gina on them and John's information for anyone to get in touch if they saw her or knew where she was. He had put MISSING at the top of the poster, which wasn't actually true but she was missing to him and it would make people take notice. He just had to speak to her to stop all this nonsense.

When John got off the train, he made his way to the street outside and immediately dumped the posters in the nearest bin. *There, job done,* he thought, *let's hope that's the last I hear about it.* He made his way to a black cab and instructed the driver to his friend's address.

Annabel was intrigued by the man who got off the train. He was very good-looking and very well-dressed. She watched him go through the station and dump a package in the bin outside. *I wonder what that package is. It didn't even look unwrapped and he's just thrown it away,* she thought.

She made her way to the bin and retrieved the parcel; it was something heavy wrapped in brown paper. It had no name or address on it. She was even more intrigued, so she ripped open the brown paper and stared in disbelief at what she saw, this day was just getting better and better.

Image courtesy of https://stock.adobe.com/uk/search?k=blonde+woman

Scotland thought Annabel, *she doesn't live in Scotland but I know exactly where she is right now.* She looked at the picture, the whore was so damn beautiful; no wonder, Neil had fallen for her but when he knew about her past that would change.

She took one of the posters and made her way home. She would ring the number and tell John that she had information on Gina.

When she arrived, she was relieved to find Edna was still out. *Thank god,* she thought, *I don't need her interfering.* She dialled the number.

"Hello," said a male voice.

"Hi," said Annabel sweetly. "I'm ringing about the poster you threw away, I have information on this woman."

"Where did you get that?" John said, slightly panicking. *This was not supposed to happen,* he thought.

"Out of the bin, you threw it away in. Why would you throw them away if her husband is looking for her?"

"It was a mistake," said John, now getting worried. "Did you say you knew where in Scotland Gina is?" He asked.

"I know where she is, but it is not Scotland," she added.

"Oh," said John, "she told her husband that she had a job in Scotland and had moved there."

"Well, she was lying because she's in Weymouth."

"Weymouth," said John surprised.

"Are you her husband?" Annabel asked.

"No, I'm his friend," he said, "he asked me to put the posters up for him and send him any information if anyone got in touch."

"Well, I can give you information," said Annabel.

"The thing is," said John. "He's in prison and he wants me to take information and pass it on to him. Can you give me your details and I'll pass them on? He can email, so an email address would be good too, but please, don't tell him I threw away the posters. It's a long story and I don't want him hurt because of where he is."

"I won't," said Annabel, thinking she was quite looking forward to communicating with this David.

"My name is Annabel, my phone number is 05612666666; my email address is Annabel325896@gmail.com."

"And you say you know where she is?" John asked.

"Oh, yes," she said. "I know exactly where she is."

"Ok, I'll pass this on to him, he's calling me in the morning," he said.

"Thank you," said Annabel and hung up the phone.

Fuck! thought John. He wasn't expecting anyone to see them let alone get in touch but at least David would think he had distributed them now.

Annabel was sitting at her laptop all day waiting for an email from David when one pinged through at 3:25 pm.

"OMG, it is him," she said.

She read the email, it was quite short.

Hi Annabel

John passed me your details and I would like to talk to you. I will need to add your telephone number to my approved call list—is that ok?

The prison will ring you within a day or two for you to give them permission for me to call you.
Regards
David

Annabel thought he sounded like a nice person, not the monster the papers made him out to be. So what if he'd hurt a few women, he sounded a bit like herself. She laughed as she thought about that. She pressed the reply button.

Hi David
Thank you for emailing me, yes, please add me to your call list and I will of course give permission.
Regards
Annabel

He didn't reply again that day. She thought he must be sorting out the phone number or he had limited time on a pc. She was surprised to find herself a little disappointed, but she would be talking to him soon enough.

Annabel went to find Edna and told her in no uncertain terms that she answer the phone for a few days until Annabel told her otherwise.

"What are you up to now?" Edna sighed.

"None of your business," said Annabel. "Just do as you're told."

Edna knew better than to do anything else. What was she up to now? She despaired of her daughter and she really had had enough of her and he nasty ways.

The next day the phone rang around 11 am. "Leave it," shouted Annabel. "I'll get it."

Edna had no intention of answering it, she had been told after all and she didn't want to feel her daughter wroth once again.

"Hello," said Annabel when she answered.

"Hello, is that Annabel?" The caller asked.

"Yes it is," she replied.

"This is prison offer Gelby from HMP Littlehey; we have a David Taylor here and he has requested your number goes on his permitted call list. Before we can do that we need your permission."

"Yes, yes, that's absolutely fine," she said.

"Ok," said the officer, "that will be added now and David will be able to call you once it's cleared in about an hour."

"Brilliant," said Annabel excitedly. "Thank you so much."

They both hung up and Annabel went back to her room and waited for David to call.

It was 1:30 pm when the phone rang again. Annabel jumped up off her bed and ran downstairs past Edna and pick it up.

"Hello," she said slightly out of breath.

"Annabel?" The caller said. "It's David."

"Yes, it's me," said Annabel. "I'm so glad you called."

Edna was in the lounge, *another lamb to the slaughter*, she thought when she heard Annabel's voice. She knew that voice, she bought it out every time a new man came on the scene.

"Thank you for accepting my call," said David. "John said you had some information for me, we can't really say too much on the phone as they monitor the calls here."

"How am I going to tell you then?" Annabel asked.

"I wondered if perhaps you would visit if I put you on the visitors' list?"

Oh, thought Annabel, *this is exciting*, she had never been inside a prison before. "Yes," she said. "I will visit you, where is Littlehey?"

"It's in Huntingdon; a long way from Scotland, but I can send you some money for your fare and a hotel for a couple of nights if it helps, at least then we can talk without being monitored too much."

Oh, he has money, thought Annabel, *that's good*. She smiled to herself.

"Ok," she said. "If you can do that, I will visit."

"Great," said David. "I'll email you the address and you send me your bank details. When you have booked somewhere, let me know and I'll book the visit."

"Ok," said Annabel, this had progressed further and quicker than she anticipated but she was really excited. He sounded so gentle and caring. She actually couldn't wait to see him in person.

Annabel arrived at HMP Littlehey at about 2:30 pm. She was booked in to see David at 3:30 pm but knew she would have to go through procedures. She had hardly slept the night before in excitement. The hotel he had sent her the money for was lovely and the bed was really comfortable but sleep had evaded her because she couldn't stop thinking about David.

What was he like? What did he look like? Was he the monster the press had made him out to be? Why was he obsessed with finding his wife? She was about to find out in about one hour. She had butterflies in her tummy; she had never done anything like this before.

Edna had given her the third degree before she left as usual but she'd told her to back off. She was going away for a few days and it was none of her business. *Why did she keep interfering?* She thought as an officer called her over for her photo and fingerprints. She felt like she was in a TV show. After all, she had only ever seen a prison on TV, let alone been inside one.

She made her way to the main building for the rest of the checks; she was still thinking about her mother. *She's always in my business and I'm sick of her. I really need to get out of that cottage as soon as I can. I may even stay here a few more days if David will pay. I'll tell him I'll visit again if he would like me to.* Whoa, she thought, *you've not met him yet and you're planning on coming again; you may hate him and never want to see him again.* Even she realised she was getting ahead of herself; she was just so desperate to get away from her mother now, she was ruining her life.

Edna sat at the kitchen table with her head in her hands. *When is this ever going to end*? She thought. Annabel had gone off again without telling her where. She had heard her booking a hotel and trains yesterday and she was gone today. She was pregnant, for god's sake, and she was going off around the country on her own again. She hadn't a clue where she was going; she only knew about the train and hotel because she was listening from the lounge. She felt bad listening in on Annabel's calls but how else could she find out what was going on? Annabel had a mental illness; someone had to try and keep a check on her.

Where has she gone? Edna fretted. Trains, hotels and obviously, a man from how she was talking on the phone the other day. She really hoped she wasn't causing trouble for someone else or even that nice couple from the Haven Hotel; she had caused them enough grief. Edna got up to put the kettle on; *maybe it's better if I don't know* she thought.

Annabel had gone all through the prison visitor checks and was sitting in the visitor's room waiting for the prisoners to come through. She looked around. It wasn't a bad place to be; it was nice and clean with a little café up the corner and even a children's play area. She never even thought it was wrong to have to bring children here. They needed to see their fathers, whatever they had done.

Suddenly she heard the clonking of locks and realised the prisoners were coming in. She hadn't a clue what David looked like until a man came over and said, "Annabel?"

"Oh, my god," Annabel said in a whisper, he was gorgeous. "Yes," she said standing up ready to shake his hand.

"No contact," shouted a guard.

"Sorry," said Annabel and sat back down.

"Pleased to meet you," said David. "And thank you for coming, how was the journey and the hotel?"

"The journey was long," she laughed. "But the hotel is gorgeous, I could stay there longer."

David laughed. "You have some information for me," he said.

"Oh, yes," she said. Annabel had almost forgotten that was the reason for her visit, she was so taken up with his gorgeous face.

"Your wife, Gina, why are you so keen to find her?" She asked.

"I'll be straight with you, Annabel; you deserve that after coming all this way," he said.

"Ok," said Annabel wondering what he was about to say.

"When I was married to Gina, we were so close and I treated her really well. I know what I did was terrible and I regret it."

"Regret what you did or getting caught?" Annabel asked.

"Both really," smiled David, "but I never hurt Gina, so I assumed she would wait for me until I got out."

"Well, she's not done that, has she?" Annabel said.

"No, it doesn't seem that way," he said sadly. "She came to see me just after Christmas."

"Did she?" Annabel asked, thinking *I bet Neil doesn't know that.*

"Yes," he said. "I thought she had come to talk about us when we got out and that she was going to start visiting me but she hadn't. She told me she never wanted to see me again; she had returned our house to the landlord and she had got a job in Scotland and was living there."

"She not living there, I live there and that's how I saw your poster," she said.

"Do you know where she is?" David asked.

Annabel was a bit irked. Now that they were talking about the bitch, she really liked David, but realised that's why she was here.

"Why do you want to know if she's told you she doesn't want to see you and why can't you just call her or her parents?" She said.

"She has issued divorce papers and a non-molestation order meaning I'm not allowed to contact her, but I really need to talk to her to sort this out. She walked out of here without letting me talk. I need to talk some sense into her, her parents won't have anything to do with me either."

"But won't you be breaking your order if you contact her?" Annabel said.

"I don't care," said David. "I just need to talk to her or even just write to her."

"Well, I don't have a number for her and if I give you the number of her work, they probably won't let you speak to her. They are really defensive where she is concerned, but I can give you the address."

"Where is she?" He asked.

"Weymouth," Annabel replied.

"Bloody Weymouth," he shouted, "that's the opposite end of the country to Scotland, for Christ's sake."

"Keep it down, Taylor," said a guard. "Or you'll be taken back to your cell."

"Sorry," he said. "Weymouth?" He asked again.

"Yes," said Annabel. "Guess, she really wanted to put you off her trail."

"Can you give me the address? They won't intercept that because they won't realise it's for her."

Annable gave David the address of the hotel. "You'll have to memorise it," she said. "They won't let me pass your paper in here."

"I know," he said. "I will, thank you, Annabel. I can write to her now and put a stop to her nonsense."

Annabel could feel disappointment rising. She wanted him to like her, that bitch wouldn't wait for him or keep visiting him but she would if he gave her a chance.

"Would you like me to visit you again?" She asked.

"Why would you want to visit me?" David asked. "I'm a monster, apparently."

"I don't see a monster," said Annabel. "I see a lovely handsome man who loves his family. We all make mistakes."

"You know something, Annabel," he said. "That's the nicest thing anyone has ever said to me for a long long time. I would love you to visit again. I can send you the money. I have plenty and I can't spend it here, it will be worth it to see your pretty face again."

Annabel was overjoyed that he wanted to see her again and he had called her pretty! Oh, this was exciting, maybe she didn't need to split up Neil and the bitch but then that would be just for fun.

She smiled. "Book me in for next Wednesday and I'll book the hotel and train again when I get home."

"Thank you," said David. "And thank you for the information."

"My pleasure," she said just as they called time, she got up. "See you next week," she smiled.

"See you next week," he replied thinking things were looking up for him finally. Not only had he got another person on his call list, but he also had a visitor, a pretty visitor who seemed keen to keep coming.

It was a busy Monday morning at the hotel when the postman arrived. There was the usual hotel post, enquiries and bills; there was some for the staff too. Gina took it all from the postman and started to pigeonhole it for everyone. There was a letter for her and a letter for Neil.

Strange, she thought, only her mum and dad knew the address and it didn't look like their writing. It would have to wait for now there was so much to do; she would open it after her shift.

"Morning, gorgeous," winked Neil.

"Morning, handsome," she replied smiling at him.

"There's a post for you," she said.

"It'll have to wait till later," he said. "Too much to do right now."

"Ok," she said. "Shall we have a coffee after my shift?" She asked.

"What time you on till today?" He said.

"2 pm," she replied.

"Perfect, I'll meet you in the dining room, can you bring my post then?"

"Sure," she said. "See you later."

Both of them went about their duties and Gina didn't think about the letter until the end of her shift. It had been a busy morning with all the Monday to Friday guests arriving so the morning had passed quickly.

Abby came to relieve her at 2 pm and she picked up hers and Neil's post and went to the dining room where Neil was waiting and so was her coffee.

"Thank you," she said as she sat down, "here's your post."

"Cheers," he said taking it from her.

They both opened their letters and suddenly they both said in unison, "What the hell?"

They looked at each other; Neil spoke first, "Who is it from?"

Gina was shaking, "David," she said. "How did he find me?"

"What does he want?" Neil asked.

"To talk," she said. "He's broken his order, I need to speak to Mike."

"Are you going to reply to him?" Neil asked.

"I am not," said Gina defiantly. "Anyway who is yours from?"

"It's anonymous," said Neil. "It's a letter telling me about your past? Who the hell would send this crap," he fumed.

"Oh my god," said Gina. "Someone has been looking me up; someone who knows where I came from. Who the hell could it be? I am so glad we all came clean the other day."

"Well, whether or not you told me, I want to know who the hell is trying to ruin our life and I want to know why that ex of yours is upsetting you by getting in touch when he's not supposed to!"

"Who has given him my address?" Gina cried.

"Don't get upset," said Neil. "My letter is from someone who is jealous of our relationship and I think I may know who, but that doesn't explain how David found out where you are?"

"Who?" Gina asked.

"Well, who wanted me to leave you to go with them?"

"Annabel." She sighed. "She's never going to give up, is she?"

"Oh, she will," he said. "Even if I have to take an order out on her crazy bitch."

Gina got up. "Where are you going?" Neil asked.

"To call my solicitor," she said. "He's not getting away with this."

Chapter 22

Moving On

By the end of March, the wedding plans were finally able to start. It had been a stressful couple of months waiting for David to sign the divorce papers but now he had, they could get started.

After she called Mike about the letter, he said he would report it. He had told her to go ahead with her plans as even if David contested the divorce, a judge would still rule in her favour, especially with his latest breech, so she would be easy on for the end of June. Still, she felt uneasy about arranging anything back then in case there were any hiccups.

A few weeks later, Mike called again to tell her that David had been called to a disciplinary hearing and they had added 180 days to his sentence for his breach of the order. He had also told the members of the panel that he would back off and sign the papers, which he did; they were back in Mike's possession now so he would be submitting them to the court.

"Why the change of heart?" She asked. "I didn't think he would give up that easy."

"Lord knows," replied Mike. "Maybe he doesn't want time to keep being added to his sentence anymore. He will have lost privileges for a while too."

"Oh," said Gina. "Do you really think it's over?"

"Looks that way," said Mike. "There may be another reason," he added.

"Really?" Gina said.

"Yes, when the governor rang me to tell me the papers were being returned to me signed, I too was curious about the change of mind and I asked him if he knew why," Mike said. "He said he had no idea, but it may be because he was now getting a regular visitor."

"A visitor?" Gina asked. "Do we know who, I can't think of anyone who would want to visit him after what he had done apart from maybe John, his old friend?"

"No," said Mike. "The governor said it was a female, but who cares, Gina, if it keeps him off your back."

"You're right," she said still wondering out of curiosity who it may be. Then she added, "Actually, Mike, you a very right, if someone is stupid enough to be taken in by him, he'll leave me alone."

"Exactly," said Mike. "I'll be in touch when it's all finalised but you go and enjoy your life now and book a wedding you deserve."

"Thank you, Mike," she said. "I will."

They both put the phone down; Gina was so relieved as she went to find Neil.

"That's fantastic," Neil said hugging her.

"I know," she said. "I can't quite believe it, is it really over, Neil?" She asked looking up at him.

"It certainly looks that way. David has signed the papers and is pulling some other poor soul into his life and I've had no more letters so it looks like Annabel has gone quiet, thank god."

"Let's start planning," she said.

"Let's do that," said Neil smiling.

David was not happy at the extra time that had been added to his sentence, six bloody months, he raged, just for writing a fucking letter! And no TV or canteen for two weeks, he would go out of his mind without the TV and no cellmate to talk to.

He realised he needed to back off with Gina, for now anyway. If he kept contacting her, he would never get out of this shithole. What annoyed him the most was that she wanted a divorce, she wasn't even prepared to talk about it!

Wayne, another inmate, walked into his cell.

"What's up, brother?" He said. "I can hear you raging from the other side of the wing."

"That bloody wife of mine, she's moved away and got a new job, apparently, another bloke and wants a divorce. I can't even write to her or speak to her."

"What did you expect?" Wayne said. "You raped other women, sis, you really think there was a chance for you two after that?"

"I never hurt her," said David.

"Not physically, mate, but she's never going to forgive you for the mental hurt you put her through," said Wayne.

"What did your Mrs do?" David asked.

"I hadn't got a Mrs when I committed my crimes, but if I did, I wouldn't expect she'd wait 18 or so years for me. You're being unfair to her in my opinion, you've put her through enough; let her have a chance at a future," said Wayne leaving the cell. "See you later when you've calmed down."

David hadn't really liked that conversation. It wasn't what he wanted to hear at all. He loved Gina and he really wanted to make it up to her. He lay down on his bed and began to think.

Was he really being unfair to her? She was out there living her life while he was stuck in this box for years on end. Suddenly, he realised how selfish he had been and was being. He had committed the awful crimes. He was ashamed and looking for someone to blame and that someone it seemed, was Gina.

She had done nothing wrong at all, yet she had been through all the problems that his crimes brought her, the arrest, the court case and the press. She hadn't driven him to what he did. She was the perfect wife, even understanding when he said he was impotent. Although that was just a cover because he didn't feel he should touch her after touching the filthy whores.

Wayne had made him see a bit of sense. He really wasn't being fair to her. If he loved her, he needed to let her go. Annabel was visiting him regularly anyway, so maybe he could build a life with her when he got out. They got on well and the conversation flowed. Ok she was a bit manic, but she was pretty enough; he wasn't overrun with options at the minute, was he?

A couple of weeks later when he had his privileges reinstated, he sent a visiting order for Annabel. He had actually missed seeing her these last two weeks. He would have to send her money again but it was worth it, maybe she would consider moving closer when she had the baby to save her keep travelling and staying in a hotel. He would ask her after the baby was born, she would have been visiting for over six months then.

David had also requested he see the governor which they allowed him to do three days later.

"You wanted to see me, Taylor," said the governor as David was escorted into his office. "What's it about?"

"It's about the divorce papers that my wife served on me," he said.

"I have them here in my office but you have refused to sign them, I was going to return them to your wife's solicitor," the governor barked at him.

"I have changed my mind," said David. "I'll sign them."

"What's changed your mind?" The governor asked.

"Does it matter?" David snapped. "I will sign them now."

"Watch your tone," the governor said as he got up to get them.

"Sorry," said David not wanting any more punishments issued.

The governor bought the papers over and gave David a pen. "Sign on pages 2 and 3," he said.

David signed the papers; it was tearing his heart out but he knew he was doing the right thing and he knew Annabel would be happy about it also.

After he signed the divorce papers, he was taken back to his cell. He lay down on his bed and tears started to roll down his face. He knew he had really screwed up his life and what for, his life was perfect before, but he couldn't stop himself from doing what he did at the time. The tears kept rolling and soon they turned into an uncontrollable sob.

It was approaching the Easter holidays and Gina was excited. Her family and her best friend Sammie were coming to stay for a whole week. Abby had said she could take a few days off to spend time with them and show them the sights.

The wedding arrangements were starting to take place; Gina really wanted to get married a St Nicholas Church in a little village called Abbotsbury. It was a short drive from the hotel but it was such a lovely church in a lovely village. Neil liked the idea of it too, but Gina knew they would have to get permission as she had been married before.

They went to see the vicar after the Sunday service which they had attended.

"Could we have a word, Vicar?" Neil said.

"Of course," he said. "Come into the vestry."

They followed him through the church to the vestry and explained to him that they would like to marry there but Gina had already been married.

"I see," said the vicar. "What happened in your last marriage?" He asked.

"Well," said Gina. "It's a long story, but if you have time, I will explain."

"I have time," he said, so Gina explained all about David, what he had done, how he had behaved with her since he was imprisoned and how he had now agreed to sign the divorce papers.

"I just want a chance at a new life," she said. "Neil and I love each other so much and I absolutely love this village and your church."

"Well, you have certainly been through the mill," said the vicar. "It's not impossible for you to get married in a Church of England church if you are divorced and some vicars will not do it at all. It all very much depends on the circumstances of the previous marriage and the reason for the divorce."

Gina and Neil sat listening with their hearts in their mouth, was he saying no? Or was he just explaining the rules? They just wish he would spit it out.

"It sounds to me," continued the vicar. "That you were at no fault whatsoever and I would be happy to carry out your wedding ceremony in my church."

He smiled at them. "What date were you thinking?" He asked.

"30 June, this year," said Neil.

The vicar got out his diary. "I can do a ceremony at 2 pm for you if that suits you."

Gina burst into tears. "Thank you so much," she cried. "That's perfect."

"I hope those are happy tears," laughed the vicar.

"They most definitely are," replied Gina smiling.

"Your bands will be read for the three weeks prior and you will be expected to attend those ceremonies. The rehearsal will be booked for the week before the wedding," he said. "Is that ok?"

"Yes," said Gina and Neil at the same time.

"Ok, let me just get some details from you both."

He took the details from them and bid them farewell. "See you in church soon," he winked at them.

Neil smiled at him. "Of course," he said.

"Oh, thank goodness," said Gina. "Let's hope our other venues go so well."

They had agreed to have the reception back at the hotel but they would have caterers in for that day as Oliver was going to be best man and all the other staff had wedding duties of their own. There were going to be around 100 guests and Abby had decided they would have a huge marquee in the grounds of the hotel.

They had the church and reception sorted. Abby was going to sort out everything for the reception so that they could concentrate on the other things such as outfits, rings, flowers, photographs and cars.

Gina wanted Sammie, Kathleen, Aunty Pat and Abby to come along to find the perfect dress so that was waiting until they visited. Neil and Oliver would be dressed in the same so they would go to the outfitters together along with Derek and Paul who were going to be ushers, bridesmaids Carol, Tracy and Sheila would go with Gina to the bridal shop in town so they could get their dresses sorted; they would sort out Sammie's when they came for their visit. Sammie was to be the maid of honour.

That just left Steven, Jenny, Peter and Janice; they were going to be the witnesses to the signing of the register. They had tried to involve everyone and of course, Abby would take pride in her place as the sister of the groom.

The porters, Keith and Troy, were going to manage the hotel on the day of the wedding, Gina felt bad they weren't involved but they had offered and said they would be there when they returned from the ceremony and then take it in turns to come into the marquee to celebrate with them. Abby was grateful and told them they could both have the next day and night off paid for their kindness.

Abby was in her element when she was organising, she made a list— Marquee, caterers, covered tables and chairs, flowers, DJ and a red carpet for the newlyweds to enter on.

The caterers were coming to the hotel over the Easter period for everyone to do the tasting of the menu samples. Abby had arranged it for when Gina's family were down as she wanted to involve them as much as possible. After that, they could decide on the menu and place the order for the cooked menu and the night-time buffet.

The list was getting ticked off bit by bit and Abby's excitement was rising. She never thought she would see the day her brother settled down and he'd picked the perfect woman to do it with.

For now, though, things would have to wait as the hotel review representative had arrived. They came every 12 months to review the hotel and give it a star rating for the hotel's guide. She had everyone check the rooms and make sure everything was clean and tidy. Not that it was ever any different, Abby had strict rules about how the hotel should be presented and she made no compromises in that department.

"Good morning," she said greeting a young gentleman. "My name is Abby and I am the owner."

"Good morning," replied the gentleman, shaking her hand. "Tom Jackson from the Hotel Review Board."

"Where would you like to start, Mr Jackson?" she said.

"Please, call me Tom," he replied. "Shall we start with the rooms?"

Abby led Tom to the room where he took notes and pictures then they covered the dining room, lounge and reception before going outside.

"The grounds are beautiful," Tom said. "And very big."

"We have my brother and the gardeners to thank for that," said Abby. "They work hard to keep it looking so nice."

"You have a lot of land here too," he said. "Do you do events here?"

"Not presently," said Abby. "But we are holding a wedding reception here at the end of June with a large marquee and around 100 guests, if that goes well, then it is something I may consider going forward."

"You should," said Tom. "It is a beautiful spot; anyone would be happy to have their reception here and it would be great for business."

"Yes," said Abby. "It is something I have thought about, but I'm going to have the trail run with my brother's wedding first."

"Would you mind if I returned on the afternoon of the wedding to take some pictures?" Tom said. "Then if you are happy, I can add them to your review."

"Of course, I don't mind," said Abby. "You can stay for the reception if you would like to. Then you can take pictures at different times. I could allocate you a room too so you get the full package for your write-up on us."

"That sounds like a good plan to me," said Tom "What date in June?"

"30·" said Abby. "The wedding is at 2 pm, so we should be back here around 4:30 pm."

"See you on the 30·" said Tom. "Nice to meet you, Abby."

"Nice to meet you too," she said shaking his hand. "Goodbye, Tom."

Abby was over the moon with how that had gone, she could be branching out soon if everything went well which would be good for everyone.

Everyone was getting so excited—everything was coming together nicely for a change.

It was the day before Good Friday and Gina's family were due to arrive anytime now. Everyone was busy and Neil and Gina were making the final touches to their rooms. She left their wedding invitations on the small table leaning up against a vase of fresh flowers. Neil had topped up the refreshments and the mini fridge and Gina added some snacks. Her dad loved snacks so he would be happy.

"I can't wait for them to arrive," she said to Neil.

"I can't wait to meet them," he replied. "I hope they like me."

"They will love you," she smiled. "Just like I do."

"I hope so," he said giving her a kiss on the cheek.

"When they arrive, I'll bring them to their rooms to unpack and settle first," she said. "Then we can all meet in the dining room at 1 pm for lunch and introductions, is that ok?" She asked.

"Of course, it is," he said. "I'll tell Abby to be there for 1 pm, we'll keep out of the way until then. I know how much you are looking forward to seeing them."

"Thank you," said Gina. "And it is so kind of Abby to give me a few days off next week for shopping with them."

"Abby knows how much you love your family; we want them to be part of our family too and she wants them to be as involved as possible," he replied.

At that, Sammie rang, "Hi, Gina," she said. "We've just got into the taxi so we will be with you soon. Aunty Pat and Uncle George are in a separate taxi but they are on their way too."

"Brilliant," said Gina. "Can't wait to see you."

"See you shortly," said Sammie. "Can't wait," and she put the phone down.

Gina made her way to reception to greet them; Troy was covering the desk until the end of his shift so she could spend time with them. Everyone here is so kind, it's like a big family, she thought.

The main reception door opened and in walked her mum and dad with Sammie. Sammie ran to her with her arms outstretched.

"This place is beautiful," she enthused. "And that driveway—wow!"

"It is lovely here," Gina replied smiling.

"I can definitely see why you're attracted to it," said Henry coming in for a hug.

"Hi, Dad," she said. "It's so good to see you all."

Gina hugged her mum. "It is a lovely place, Gina, you have dropped lucky here."

"I know, Mum," she said. "I am very lucky."

Aunty Pat and Uncle George came through the doors and more hugs and greetings were exchanged.

"When do we get to meet this young man?" Henry said.

"All in good time," she said. "First, I'm going to show you to your rooms so you can unpack and get settled. Then we have a table in the dining room at 1 pm for us all, Neil and Abby; you will get to meet the others over the week when they are working."

"Sound good," said George. "Lead the way."

The first stop was Kathleen and Henry's room. Gina opened the door and let them in.

"Jesus, it's a suite," said Henry. "Very nice indeed and do I spy snacks?"

Gina laughed. "Yes you do, we couldn't leave you without your snacks, could we?"

Kathleen rolled her eyes. "You and your snacks," she said.

"The mini bar is fully stocked and there is tea, coffee and drinking chocolate by the kettle and cups," said Gina. "Don't eat those snacks and ruin your lunch," she laughed. "Your invitation is there too."

"I don't need an invitation; I'm giving you away," he replied.

"Henry," scolded Kathleen. "I will want to keep that invitation in my keepsake box!"

"Ok, ok," he said. "Thank you, sweetheart. I think I'm going to like it here."

"See you in reception at 1 pm," she said closing the door.

She showed Aunty Pat and Uncle George their rooms; it was the same as her parents' room with everything stocked up for them.

"Thank you," they both said, "it really is lovely."

She then showed Sammie to her room; it was a suite but a smaller one for single occupancy.

"Oh, this is lovely," said Sammie. "I'm going to love staying here."

"You will love this place," said Gina. "It really draws you in."

"I'm already drawn," said Sammie making her way over to where her invite was sitting. She picked it up and squealed 'Maid of Honour'; she said, "Oh, Gina, thank you, thank you, thank you."

They both started to cry happy tears and hugged each other so tight Gina thought she might stop breathing. They broke away and laughed. "I'll let you settle in and see you downstairs at 1 pm."

Everyone was in reception just before 1 pm. "Did you all settle in your rooms ok?" Gina asked.

"Your Uncle George got a bit too settled," laughed Pat. "I had to wake him up."

"Yes, the bed is very comfortable." Her dad laughed. "I nearly nodded off myself."

"Let's go into the dining room, Neil and Abby are waiting for us."

They all followed Gina into the dining room and Gina did the introductions.

"It's so nice to meet you all," said Abby. "We have all heard so much about you."

"All good I hope," said Kathleen.

"All very good," replied Neil. "It's good to finally meet you all and I hope you enjoy your stay."

"Everything is great so far," said Henry. "If I may say, Abby, your hotel is beautiful and you have impeccable taste."

"Thank you so much," replied Abby. "It's down to the team too, we all work together to bring the best experience for our guests."

"Well, whatever, you all doing you are doing a great job," said Henry.

Oliver came out of the Kitchen, with the starters. "This is Oliver," said Gina. "He will be Neil's best man; they have been friends for a very long time." She decided to leave out the bit where they had fallen out, there was no need for anyone else to know about that at the moment.

"Pleased to meet you all," said Oliver. "Welcome to the Haven Hotel and I hope you all enjoy your lunch."

With pleasantries exchanged, Oliver returned to the kitchen to cook the main meal and everyone tucked into their food.

"That was delicious," said Kathleen cleaning her plate.

"Absolutely beautiful," said Pat.

"Oliver is a top chef," said Abby. "We are so lucky to have him here."

"I understand the wedding plans are underway," said Kathleen. "Abby, it is very kind of you to hire the marquee and have the reception here."

"I wouldn't have it any other way," said Abby. "We all love Gina and we are so happy about this marriage."

"She deserves someone good," said Henry. "After what that piece of scum did to her."

"I will look after her, you have my word," said Neil.

"Yes, lad, I believe you will," Henry replied.

Neil was relieved; they liked him and he so wanted them too. He liked them too and was glad there were going to be his family. He looked at Gina; she was radiant, and she really did love them all so much. She was a beautiful sole.

"Yes," Gina cut into his thoughts. "We have the church sorted; I was so relieved the vicar agreed to marry us. Mum, you will love it; it is so beautiful and in a lovely little village not far from here."

"I'm sure I will," said Kathleen. "If you like it so much it's got to be good."

Gina continued, "Abby is sorting out the reception for us. We have sorted the cars, there will be a car for Neil and Oliver, a car for the bridesmaids and you, Mum, a car for Abby, Aunty Pat and Uncle George and obviously one for you and me, Dad."

"Oh, we are in a wedding car," exclaimed Aunty Pat. "Oh, lovely."

"Of course, you are," said Gina. "Neil and I are going into town after Easter to sort out the flowers, rings and gifts, and I will go with the bridesmaids to sort their outfits."

"Who are the bridesmaids?" Her mum asked.

"Carol, Tracy and Sheila," Gina replied. "They have become very good friends to me since I have been here."

Kathleen looked a little awkward as she asked, "What about Sammie?"

"Sammie is going to be my maid of honour," said Gina.

Kathleen looked relieved and Sammie was smiling from ear to ear.

"That just leaves mine and Sammie's dress which I was hoping you and Aunty Pat and Abby would help me with while you are here."

"How lovely," said Pat.

"I will love that," said Kathleen.

Oliver came out with the mains, and once again, they all started to tuck into the delicious food he'd served.

"Where are you going to love once you are married?" Sammie asked.

"We thought it made sense to stay here to start with," said Neil. "We both work here and love it here so much plus it will enable us to save for our own place, which is our ultimate goal."

"Makes perfect sense to me," said George. "It's not cheap to start out nowadays so a little help is always welcome. Where are you going on honeymoon?" He asked.

"We want to go to Dubai for two weeks if we can save enough," said Gina. "Neither of us has ever been but we both would love to go."

"We would like to contribute towards that as a wedding present," said Aunty Pat.

Gina and Neil looked shocked. "Really?" Gina said. "That would be so kind of you."

"Very kind," said Neil. "Thank you so much."

"And your dad and I want to pay for yours and Sammie's dresses," said Kathleen.

"Oh, my god, you all don't have to do that," cried Gina.

"We want to contribute; Abby has the reception covered, so we will cover the honeymoon and dresses between us," said Henry.

Gina went round and hugged them all. She couldn't believe it and neither could Neil. They were going to be able to have a dream wedding now that was for sure. They were lucky to have such lovely families.

Easter went really well. "It's like old times having my family around at times like this with the added bonus of having you two in my life as well." Gina smiled to Neil and Abby.

"We are lucky to have you, Gina," said Abby, "and your family is lovely."

"Yes, they are," said Neil. "We will be one big happy family after the wedding."

"I wished they lived closer and Sammie," said Gina.

"They can stay here and visit as often as they like," said Abby.

"And we will go and see them often," said Neil. "You won't have to spend another Easter, Christmas or Mother's Day without them from now on."

Gina couldn't believe how life had changed; she was so happy. Both families got on so well and she was marrying the man of her dreams. How did she get this lucky, she thought.

"Taxi is here," said Abby interrupting her thoughts.

"Oh, let's go," said Gina excitedly, it was dress hunting day.

All the ladies got into the taxi which took them into Weymouth town. The town had three bridal shops so they were hoping to be able to find what they wanted. There was plenty of time for alterations if they were needed.

They tried the first shop they came to but nothing really stood out, the second one had one possibility but it didn't excite Gina that much.

"Let's try the last one," said Kathleen. "If there is nothing in there that you like, we can go further afield tomorrow. We need to get yours first so that Sammie's will compliment it."

"Ok," said Gina, by now feeling a little deflated. "Let's go."

They walked across town and came across the last bridal shop; this looked more promising. It was huge and the dresses in the window were gorgeous.

They walked in. "Can I help you?" A friendly assistant asked.

"I hope so," said Gina. "I'm looking for a wedding dress, preferably in ivory." She didn't want to wear white; she'd worn white at her first wedding and this one had to be different. "And we need a maid of honour dress for my friend to compliment my dress," she said.

The assistant looked them up and down, "Ok, size 12 for a maid of honour and size 10 for the bride," she said.

"How did you know that?" Gina gasped.

"I've had plenty of practice," the assistant laughed. "My name is Trina, by the way. I'll look after you, all take a seat over there for a moment."

They all sat down and waited, five minutes later, Trina returned with a tray of prosecco for them all.

"Thank you," they all said as they took their glasses.

"Now give me 10 minutes," said Trina. "And I'll bring you a selection of wedding dresses that I think you will love."

"What a service," said Sammie. "I could get used to this."

True to her word, Trina returned with a selection of dresses and held them up one at a time for Gina to see.

Gina was in awe; they were all so beautiful but the second one she was shown blew her away. "They are gorgeous," she said a bit dumbstruck, "How much is the second one, please?"

"We are not worrying about the cost, Gina," scolded her mum, "go and try on the one you like best first."

Gina went with the assistant who helped her into the dress; it wasn't a perfect fit but it was stunning. It had a beaded corset and was straight-fitting with a long train at the back. Trina had bought some tiaras and she found one that she knew Gina would love with that dress.

"We can do your alterations free of charge," said Trina as though she was reading her mind. "Here, let me pin the back so you can see what it looks like with the right fit."

"It's perfect," said Gina. "Can I show the others?"

"Of course," said Trina. "That's why they came, after all."

Gina walked out to where the others were waiting and both her mum, Abby and Aunty Pat burst into tears.

"You look stunning," said Sammie, "that is definitely the dress for you."

"You look gorgeous, sweetheart," said her mum through her tears. "I've never seen you look so radiant."

"So beautiful," added Aunty Pat still snivelling.

"You all like it?" Gina asked.

"It's stunning," said Abby. "You are stunning," she added.

"We all love it," squealed Sammie who also now had tears in her eyes, "my beautiful, stunning best friend," she said.

Trina smiled, her work on the wedding dress was done. "Is this the one?" She asked Gina.

"This is definitely the one," answered Gina. "I'm in love with it; you will get it altered for me right?" She asked.

"We will," said Trina. "Now, let's get you out of it and get the other dress sorted."

Gina was back with her family as Trina bought out some dresses for Gina to choose for Sammie.

"Which one do you like?" Gina asked Sammie.

"I like them all," laughed Sammie. "But I think the pale blue one would complement your dress beautifully."

They all agreed with Sammie, and Sammie went off with Trina to try it on. When she returned to the room, Gina gasped. "It's a perfect fit!" she exclaimed, "Sammie, you look gorgeous."

"It does feel pretty special," Sammie replied. "I shall just have to make sure I don't put any weight on." She laughed.

"Will you be here for a few days before the wedding?" Trina asked.

"Yes, I think so," said Sammie.

"Well, if you pop in for a fitting a few days before, we can make any alterations in plenty of time."

"Oh, great," said Sammie. "That's a relief."

They decided on the two dresses and Kathleen paid the deposit; the balance would be paid when they picked them up.

"Was it very expensive?" Gina asked her mother.

"That's not for you to worry about," said Kathleen, "the dress is perfect for you, price is not a problem."

They all made their way back to the hotel very happy. Gina felt like she was on a cloud she was so happy. She just hoped nothing would come along to knock her off it.

Everyone enjoyed their time together over the Easter break and soon, it was time for everyone to go home.

"I wish you were here longer," Gina said.

"So do we," said her mum. "But you have work to do here, you can't keep spending it all with us."

"We will be back before you know it," said her dad giving her a hug. "Only a couple of months."

"I will miss you so much," said Sammie, giving her a hug, "but I'm so happy things are working out for you now."

"I will miss you too," said Gina. "I wish we were closer."

"You are in the right place for you now, Gina," said Sammie. "Away from that scumbag. I will visit as often as I can and you will come to us, won't you?"

"You bet we will," said Neil. "I'll look forward to your return visit," he said meaning every word.

"You are all welcome here anytime," said Abby. "It's been a pleasure meeting you all."

"Same here," said Henry. "We will all go away knowing you are in safe hands now; you're a good lad, Neil."

"Thank you, Henry," he replied. "And yes, she is in very good hands."

"Call me when you get home," she said to them getting a bit teary.

"We will," they all replied and with that, their taxis pulled up.

They all said their goodbyes and got in their taxis. Gina, Neil and Abby waved them off until they were out of site.

"You have a lovely family, Gina," said Neil. "I'm so happy that I'm going to be part of it."

"A very lovely family," added Abby. "It's been such a pleasure to get to know them."

Gina smiled; everything was really working out well. She turned to Neil and smirked. "Shopping day for us tomorrow."

Neil hated shopping usually but this time he was looking forward to it.

"Yup," he said smiling, "time to get the rest of this show on the road."

They all went back into the hotel and set about their duties with a definite spring in their step.

Chapter 23

Wedding Bells

29 June: Day Before the Wedding

Everyone was very busy at the hotel today getting everything perfect for tomorrow.

Abby had decided to close the hotel for guests that weekend. It wasn't fair on her staff to expect them to be dealing with them at such a special time. Everyone wanted to be involved in the organising; after all, this was the biggest event the hotel had ever held. She decided she needed all hands on deck and guests would just be in the way, so when her Monday to Friday checked out there would be no one arriving until Monday.

Abby was outside with Neil and Oliver, overseeing the erection of the marquee, it was looking magnificent already.

"Blimey, it's huge," said Neil.

"We have 100 people to accommodate," said Abby. "It needs to be huge."

"Glad, I'm not cooking this weekend." Oliver laughed.

"You have more important tasks this weekend, Oliver, like not losing the rings," she smiled.

Once the marquee was up, Derek, Paul and Steven set about placing all the tables and chairs they had hired with a table for 9 as the top table. They would also be erecting a temporary stage for the DJ and Singer.

Abby was busying herself with placing the ornate vases and other bits ready for the flowers.

Neil, Oliver, Henry and George went out the front to decorate the fencing on the driveway up to the hotel while all the ladies were doing their bit inside decorating the reaction area and making sure all the bathrooms were clean and fully stocked.

The rest of the staff were checking the bedrooms and ensuring everything was stocked and ready.

Neil came back to the marquee. "Abby, it looks great," he said.

"I know," said Abby. "If this all goes well, this could lead to us doing more of these events for paying customers."

"It's definitely something we should look into," he said.

"Well, I've invited the hotel reviewer to the reception tomorrow, so he can get pictures of it in full swing. He's already saying great things about the hotel itself but said he would hold off on publishing until after the wedding so he can review our event too," she said.

"That's great!" said Neil.

"I know," she said. "I am really quite excited."

Neil was happy to see Abby happy; she was in her element with this event and he believed she would really shine if she added it to their charter.

At 2 pm, the bridal shop staff arrived with the wedding gowns and bridesmaids' dresses which were put upstairs in the master suite and laid out. Gina looked at her dress and still couldn't believe how gorgeous it was, Sammie read her mind.

"You are going to look stunning in it," she said to Gina.

Gina smiled at her. "I am so glad you are here."

"Where else would I be?" Sammie laughed. "You are best friend and this is going to be some event, I wouldn't miss it for the world."

"It means so much to me that you all came early," said Gina.

"We want to spend as much time with you as possible, plus there's lots to do," she said.

"I can't wait for tomorrow now," said Gina.

At 3 pm, Abby called for all the staff to meet in the staff dining area and they all arrived promptly.

"Right," she said, "I think everything is covered for today. The marquee is as ready as it can be for now. The florist is arriving around 9 am with our flowers and she will decorate the marquee too. The room dressers are arriving at about 9:30 to cover all the tables and chairs and lay the table decorations and the caterers will be here from 10 am, preparing for the wedding breakfast when we return. Does everyone know what the plans are for tomorrow?" She asked.

"Think so," said Oliver. "Neil and I will get ready in Neil's room, the cars are arriving at 1:30 when Neil and I will leave for the church."

"Yes, that's right," said Abby. "For the ladies, the hair and makeup ladies are arriving at 6:30 am, they have a lot of us to get through and they need to be finished by 12:30 in order for us all to get dressed. All of the bridesmaids, myself, Gina and Sammie will be getting ready together in the master suite, Kathleen and Pat are getting ready in Pat's room."

"6:30!" said Neil. "I'm glad I don't need makeup." He laughed.

"Yes, 6:30," said Abby. "There are eight of us for them to do so it needs an early start. When we know the coast is clear after you and Oliver have left, we shall come down at get into our respective cars. Once we have left for the church, I have someone coming in to clear the master suite and clean it as, Neil and Gina, this will be your room after the wedding."

"Wow, thank you, Abby," said Gina. "That's very kind of you."

"Yeah, thanks Abs, that's great," added Neil.

Abby smiled at them both. "My pleasure," she said. "The DJ will arrive while we are out to set up for the music. I have discussed what we wanted and he's happy with that."

They had chosen soft music for the afternoon playing in the background; then he would do an hour of more chart music up until around 7:30 pm when he would take a break When he took his break, the live singer would be on for a couple of hours. It was a tribute act that would do 2×45-minute slots, then that would be followed by the DJ until 1 am.

"It's going to be a great day," said Sheila excitedly.

"My kids are going to love it," said Tracy. "Roger is bringing them around 7 pm if that's ok."

"Absolutely fine," said Abby. "I shall look forward to seeing them. Right, what are everyone's plans for this evening?"

"Gina and I are going to have a pamper evening in Gina's room, facials, nails, the works," said Sammie.

"Oliver and I are just having a few drinks in the bar here," said Neil. "Anyone else is welcome to join us."

"That would be grand," said Henry. "You in, George?"

"Yup, count me in," he said.

"Pat and I are going to have a couple of drinks in the room then get an early night; it's going to be a big day tomorrow," said Kathleen.

"Yes, it is," said Abby. "And for that reason, I am going to have a long soak in the bath and have an early night myself. Carol, Tracy and Sheila, can you be back at the hotel at 6:15 in case they want to start with you in the morning?"

They all agreed they would be and set off home to prepare themselves for a very exciting day. Everyone else went to their respective places to enjoy a relaxing evening, everyone was buzzing with excitement.

30 June: The Wedding

Everyone was up by 6 am, none of them had slept with the excitement of what was to come today.

Sammie had stayed in Gina's room; they we up talking half the night but they we both wide awake at 5:30 am.

"Well, your day has arrived, madam." Sammie laughed.

"I am really doing this, aren't I?" Gina said.

"You are, indeed," said Sammie, "and I for one, couldn't be happier. He is your soulmate, everyone can see that."

Gina smiled and thought he definitely was. "I'm excited for our future," she said.

"Well, let's get today done first," laughed Sammie. "You go in the shower first."

Gina showered and then Sammie went in. There was a knock at the door; it was Abby.

"The hair and makeup team have arrived," she said.

"Team?" Gina asked.

"Yes," said Abby. "Three hairdressers and three makeup artists."

"Oh, ok," said Gina.

"I thought I'd send two hairdressers and two makeup artists in here as there is more of you and the others can do your mum, aunt, if they finish us they can come up here to help finish off here."

"Sounds like a plan," said Gina.

"Are you and Sammie showered and ready for them?"

"Yes, we are ready," she said.

"Then I'll bring them up and check with your mum and aunt if they are ready."

The team arrived and quickly got to work on the bridesmaids first, applying their makeup to perfect and styling their hair in beautiful curls apart from Carol who had short hair. For her, they had put a flower ribbon band across the front of her forehead, it looked stunning.

Next, it was Gina and Sammie's turn; they had a team each. One applied makeup while the other put rollers in their hair.

"What sort of look are you after?" Tina, the makeup girl, asked. "Natural but radiant?"

"Yes, please," said Gina. "I never put a lot of makeup on, so I don't want to look overdone."

"Oh, you won't, you will look beautiful, you have great cheek structure," said Tina.

"Thank you," said Gina.

She looked across, and Sammie, and her makeup girl, Sherry was busy working on her pretty face.

When Tima was finished, she gave her a mirror. "Wee, what do you think, if you don't like it just say."

"I love it," said Gina. "it really does look natural and radiant," she smiled.

"I'm glad," said Tina. "Now with everyone done in here, I'm going to see if they need help in another room. I'll see you later when your hair is done, we like to take pictures for our portfolio if that's ok with you."

"Of course," said Gina.

Tina left and Michelle, the hairdresser, asked her if she had anything in particular in mind for her hair. "It's all curled and bouncy now," she said. "So, I can do whatever you like."

"I'd like it put up," said Gina. "But I'll leave the rest to you."

"Where is your tiara?" Michelle asked.

Carol paced Michelle the tiara. "Great," said Michelle, "let's do something special."

When Michelle was finished, Gina looked in the dressing table mirror while Michelle held a mirror up behind her. Gina was blown away; it was so intricate and looked more beautiful than she had ever seen her hair look.

"Gina!" said Sammie. "That looks amazing. Michelle, you are a genius."

Sammie's hair was just being finished; she'd opted for a curled ponytail and it looked equally as stunning.

"Your team has done a brilliant job on all of us, thank you so much," Gina said.

"It's our pleasure," said Michelle. "Now, I'll go and see if anyone requires my help. See you all later when you are dressed and ready to go."

It was 12:15 pm by the time everyone was done and they had all come up to the master suite.

"Everyone looks so beautiful," said Kathleen. "Gina, you will look like a princess when you walk down that aisle; you make your dad and me so proud."

"Stop, Mum," Gina said. "You'll have me crying and I'll ruin my makeup."

Everyone laughed; everyone was happy for a change. "Let's all have a glass of bubbly," said Abby. "Then we can all get dressed; everything is going to plan downstairs and I have the flowers in my lounge, so I'm not needed for anything right now."

Sheila poured everyone a glass. "To Gina and Neil," she said raising her glass.

Everyone raised their glasses. "To Gina and Neil," they chorused.

The cars arrived just before 1 pm. Neil and Oliver were waiting in reception in their matching three-piece suits. They had both shaved and scrubbed up and they both looked very handsome.

"Nervous?" Oliver asked. "Your first wedding." He laughed.

"A bit," said Neil, "but I'm also very happy and still actually can't believe my luck. I keep thinking something is going to happen to stop this wedding."

"Nothing will happen," said Oliver. "Her ex is locked up and that creep of a girl is hopefully in a mental institution by now."

"Oliver!" said Neil. "She was nuts, but I don't wish that on her."

"Sorry," said Oliver. "That was a bit harsh but nothing is going to ruin this wedding; you two are made for each other," he said.

"I love her so much," said Neil. "I really do."

The chauffeur of their car came in to collect them.

"Here goes," said Oliver with a smile.

"Oliver," said Neil. "I'm so happy we made up and you're here today."

Oliver smiled. "Get in the car, you soppy sod."

They made their way down the decorated driveway and got in the car; it drove them away from the hotel and towards Abbotsbury.

Abby went and knocked on Gina's door. "Neil and Oliver have gone now," she shouted through the door.

Sammie opened the door and when Abby saw Gina her jaw nearly hit the floor. "Oh, Gina, you are a vision," she said. "You look so beautiful."

"Thank you," said Gina, "I actually feel it." She was wearing a beautiful ivory dress; it had a lace bodice and straight full-length skirt and a long trail behind it. On her head, she wore a tiara and veil on her perfectly styled hair. She felt very special at this moment and couldn't wait for Neil to see her.

Sammie helped her down the stairs to everyone in reception who was waiting for her, she heard gasps and saw tears in her mum's eyes.

"Mum, don't cry!" she said. "Your makeup will run."

"Oh, Gina," said her mum. "Even I didn't envisage you would look this beautiful."

"Thanks." Gina laughed.

"You know what I mean." Her mum laughed.

Everyone was looking around the dress in awe of it and Gina's beauty when Abby announced it was time to get in the cars.

"Kathleen and the bridesmaids, you go into the first car," she said. "Pat, George, Sammie and I will take the second car and obviously, you and your dad will go in the third car."

Everyone got into their respective cars and they started to pull away.

"I am very proud of you, Gina," said her dad when they were alone. "You look like an angel."

"Thank you, Dad," she said looking at him. "I am doing the right thing, aren't I?" She asked, always looking for her dad's approval.

"Of course, you are," he said. "You two are a match made in heaven; it is clear to see how much he loves you."

"I know but after last time..." Gina started before her dad interrupted.

"Last time was very different, Gina, your mother and I were against that marriage from the start. He was very shifty, only seeing you every two weeks and never letting you go to him. Yes, he was nice and pleasant enough on the surface but I always felt there was something wrong with him, and I was right." Henry liked being right and was always quick to tell anyone who would listen.

"Neil is different," Gina said.

"Very different," said Henry. "For a start, you see him every day, so he's definitely not hiding anything. He's told you all about his past and you have told him about yours. Neil is a good lad and I think he will make you very happy."

Gina was overjoyed to hear her dad talk about Neil like that. "He will," she said. "I know he will. I guess I just wanted your approval this time."

"Well, you have it and your mother's," said Henry.

It was about a 20-minute drive to St Nicholas Church so they sat back and took in all the pretty scenery they were passing on the way.

When they arrived at the church, Gina could see everyone waiting on the church steps, Kathleen, Pat, George, Sammie, Sheila, Tracy, Carol and Abby. All the guests were inside, as were Neil and Oliver.

Sammie and her mum came towards the car to help her out; her dad held her hand and she stepped out.

"Go and stand on the second step," said Sammie. "And I'll straighten out your train."

She did as she was asked and Sammie and her mum laid out her train behind her.

Kathleen, Abby, Pat and George went inside to take their seats. Sammie, Carol, Tracy and Sheila would go in next with Gina and her dad behind them. Sammie signalled that they were ready and the organist began to play the music.

As they walked down the aisle, Neil couldn't get a clear look of Gina, until the bridesmaids moved aside.

"Oh, my god," he said to Oliver. "She looks breathtakingly beautiful."

"She sure does," replied Oliver. "You are one lucky bastard."

Gina took her place by Neil giving her bouquet to Sammie, her dad sat down by her mum.

"You look beautiful," Neil said.

"You don't look so bad yourself." She smiled.

The vicar started to speak by welcoming all of the guests to St Nicholas parish then gave a statement about the sacredness of the union and the vows they are about to exchange.

He then continued with the wedding vows. Gina and Neil had opted for the traditional vows, not the modern-day ones.

"Neil, repeat after me," he said.

I, Neil Adams, take you, Gina Louise Taylor, to be my lawfully wedded wife. I promise to love and cherish you, in good times and in bad, in sickness and in health, for richer for poorer, for better for worse, and forsaking all others, keep myself only unto you, for so long as we both shall live.

Neil repeated the vows and then it was Gina's turn.

"Gina, repeat after me," said the vicar.

I, Gina Louise Taylor, take you, Neil Adams, to be my lawfully wedded husband. I promise to love and cherish you, in good times and in bad, in sickness and in health, for richer or poorer, for better for worse, and forsaking all others, keep myself only unto you, for so long as we both shall live.

Once both Gina and Neil had repeated their vows, they had to exchange the rings. Neil went first then Gina placed Neil's ring on his finger both reciting the ring exchange script.

I give you this ring as a sign of our marriage, and I promise.
I give you this ring as a symbol of my love.
I give you this ring as a token of my love and a sign of our marriage.
I give you this ring as a symbol of my love.
I give you this ring as a symbol of my love.

Then came the part everyone was holding their breath for; after recent experiences, they really hoped this would go well. Gina and Neil looked at one another as the vicar read out:

If anyone knows of any reason why these two should not be married, speak now or forever hold your peace.

A couple of minutes passed and everyone breathed a sigh of relief. *Thank you*, thought Neil and Gina.

I now pronounce husband and wife. You may now kiss the bride.

Neil had no problem with that part and neither did Gina; when they broke away from each other, Neil said, "Hello, Mrs Adams."

Gina smiled at him. "Hello, Mr Adams," she said. She was so happy; everything had gone smoothly and now they were husband and wife. She felt she should pinch herself to make sure she wasn't dreaming. Neil turned to look at Oliver who winked at him and gave him thumbs up. *This is really the best day of my life,* thought Neil.

They went through to sign the register with their chosen witnesses, Steven, Jenny and Peter, and then walked back down the aisle as man and wife. Everyone was clapping them as they walked past and out of the church where they both got covered in confetti.

Abby looked at them and was beaming; life was turning out so good for them all now. What a bonus it was that she had given Gina the receptionist job, she never dreamt it would turn out like this. With all their pasts laid to bed, she knew the future was going to be special for all of them.

After the photographs were done on the grounds of the church, everyone headed back to the hotel. Gina and Neil rode back together and the others utilised the other three cars to get back.

"How are you feeling, Mrs Gina Adams?" Neil asked smiling at her.

"Like I'm in a dream, Mr Adams," said Gina.

"Same here," replied Neil. "But we did it, and it is the happiest day of my life."

"Mine too," she said and they both leaned in for a kiss.

When they arrived at the hotel, they were told to wait in the car for ten minutes while all the guests took their seats in the marquee. Then they could make their entrance. They duly obliged, spending time alone wasn't a problem for them at that present time.

When it was time, Abby came out for them and they followed her up the driveway, through the hotel and onto the marquee. Everyone cheered when they walked in; they were both taken aback by how stunning the marquee looked.

They took their seats at the top table with her parents, Sammie, her aunt and uncle and of course, Abby. Everyone was chatting and enjoying their welcome glass of champagne. Gina was looking around the marquee in awe.

"Abby, this is a beautiful venue," she said.

"You like it?" Abby asked.

"I love it," replied Gina.

"We could make a business with this," Neil said. "If we get the advertising right."

"Well, Tom is over there chatting to Alan from the village. Hopefully, he'll get some good photos and be able to provide a good review. He's staying over tonight, so I will have a chat with him in the morning before he leaves," said Abby.

"Good call," said Neil. "You have done a fantastic job, Abby. Proud of you."

Abby smiled; yes, she had done a good job. She knew it and she was excited for future bookings if it all came to fruition. She was never happier than when she was organising something.

The DJ was beckoning for Gina and Neil to do their first dance before the dinner could be served. They got up and started to move to the sounds of Amazed by Lonestar. They had chosen that song because the words meant so much to them and were relevant to how they felt.

When it was over, they sat back down and soon the waiters and waitresses were starting to serve the first course of the dinner, duck pate with pickle. The main meal was bought out next; this was either beef or pork depending on everyone's own tastes. Finally, the dessert of crème Brulle or black forest gateau was served followed by coffee for those who wanted one. Other waiters and waitresses were topping up wine and prosecco glasses or fetching beer from the bar area.

Next, it was speech time. Her dad got up and gave a lovely speech about her that brought tears to her eyes. Abby got up on behalf of Neil; then Oliver got up for his. His speech was so funny. He had everyone in stitches. He had known Neil for a long time; they had got up to all sorts of mischief and it all came out. Everyone loved it and Gina's tummy was aching from so much laughing, she really was glad they were friends again.

After the toasts to the couple, the gifts were given out by Neil and Gina to the parents and bridesmaids. Everyone enjoyed the music that the DJ was playing. It was all going really well and Gina noticed that Oliver had gone over to sit with Janice.

"Those two look cosy," she said to Neil.

"They do, don't they?" He said. "Go on, my boy, it's about time he got himself back out there."

"Neil, they are only talking," she said.

"I only talked to you when you arrived," he winked.

The whole day and evening went without a hitch; the live singer had been amazing. He'd got everyone up dancing and everyone continued dancing when the DJ came back on when he'd finished.

Abby was talking to Tom about the hotel review.

"Abby, what an amazing event you've put on here, I have had the best time," he said.

"Does that mean you'll include it in your review?" She asked.

"You bet, I will," he said. "I've taken loads of photos so I can pick the best ones for the spread, which will be a double centre page by the way."

"Really?" Abby said. "That's amazing; thank you, Tom."

"Nothing short of what you deserve," he said. "I bet they'll be queuing up to hold events here after it's published."

"I'm so happy, Tom; I can't tell you. When will it be published by the way?"

"Next week," he said. "So, saddle up for the ride."

"Oh, I'll be ready," she said. "I'll be ready."

"I'll speak to you in the morning. I think I'm going to head up to my room if that's ok, but thank you again for asking me. I really have had a good time."

"Of course, it is ok," said Abby. "Goodnight, Tom, you are more than welcome."

She went off to find Neil to tell him the good news; he was over the other side of the room talking to his new wife. She smiled and made her way over.

"Shall we retire to our marital room?" Neil said to Gina. "It's 11 pm and the taxi is coming at 8 am to take me to a location where I spent two blissful weeks alone with my new wife."

"Yes," said Gina. "I am rather tired now."

"Oh, I wasn't thinking about sleep." He winked.

"You are intolerable," she laughed. "Let's find Abby and head up."

Abby got to them first and told them about the conversation she had had with Tom.

"That's fantastic," said Neil.

"It's very exciting," said Gina. "Well done, Abby."

"Well, I shall need both your help, but I am very excited about it," Abby said.

"Goes without saying," said Neil. "We are a team, a family team now."

"Of course," said Gina. "It is exciting news for us all, and Abby, thank you again for today; it really has been spectacular."

"It's my pleasure," said Abby. "Welcome to the family, Gina. We are really happy to have you be part of it."

"Thank you," said Gina. "I am very happy to be part of it."

"We're heading up, Abby," said Neil. "Early start in the morning."

"Oh, really," winked Abby.

Neil smiled. "We're off to say goodnight to Gina's family and Sammie then up to bed."

"Goodnight, both, see you in the morning before you go," said Abby and gave them both a kiss on the cheek.

Neil and Gina went off to find Gina's family and said their goodnights.

"It's been a cracking day," said Henry. "We'll be in reception in the morning to see you off," he said.

"I've had a fabulous day," said Sammie giving Gina the biggest hug. "I've been getting on quite well with Paul the maintenance guy," she winked.

"Glad you've all enjoyed it," said Neil. "Goodnight, all."

They left the party which was still going pretty strong and headed to their new room. When they arrived, they found it had all been cleared, cleaned and a bottle of champagne was on ice and there were strawberries in the fridge.

"Looks like our night is just beginning," smiled Neil.

"Doesn't it just," smiled Gina.

"Come here, Mrs Adams," he said. "I've been waiting all day to get you on your own."

Gina obliged his request willingly and they fell onto the bed in each other's arms.

The next morning, they were woken by the alarm clock. The limousine would be arriving in one hour to pick them up to take them to the airport.

"Good morning, Mr Adams," smiled Gina. "Time to wake up, Dubai is calling."

"Good morning," replied Neil. "You look just as beautiful as you did last night."

Gina laughed. "Are you sure, you awake? I have bed hair."

"You look beautiful to me," said Neil pulling back the covers to get out of bed.

They both got ready and added the last few things to their cases; they were both looking forward to spending some time alone on their honeymoon. They had chosen Dubai as neither of them had ever been and they both longed to go, so it was the perfect place for them to visit together for the first time.

When they arrived in reception, everyone was already there.

"You are all early birds," said Neil.

"You don't think we would have let you slip away without saying goodbye did you?" Sammie said.

"How long are you staying?" Gina said.

"We are all leaving tomorrow," said her mum. "We're spending some time with Abby today, with everything being so busy, we haven't had the chance to have a proper catch-up."

"Yes," said Abby. "We are all going to have some breakfast, then we are going into Weymouth town for the day and having dinner at Oliveto's."

"Oh, my favourite Italian restaurant," said Gina. "Have a lovely day."

"Don't leave it too long until you visit again," said Neil.

"We won't," said Henry. "But you are also welcome at our house anytime."

"I'll hold you to that," said Neil.

"Please do," said George.

They all said their goodbyes and hugged each other tightly then went out to the waiting limousine.

"Going in style," said Kathleen excitedly. "Safe travels both."

"Only the best for my wife," smiled Neil. "See you all soon."

With that, the limo pulled away slowly, everyone waving until it was out of sight.

"I'm so excited for this holiday," said Gina. "I have always wanted to go to Dubai and I can't think of anyone I'd rather see it with."

Neil smiled. "Same," he said. "It's going to be a long journey ahead though."

"I know," said Gina, "but we have a stop-off on the way and anyway, it's all part of the experience."

Neil laughed. "Ever the optimist," he said. "But yes, let's make the most of every minute."

They were getting the limo to Bournemouth Airport and getting a flight to London Heathrow where they would spend the night. It would be a long, long day if they travelled straight through to Dubai, so they had booked a room at Heathrow's Premier Inn. For the next flight, they had booked the Plaza Premium Lounge while waiting for their flight.

There was no expense spared on this honeymoon, with the family paying for the flights and the hotel, Neil and Gina were able to pay for the extras to make it extra special.

The room at the Premier Inn was lovely and the bed was really comfortable. They had dinner downstairs and then headed up to the room. They sat chatting for a while.

"It's so nice to be way, isn't it?" Gina said.

"It sure is," said Neil. "It feels like all the shite is behind us now and I'm looking forward to our future."

"Me too," Gina mused. "Isn't it strange how both David and Annabel have gone so quiet for so long? I hope it stays that way."

"They've got the message," said Neil. "They won't bother us again."

"I hope you are right," said Gina. "Annabel is due soon, that might stir her up and I'm still intrigued how David found out where I was, but he no longer worries me. He's safely out of the way and if he bothers me again, he'll be out of the way even longer."

"Well, they can't get to us here so let's just forget them and enjoy our honeymoon," he said.

"You're right," said Gina.

The next morning, they headed downstairs for breakfast and then made their way to the airport terminal. All checked in, they went to the Premier lounge to wait for their flight.

"Good morning, sir, madam, my name is Tina and I will be looking after you while you are in the lounge," said the concierge as they entered.

"Good morning," they both replied.

"May I see your passes, please?" Tine said.

Neil showed her their passes and she showed them to a table overlooking the airfield.

"There is free Wi-Fi, complimentary snacks, beers, wines and spirits, speciality teas and coffees, soft drinks and fruit juice," said Tina. "What can I get you? We also have hot food to order if you prefer."

"Oh, we've just had breakfast," said Gina. "We can help ourselves to snacks if that's ok, I'll have a Bucks Fizz," she added.

"I'll have the same," said Neil.

"Not beer?" Gina asked.

"No, we're celebrating, let's do Bucks Fizz," he said.

"A celebration?" Tina asked.

"Yes, our honeymoon," replied Gina. "We were married just yesterday."

"Oh, how lovely," replied Tina. "I'll let our flight crew know then you'll get more complimentary drinks." She winked as she went to fetch the drinks.

"This is definitely the way to travel," said Neil. "Bucks Fizz at 10 in the morning and being waited on hand and foot."

Tina returned with the drinks and put them on the table. "We also have magazines and newspapers, there are showers over there if you want to freshen up before the flight and we also offer spa treatments if you fancy a nice massage," she smiled and left.

"Wow," said Gina. "Is there anything that they don't do? I could get used to this."

They had a few drinks and some of the complimentary snacks while they were watching planes land and take off. After a couple of hours, the Tannoy announced that their gate was open so they made their way there. They went through and found their seats on the plane, Gina looked at Neil, she had never felt so happy in all of her life.

Neil was deep in thought, thinking how lucky he was to have found Gina. If she hadn't come for the job his life may have been very different. This was the beginning of a great future, he just knew it. He looked at Gina, and he had never felt so happy in all of his life.

It was mid-July and Annabel looked fit to burst; she was so big. She was due very soon and she wished the baby would just hurry up. Nobody wanted her looking like this and she hadn't slept with a man in months. As soon as they saw her stomach, they moved on. She needed to give birth, so she could pursue Neil. She wanted the life she'd dreamt of at the Haven Hotel and once this child was born, he was going to find it hard to refuse her.

She was sitting in the kitchen with a cup of tea and reached for the Hotel Review magazine. She wasn't really interested but she was bored. She wondered if Sunny Cottage had a review this month and started to flip through the pages when suddenly she stopped and shouted, "No!"

Edna rushed in. "Whatever is the matter?" She asked.

"Look at this! How could he?" Annabel shouted.

Edna looked at the magazine article and her heart sank. Annabel hadn't mentioned Neil for some time and she had hoped she had let it go but obviously not.

"Annabel, Neil is entitled to marry his girlfriend," she said.

"Not when I am carrying his baby," shouted Annabel.

"We both know it is not his baby from the dates," said Edna.

"What do you know, you stupid bitch? Of, course it is his and when it is born, he will have to ditch the whore and take his responsibilities," she shouted pacing around the kitchen. "How dare he get married and rub it in my face like this?"

She got the magazine and started to rip it to pieces; she was in a frenzy ripping and shouting.

"Annabel, calm down," said Edna. "Think of the baby."

"Fuck off," shouted Annabel and then screamed out in pain and was clutching her tummy.

"What is it?" Edna said panicking.

"The pain," cried Annabel. "It's unbearable, I can't stand up."

All of a sudden, a flood of water fell from her onto the kitchen floor.

"Oh, my god," said Edna. "You're in labour."

"I'm not due until next week," shouted Annabel.

"You've worked yourself up so much that you've bought it on early," cried Edna. "I'll call an ambulance."

The ambulance arrived quite quickly and confirmed Annabel was in labour but there seemed to be a complication. "We need to get you to the hospital straight away," said the paramedic.

"I'll follow in my car," said Edna. "I'll meet you there, Annabel."

"I don't want you there," growled Annabel.

"I'm sure you will need someone when this pain gets worse," said the paramedic. "And I don't see anyone else offering," he didn't like the way Annabel spoke to her mother at all.

They lifted her into the ambulance and Edna followed in her car. She was dreading this. She knew that Annabel would not rest until she had Neil's DNA and even then she doubted she would believe the results.

Annabel wanted Neil to be the father so she could go off and have an easy life with him and she knew Annabel would not stop until she got what she wanted. *Jesus, we are in for another roller coaster ride*, she thought with her heart sinking further and further down to her boots.

When she arrived at the hospital, she went to the reception and asked the receptionist if she knew where her daughter had been taken.

"I'll find out for you," the girl smiled. "Just take a seat over there."

A few minutes later, the receptionist let her know that Annabel had been taken in for a caesarean section and when she was out of theatre, the doctor would come and see her.

Edna sat and waited for what seemed like ages. In fact, it was nearly two hours and she was getting very worried! A doctor came through to the waiting room, called her name and beckoned her to follow him to a side room.

"Is Annabel ok?" Edna asked.

"Well, it depends on how you define ok," said the doctor. "The cord was wrapped around the baby's neck, so we had to take her in for an emergency caesarean, the baby is fine and in an incubator for now to be on the safe side; she is being closely monitored but your daughter is another matter."

"What do you mean?" Edna asked startled. "And it is a little girl."

"Yes," he replied. "A bonny little girl weighing in at 7lbs 6ozs, a very healthy weight and we can find no issues with her. We are just airing on the side of caution because of the complication of the birth."

"And Annabel?" Edna asked warily.

"Well," he said. "We tried to give her baby to hold and she started screaming, saying it wasn't hers and we had swapped them and given her the wrong child."

"Oh my god," said Edna. "This is another level for even Annabel, why was she so adamant it wasn't hers?"

"She said it was the wrong colour," the doctor answered.

"Wrong colour!" said Edna shocked. "What colour is it?"

"It's mixed-race," said the doctor. "Is her boyfriend mixed-race?"

"She hasn't got a boyfriend. She has convinced herself it is a guy she slept with when he visited our guest house but he is white. She has envisaged a lovely life with him and now she knows it can't be his. There was never any chance it was his anyway but, Annabel, well, she was different."

"Yes, I see from her medical records that she has been sectioned for mental health in the past."

"Yes, she has," replied Edna sadly.

"The episode she has just had was a sign of psychosis, her perceptions aren't real and she's having delusions, we have had to sedate her and if she wakes up in the same state we will have to section her for her own safety."

"Can I see her?" Edna asked.

"Yes," said the doctor. "Would you like to see your grandchild first?"

"Yes, please," said Edna and got up to follow him to the nursery.

"She is beautiful," said Edna, "and perfect."

"She is a bonny little thing," the doctor said. "Do you know who the father may be, would he need to be told?"

"Not really," said Edna. "My guess is it was one of the boys who stopped by when they were working on a building site up the road from us, he is well gone. Unfortunately, my daughter has a way of getting them into bed believing she's going to get her happy ever after but they simply move on at the end of their contract and don't give her a second thought."

"Oh, I see," said the doctor. "If Annabel is sectioned, will you be able to look after the baby?"

Edna looked startled. "Doctor, I am 72 years old with a guest house to run. I don't think I would cope."

"Then we might have to ring social services about a foster family," he said. "Let's go and see how Annabel is doing?"

She followed him to a side room. Annabel was crying.

"Annabel," said Edna. "Are you ok?"

"Of course, I'm not fucking ok, they have swapped my baby; Neil will never take responsibility for a baby that is not his or mine!"

"But Annabel, we always knew it wasn't Neil's," said Edna. "The dates were out."

"Get the fuck out," screamed Annabel. "You don't know what you are talking about, you dozy bitch. I don't want that freak of a baby anywhere near me. Now get the fuck out of here."

With that, Annabel got out of bed and launched herself at Edna, landing a hard punch on the side of her head. Edna was knocked off balance. She couldn't believe what just happened. Annabel had always been nasty, but she had never hit her before.

The doctor and two nurses were restraining Annabel on the bed while another nurse took care of Edna. Annabel was screaming like a wild banshee while Edna looked on in disbelief.

The doctor took Edna out of the room. "We are definitely going to have to section her," he said "for her safety and yours and the baby."

"I can't believe what just happened," said Edna. "This is the worst she has ever been."

"She believes she's been cheated and her mind has switched to this, don't take it personally. Psychosis can be treated but under strict conditions. I will sort out an institution for her to stay in for a while and she'll get the treatment she needs."

"Can you try and get her close so I can visit?" Edna asked.

"I'll do my best," said the doctor.

Edna was quite relieved actually. She would get some peace; she would visit Annabel, but if she got abusive she could just leave.

"And the baby?" Edna asked.

"We will contact social services to get her put into foster care. We can reassess the situation when Annabel's had her treatment."

"To be honest, doctor, I think that is the best solution. Annabel has given me a life of hell for the past 17 years. I would wish that on the poor little might. That baby deserves to be with a young family who will give her the love she needs."

Edna left the hospital for home; the doctor said he would ring with all the details. She had lost a daughter and granddaughter in one day and it had hit her hard.

She got in her car and started the drive home. *At least I'll get a bit of piece for a while,* she thought.

A few weeks later, Annabel was sitting in her room at Westhaven Hospital, in the Linden Unit for acute mental health needs. She really didn't understand why she had been put here to live. She'd done nothing wrong; it was the hospital that got the babies mixed up.

They had told her that her baby had gone to foster parents while she was having treatment, but if they tried to give her that mixed-race baby back, she would refuse it. It wasn't hers and she wouldn't have it. She started to cry thinking about the life she had lost with Neil because of their stupid mistake. There is no way she could have a life with him now.

"Stupid fucking hospital," she shouted.

Her carer came in. "What's wrong, Annabel?"

"I'm fucking angry that the hospital switched my babies, that's what is wrong," she growled.

The carer knew better than not to agree with her while she was in this state.

"It will all get sorted," she said. "Now, let's give you your medication, it will help to calm you down."

Annabel had her medication and felt a bit calmer; she turned her thoughts to David. She needed to write to him and let him know why she hadn't visited. She needed to keep in contact with him; after all, he was her only hope of a happy life now. Ok, he has 18 years to serve but she was only 22 years old and if she waited, she could have a perfect life with him when she was 40.

She didn't want him to have any other visitors that he may grow close to, so she sat at her writing desk and began to write.

Dear David

I'm sorry I haven't visited for a while but I have been a bit tied up. I had the baby but the hospital switched them and tried to give me a mixed-race baby. I knew it wasn't mine and I went mad at them. I told them I didn't want a freak of a baby.

My evil bitch of a mother turned up talking nonsense so I ended up punching her in the head, she did deserve it though but because of this they have sectioned me to Westhaven Hospital for treatment; waste of time really because there is nothing wrong with me. I only freaked out because they gave me the wrong baby and my mother insisted that one was mine.

The baby has gone into foster care; they said they will see how I am after treatment to see if I can have her back. I told them I didn't want her she was not mine!

I will continue to write to you regularly and when I get out of here, I will start visiting again. I'm not going back to my mothers, I never want to see that witch again! I will ask them to rehome me somewhere nearer to the prison and I will wait for you I promise and hopefully we can start a life together.

The address here is
The Linton Wing
The Westhaven Hospital
Radipole Lane
Weymouth
DT4 0QE
Yours lovingly
Annabel
PS: I thought you should know that Gina and Neil got married a few weeks ago…

That should stop him thinking about that whore, she put the letter in an envelope and addressed it. She called the carer and said, "Can you post this for me as soon as possible?"

David was having breakfast in the canteen when the post was distributed to the cells; he hadn't heard from Annabel for weeks. Something must have happened for her not to write. Had she found out he had written to Gina and got extra time for it? Had she had the baby and there were problems? Or had she simply gone off the idea of having anything to do with him?

He missed her visits; he so looked forward to them. He walked into his cell and saw a letter on the cabinet; he picked it up and could see it was her writing. He was relieved and apprehensive. She hadn't written for a while, was this a goodbye letter?

He opened the letter and began to read, his eyes wide in shock at her words. She'd had her baby and they had switched them at birth. When she confronted them about it, they had locked her in an institution. He had no reason not to believe her and he was angry at the way she had been treated.

Wayne walked into the cell. "Oh you've had a letter, is it off the luscious Annabel." He laughed.

"Shut your mouth," said David still angry.

"What's up? I thought you'd be happy after receiving a letter, you've been on about it for weeks," said Wayne bewildered.

"I am happy for the letter, but not the contents," said David.

"Ditched you, has she?" Wayne smirked.

"No, the opposite, but she's been treated really badly and they have locked her up in a Mental Health Hospital," said David.

"Well, they don't do that for no reason, there must be something wrong with her," Wayne replied.

"Shut up and get out of my cell. There is nothing wrong with her. She's been cheated out of her baby and treated awfully," David said.

Wayne got up to leave. "Whatever," he said as he left.

David read on. They had put the baby into foster care and Annabel said she didn't want it. He was surprised at how relieved he was when he read that part. He'd never really been a kid person but he would have accepted anything now just to have someone in his life.

He was glad she was going to move nearer and he was over the moon when he read, *I promise and hopefully, we can start a life together.* Oh my god, this woman was sent from heaven. He would have something to keep going for, she wasn't bad-looking and they did get on. He would get regular letters and visits which would make his sentence so much easier to bear.

When he read the last sentence, he nearly blew with rage, Gina and her bloke had got married! That's why she was so keen on the divorce. She had omitted to tell him the reason because he didn't believe for one minute it was because of what he had done.

How dare she deceive me like that? He thought. He would never have signed for her to remarry; he would get his own back for this one day.

David went over to the table and got his stationary out to write back to Annabel.

Dear Annabel

It was so good to receive your letter, I was getting worried that I had upset you but I can see now you were unable to write.

You have been treated terribly, how dare they switch your baby and try to offload someone else's on you? It is disgusting and I can understand why you don't want it, there is no judgement from me (he would add that in as he didn't really want to come out to kids).

I am sorry that you have been sectioned. Hopefully, it won't be for too long and you can get out and move closer, then maybe visit more than just once a week, I would love that.

It lifted my heart to read that you will wait for me. We will have a good life together when I am out, and I promise you that. Just keep your head down and we will soon see each other again.

Thanks for letting me know about the wedding, Gina was a bit deceitful but I'm not too bothered since my feelings have grown for you.

Take care and hope to hear from you soon
All my Love
David

He addressed the envelope and then took it to the office for it to be posted. He wasn't sure he had feelings for Annabel but he needed to keep her sweet. She was his only contact with the outside world. He was very bothered about Gina getting married but he didn't want to disclose that to Annabel, if she thought he still loved Gina, she might cut all contact with him.

Thinking about Gina, he felt he needed to write one last letter to her. It may not get through the system and if it did, he would probably end up with extra time on his sentence. *What the hell*, he thought, *I need to do this and Annabel will wait.*

Once again, he sat at the table and started to write.

Dear Gina

I believe you have recently married, if I said I was happy for you, I would be lying. You deceived me into the divorce, I can see that now.

Do you think I would have signed those papers had I known? Of course not, why should you get to live your happy ever after while I'm in here?

I won't be in here forever, Gina, and when I get out, I will get even with you for this.
David

David had addressed the envelope to Gina Taylor, so he hoped it would slip through. He wouldn't contact her again now, but that would unsettle her new marriage a little he hoped.

Chapter 24

Two Years Later

It was early July and the weather was beautiful as Gina sat in the garden watching her son play. She was reflecting on the past couple of years since the wedding. It had been eventful but luckily, everything had settled and she was enjoying being a wife and mother very much; she had never really wanted kids in the past but Teddy had made their lives complete.

The honeymoon was absolutely amazing and did nothing but cement their love. They'd had complimentary champagne and strawberries on the flight and landed in one of the most amazing countries she had ever visited, not that she had visited many.

They stayed in the honeymoon suite at the Marriott Resort Palm Jumeirah; they dined in style in countless top-class restaurants and tried all the different cuisines during their two-week stay, Italian, Korean, Peruvian, Japanese and Mexican, to name a few. They enjoyed the days either on the beach, by the pool or sightseeing. They had spent heavenly nights in their suite overlooking views of the Arabian Gulf.

Gina had visited the spa a couple of times while Neil had gone to the hotel gym. It had been a wonderful experience for them both.

When they returned, everyone was eager to hear all about it and they were both happy to fill them in. They had asked Abby if she had heard anything about Annabel and if she had had the baby but at that point, she had not. Edan had visited just before that Christmas though and that was a very interesting visit indeed!

They had settled back into their jobs with ease and everyday life returned to normal. They had decided to live at the hotel while they saved for a place of their own in town; they wouldn't move far because they fully intended on working at the hotel. It was a family business now.

She then thought about the letter David had sent. The postman had arrived as normal and Gina was sorting the post she had delivered, placing each one in the correct pigeonhole for everyone when she suddenly saw the one addressed to her. It was addressed to her married name, who would be writing to her with her married name? Then she recognised the writing and her heart sank. He was cute; she would give him that, using her married name had obviously let it slip through the sensor but how on earth did he know she had got married? She was sure that the prison didn't issue the Hotel Review magazine to the inmates, they weren't going anywhere, after all. Who was telling him about her life and movements? It unnerved her and she called Neil to be there when she opened it.

It still gave her chills when she thought about it. It was a threat, ok. He was in prison for a long time but he would get out eventually and she didn't want to be his obsession.

Neil told her to ring Mike, which she did, who duly reported it on her behalf. A couple of weeks later, she heard David had had an extra six months added to his sentence; at this rate, he would never get out! Fortunately, though, she had not received anything else from him or about him, so she hoped that was the end of it.

A few weeks after arriving home, Gina realised her monthly was late and after testing, she found out she was pregnant. She didn't really know how she felt, she'd not even thought about kids and she thought they had been careful. Neil, however, had been over the moon about the news.

"This is amazing," he had said. "This will complete our family."

Teddy was born on Easter Sunday and Gina had never felt a love like it. He was gorgeous with little blonde wisps of hair and big blue eyes. For a while, they stayed at the hotel but continued to save until they had enough for a deposit on this place. It was a lovely little cottage but needed plenty of work. Before they moved in, they made sure Teddy's room was done and all the electrics and heating were up to scratch. The rest was and still is a work in progress. She loved her little home and she loved her family very much.

Neil still worked at the hotel full-time and Gina was now working part-time just doing afternoon shifts; her mornings were taken up with mother and toddler groups and meeting other mothers and when she wasn't doing that, she was happy at home. Teddy went to work with her and his Aunty Abby loved having him there as much as he loved being there; everyone fussed him so he had a big extended family. All the original staff was still at the hotel; no one was in a rush to move on, but why would they? It was more than just a job to them all and Abby treated them all well they were very loyal to her.

She thought about Abby and smiled. She had now got a 'companion' she had met him through a dating site which Gina and Neil had urged her to go. They both felt she deserved some happiness after what she had been through. She seemed apprehensive when she told Neil and Gina about him but they were both over the moon for her and asked if they could meet him.

Abby arranged an afternoon tea at the hotel for them all to meet and Neil and Gina really liked him. Abby had been honest with him about Harry, no more secrets; she had said but Terry assured Neil he really liked Abby and he would look after her if she would let him. They took things very slowly to start with, only seeing each other once a week for dinner but things were moving on now and they were getting very close. Gina was happy for her and so was Neil.

Gina's mind then went to Oliver and Janice. She knew they were getting close at the wedding; she had told Neil so, but it turned out they had been secretly dating for a while! They said they didn't want to say until after the wedding as that was Gina and Neil's special day but when they had returned from honeymoon, they told everyone they were a couple. Everyone was delighted for them; they made a lovely couple. Twelve months later, they moved in together in a private rented flat not far from where Gina and Neil lived. More recently, they got engaged and the wedding was planned for next May. Neil was going to be the best man; Gina, the maid of honour and little Teddy was going to be the cutest little pageboy.

Kathleen and Henry had visited when she had Teddy and Sammie had come along too. They adored him, and they planned a return visit for the christening.

After the christening ceremony, they all headed back to the hotel for the afternoon. Kathleen and Henry had asked if they could speak with Gina, Neil and Abby before they left in the morning. Gina thought there was something wrong like one of them was ill. She begged them to talk to her then and there but they said she would have to wait; they were smiling so that was a good sign she supposed.

The next morning, they were all in the lounge and Henry started to speak.

"We've been thinking," he said. "Whenever we want to see you, it is quite a trip for us and for you, if you come to us. We are not getting any younger and we want to see our grandson growing up," he continued. "We have been thinking about selling up and moving down here, what do you think?"

Gina was delighted. She never thought they would move from their house, they had been there for years and years but Gina would love them to be close.

"We could do a bit of babysitting for you," said Kathleen. "We were wondering, Abby, when we sell the house, could we rent one of your rooms while we look for somewhere to buy."

"Of course," said Abby. "I am delighted with this news; all the family will be together."

Their house sold quite quickly as it happened and they moved into the hotel. They were only there three months before they found a lovely house in between the hotel and Gina's cottage. It was perfect and it was so good to have her family close.

Sammie continued to visit often; she loved Teddy and she was his godmother. She told Gina after a few months that she really missed her and everyone she loved was now in Weymouth. She said that she and Paul had been texting and he was taking her out for dinner each time she visited.

Gina was shocked. "How did I not know this?" She gasped.

"I wanted to see how things went first," said Sammie. "But I really like him, Gina and he likes me."

"Well, I'm really happy for you," said Gina. "But what about the distance?"

"Well, about that," Sammie said smiling. "I have applied for a transfer to the local hospital down here and as soon as that is sorted I'll be moving down, I'll get a rental easy enough."

Gina had started to cry, happy tears; life was complete in Gina's eyes and she had never felt this happy in her entire life.

Gina was disturbed by Teddy, "Mummy, we go and see Aunty Abby, pleeease."

Gina laughed, "Yes Teddy, it is time for us to go, come on, let's get you ready."

Abby often thought how life had changed, for the better, she was pleased to say. A few years ago, she had an abusive husband, a failing motel and a rogue brother she had to look after. Things were definitely better now.

She blessed the day that Gina had walked into their lives. It was all down to her that they were all in such a good place now and she was thankful she had stood by Neil through a difficult time. She had, of course, been through a lot herself, but now they were a big happy family she knew they could pull through anything.

Gina and Neil were so happy in their little cottage and Abby still got to see them every day with them still working at the hotel. When Teddy was born, she was delighted; he was such a bundle of joy and he was what everyone needed after everything that had happened.

Abby had decided to make Neil and Gina shareholders in the hotel; that way, they would always have a secure future for themselves and Teddy. They were the picture of the perfect family and she felt that they actually were.

She thought back to the episode with that Annabel girl, what a time that was! Little did they know at the time just what was going to happen with her but when Edna visited, it all became clear and answered a few questions.

Edna had visited the hotel for a week in early December the year of the wedding. When she rang to book, Abby was sceptical until she knew Annabel wasn't going to be with her.

"I need a break, Abby," she had said. "A lot has happened in recent months and I loved it at the hotel with the exception of my daughter. I would love to come and stay; I have things to fill you all in on too."

"Of course, you should come, Edna, it will be nice to see you have a break," replied Abby.

When Edan arrived, she said she would unpack but would they all meet her for dinner as she had some things to tell them?

They met in the dining room at 7 pm. Tracy was looking after Teddy for a while. Edna began to talk. "Annabel had a bonny little girl," she said.

"I was expecting a call for DNA," said Neil. "Even though we knew it wasn't mine."

"There was no need," said Edna. "The baby was mixed-race."

Everyone looked shocked. "Mixed-race," said Abby, "Annabel obviously realised then it wasn't Neil's."

"If only it had been that simple," sighed Edna.

"What happened?" Gina asked.

"Annabel was convinced that the hospital had swapped the babies and there was a conspiracy going on to keep her from Neil. They had to sedate her several times, she was wild and no one could settle her."

"Oh, my goodness," said Abby. "That must have been awful for you."

"Yes," said Edna. "It wasn't a pleasant scene, anyway, she ended up being sectioned for her own safety."

"And the baby?" Gina asked.

"Well, I am too old and have Sunny Cottage to run. It's too big a responsibility for me, so it was decided that she should go into foster care until Annabel was assessed."

"Did she get her back?" Abby asked.

"No," said Edna. "She said she didn't want her; she wasn't hers and she could stay where she was. To be honest with you all, I think it is for the best. Annabel has given me a terrible life and I wouldn't wish that on anyone, especially a child. The child will be bought up by a loving, stable family who actually wants her."

"Have you seen her? She is your grandchild," said Neil.

"I saw her at the hospital but it was mutually decided that it was best to give the child a fresh start with no confusion."

"I'm so sorry, Edna," said Abby. "How is Annabel now?"

"You guess it as good as mine," said Edna. "That's another story. I went to visit her at the institute a few times. On one occasion, she asked me to post a letter. When I looked, it was to a prison."

"A prison?" Gina asked, suddenly getting uncomfortable.

"Yes," said Edna. "This is where the story gets difficult for me to tell you."

"Go on," said Gina.

Edna continued, "I challenged her as to who it was. I got the usual it's none of your business and all the names thrown at me but I told her I would take it and not post it if she didn't tell me. After a lot more shouting and abuse, she told me. I'm really sorry, Gina, but it was your ex-husband, David."

"David!" said Neil and Gina at the same time.

"Turns out she had been visiting and writing to him when she was pregnant. She had written to him to tell him that she would wait for him and now she is out of the institute, she is living in a flat nearer to where he is, so she can visit more often. I haven't seen or heard from her in over nine months."

"Oh, Edna," said Abby. "I'm so sorry, you didn't deserve this."

"Abby," said Edna "my life has been far more settled since she's left. I'm not walking on eggshells every day and Sunny Cottage has a much better atmosphere."

"Who's looking after it?" Abby said.

"I've closed it for this week. I felt I needed a break. I have got a young girl who works for now though. Shelly is a breath of fresh air. There is more though, Gina, I'm afraid."

"More?" Gina said.

"Yes, apparently, your ex-husband put posters up in Scotland reporting you missing. Annabel saw them and that's why she wrote to him."

"Missing posters," squealed Gina. "My god, the lengths he went to is frightening."

"I know," said Edna. "But Annabel arranged a visit and told him where you were living."

"Oh my god, that is how he found out," said Gina. "Do you know if she told him about the wedding?"

"I'm guessing so; the day she went into labour, the Hotel Review guide was open at the kitchen table on the pages where the wedding was featured."

"Well, that answers a few questions, doesn't it?" Abby said.

"It does," said Neil. "Well, let's hope if they find happiness together, they will leave us the hell alone."

"Have you heard anything from them since?" Edna asked.

"I received a threatening letter from him last year after the wedding but he got extra time added and I've not heard anything since. I hope it stays that way," said Gina.

"Me too, Gina," said Edna. "I'm only sorry she's caused so much trouble."

"It's not your fault," said Abby, "you have had as much trouble as anyone and I hope this break does you good, if you need anything, just shout," she said getting up to leave.

"Thank you," replied Edna. "I'm looking forward to some nice walks."

Abby came back into the room from her thoughts with a knock at the door, it was Terry. She had met Terry on a dating app, would you believe? She was very unsure about using it or accepting any invitations but Neil and Gina had badgered her to give it a go. In the end, she thought what the hell, she deserved a bit of happiness after what Harry put her through.

Terry was a match on the app and he looked so kind that she accepted the invitation to chat. They had a lot in common and eventually, agreed to meet. They hit it off immediately and even though Abby was smitten, she made it clear to him that she wanted to take things slowly, to which he agreed. At first, they saw each other once a week for dinner but now it was like he was part of the family. She could see a future with him now and that made her happy.

Yes, thought Abby as she gave Terry a kiss on the cheek; things had turned out very well indeed.

Neil was sitting in the hotel gardens with Oliver; it was a warm day and they were both on a break. They were talking about how life had changed over the last few years.

Neil was so happy that they were best friends again; everything in his life had changed for the better and it was made even better by having Oliver to share his good fortune with.

Neil loved the cottage and he equally loved doing it up for his little family. Teddy had made everything complete. When Gina told him she was pregnant, he couldn't believe how lucky he was. He was determined to get them their own place and live a perfect family life. That was turning out brilliantly so far.

Little Teddy had brought so much joy into their lives and he really missed him when he went to work; he couldn't wait for Gina to start her afternoon shifts so he could see him. Everybody wanted to look after him but occasionally, Neil had him in the gardens with him for a couple of hours and he loved every minute.

When Abby had made them shareholders, he couldn't thank her enough. It secured their futures and ensured they all had a loyalty to make the hotel work.

It was certainly working. After the magazine article, they held a large reception twice a month. They had bought their own marquee and had come to arrangements with all of the services that supplied their own wedding. It was working beautifully and they were very comfortable with money, so comfortable, in fact, that Gina kept on to him to get some people in to help renovate the cottage rather than do it all himself after work. He wouldn't, however. He could do the work; he enjoyed doing it for them and it gave him so much satisfaction. There was no rush, a lot of it had been done now and the rest wouldn't take too long. He had promised Gina it would be finished within two years of them buying it and he was well on schedule.

"Have you ever heard anything else of that Annabel?" Oliver asked interrupting his thoughts.

"Nothing," said Neil. "I told you about her mum's visit and what she said."

"Yeah, poor woman," said Oliver. "That girl was crazy, man, anything off Gina's ex?"

"Sure was and no nothing," said Neil.

"Let's hope it stays that way," said Oliver. "Things have turned out well for you, Neil, you have a beautiful wife and gorgeous son."

"I'm lucky," said Neil. "How are things with you and Janice?"

"All good," replied Oliver. "Flat is coming together and the wedding plans are well under way."

"Who'd have thought it, hey," said Neil. "Years ago, we would have run at the first sign of commitment and now look at us."

"Yeah," said Oliver. "But I couldn't be happier, great job, great girlfriend soon to be wife, great flat and hopefully, a family in the future," he said.

"Same," said Neil. "I didn't think I could be this happy ever but here we are."

"Here we are," laughed Oliver. "Two very happy reformed characters. Come on, time to get back to it."

Neil smiled and followed Oliver into the hotel. *Oh yes*, he thought, *I am a very happy reformed character.*

Edna was busy sorting things out in Sunny Cottage ready for her guests evening meal. The bed and breakfast was really busy this summer; it was great to have all the rooms full. She had a lot of returning visitors from last year, something she hadn't had before.

She knew the reason, Annabel! She hadn't really made people feel all that welcome and serving them their food was more of a chore to her than a pleasure, and she wasn't afraid to show it either.

After the events of the baby's birth and Annabel going her own way, things had been much easier on Edna; she hated to admit it but the kindest thing Annabel had ever done for her was leave.

At first, Edna had been really distraught by the idea of Annabel fending for herself, especially as she was involved with a prisoner, and more so the idea of her causing problems elsewhere when Edna wasn't there to sort things.

She had visited Dr George after a few weeks of Annabel being discharged and told him of her fears and anxiety. Dr George had told her she couldn't keep worrying about Annabel, what will be will be and that Edna had done nothing but stood by her, so she wasn't to blame for any of it. If she did cause trouble then so be it. She was an adult who refused help, so she would have to sort it out herself.

He gave Edna some pills to help her sleep and told her to take a break away and in time, she began to feel better. He was right, no matter how she tried to help Annabel, she always threw it back in her face. She was an adult, he was right, she had to step back and live her own life now. If Annabel didn't want to stay with her and go off and fend for herself to be close to a criminal then she would have to get on with it.

Once Annabel was discharged, Edna had not seen or heard of her. The institute couldn't tell Edna where she had gone because of patient confidentiality and Annabel had made it clear she didn't want them disclosing her whereabouts to her so what could she do?

During the winter, after her visit to Haven Hotel, Edna had decided to get the decorators in and give Sunny Cottage a makeover. Once they were done, Edna laid out new furnishings and ornaments and asked the hotel reviewer to visit to see if they would do a piece on the changes they made, which he did.

The article was excellent and it didn't take long for the phone to start ringing for bookings over Easter. Edna was amazed when she had to tell one caller they were fully booked; it had never been known. She knew she would need to hire someone, so she advertised for a receptionist, a chef and a waitress.

After the interviews, she decided on Sherry for the receptionist, what a breath of fresh air she had turned out to be. She was more like Edna's right-hand woman than a receptionist and had certainly relieved a lot of the pressure. Edna was able to take the odd day off now; Sherry was more than capable of running the place without her. Dan had begun as the chef and Caroline helped him in the kitchen as well as wait tables although Dan wasn't averse to waiting on the guests too when needed. The two of them certainly cooked some delicious dishes and their service was second to none.

It was the best thing Edna had ever done, hiring those three. The hotel was busier than ever and their positive attitudes and friendly service guaranteed returning guests, in fact, some guests were booking for next year before they actually left!

People in town commented on how well Edna looked and some even said she was looking years younger. Edna knew the reason why; no one asked about Annabel anymore and she was glad about that.

Yes, she was in her 70s, but she was enjoying life and had finally found the happiness she had desired for so long.

David had been moved twice in the last two years; he never knew why they needed to do it. They just appeared, told him to pack his stuff then shipped him out. Time went really slowly in prison and he hated this one more than any of them. HMP Portland was his fourth prison and it was really tough; some of the worst of the worst were there and he had his fair share of bullying from them, nothing major but some pushing and shoving and verbal abuse. His crimes against women didn't go down well with hardened criminals and they weren't shy in showing him that.

He tried to keep his head down and get involved with activities to stay away from the other inmates but it wasn't easy. He wished they had left him in HMP Bristol, he was ok there; the last one hadn't been too bad either. HMP Guys Marsh was pretty easy-going for a prison but they moved him from there after only six weeks.

A few weeks, he was confronted in the laundry room, a long-time prisoner had sneered at him and verbally abused him about being a coward by raping women. David hadn't retaliated. He knew better but this only seemed to antagonise the other inmate even more! He had grabbed David from behind and threatened to put his arm under the steam press if he saw him look at him again. David was petrified but readily agreed to the other inmates' terms. This bloke really had it in for him and he knew he had to keep a distance. He asked for a transfer to the kitchen or the library, he couldn't say why as that would be grassing, so he just said he found the work too difficult.

The guard had laughed at him. "We're not here to make things easy, lad," he had said but by some stroke of luck, they moved him to the library the following week.

David liked working in the library; it was a peaceful place and he only had to see the others to hand books through their bars, this suited him much better.

Annabel was still visiting every week, if not twice a week. When she left the institution, she found a flat near HMP Bristol, so she could see him more. It was a bummer when he got moved but she managed a weekly trip to HMP Guys Marsh as it was less than two hours away when he was moved here, it was over

2½ hours away from her, so she had written to him to tell him that she was looking for a flat nearer to Portland and she would visit as soon as she could. He realised just how much he missed seeing her when she couldn't visit but bless her, she had moved ten minutes away from the jail and visited twice weekly again.

David also realised that he had fallen in love with Annabel and they often discussed what life would be like when he got out. They would find a little place of their own and maybe start a family; he wouldn't be too old and neither would she. He was still really angry about what they had done to her with her baby and he wanted to help make up for that somehow; besides, he would be a good dad, he knew it.

They had also talked about getting married. Annabel pointed out that it was possible to do it in prison but he had wanted to give her a proper wedding. Annabel said she wanted to be his wife to cement the bond they had and they may give them a conjugal visit. David was unsure but decided that it could be a good idea, even if it was just to keep Annabel from straying from him and ensure she waited for him, so he agreed on the understanding they would have a renewal ceremony when he got out.

Annabel was so excited, but it hadn't happened yet. The prison had agreed to it but kept delaying it for one reason or another. She wasn't happy about it and neither was he but they couldn't do anything about it. It is due to go ahead in about six weeks and hopefully, they won't delay it again; after all, they were both free to marry after Gina had got her bloody divorce, she had moved on so why shouldn't he?

He was still angry about Gina's deceit. He still found it hard to believe she had got married and had a baby. It was always her that was so against kids but he wondered now if it was because he had told her he was impotent. He had made that up, of course, he couldn't face having sex with his wife after he had sex with those dirty women and he was exhausted when he got home. Gina had accepted it and said she didn't want children anyway; was she just being kind or was it just him she didn't want any with?

He still found he had a rage inside when he thought about Gina and what she had done to him. He would never forgive her, but for now, he needed to concentrate on his new love.

Karma is a bitch and he knew Gina would be served hers one day.

_____S

Annabel was sitting in her flat stroking Thomas; she'd had him six months and she loved him so much. He was a Ragdoll kitten when she had him and he showed her nothing, but love and affection, something most males didn't do, she thought.

She liked her latest flat; she had rented in a hurry, so she could visit David again, but it turned out to be a very good move. It was a good size and they allowed pets, so she had taken it instantly.

She looked forward to her visits to David. He was someone who really cared about her and was going nowhere, and he could hardly cheat on her where he was. She had grown to love him and promised she would wait for him for as long as it took. He had been sentenced to 18 years but he'd recently found out he could apply for parole after he had served half of his time, so nine years wasn't that long really.

He had agreed to marry her in prison and she had been so excited, however, the bloody governor kept delaying it. They were on their fourth delay now and she really hoped the next one would happen. They would be given a conjugal visit which would cement their love for each other.

Annabel hadn't been short on sex; she had picked up a few men in the last couple of years she had said she would wait for David but she wasn't prepared to wait nine years for sex, she loved sex! She hadn't told him, of course; she didn't think he would like it but she needed to make money and he would never need to find out. When he got out, she would find them a place away from this area, so they could make a fresh start then she would be faithful to her husband.

She smiled. "It's nice having a little secret," she said to Thomas and then started to laugh. There was no one to dictate to her at the moment; she'd left the institute and started a life without that stupid cow. She did miss her mum sometimes but not her constant nagging. Annabel wasn't keen on having to do all the household chores for herself; that was Edna's job but it was a small price to pay to be rid of her. *I bet Sunny Cottage has gone right downhill without me there*, she thought, *I used to do everything.*

Annabel hadn't really changed much over the last two years; she still had anger inside her but she was able to control it a little better with the meds. There was no way she was going back to that institute, no way on earth; she had only ended up there because of the hospital and their mistake. She had gone to a solicitor to try and sue them but he had asked for DNA. When he got the results, he said he couldn't represent her, what was all that about? She tried another two solicitors but the same thing happened. In the end, she gave up, she didn't want that freaky baby anyway, but a pay-out would have been nice.

She was doing ok for money with her little 'job'. The men paid decent money for her services so she got by ok. When David asked if she needed money, she always said yes just to stop him from asking how she was surviving.

Of course, she thought, it should never have had to come to this if Neil had taken responsibility for his child; he would have been there at the birth and they wouldn't have been able to swap it. Damn, Neil and that whore, they were living happily ever after and she was living alone while waiting for her ex to get out of prison!

Karma is a bitch and she knew Neil and Gina would be served theirs one day.

Epilogue

David and Annabel were right. Karma is a bitch and it was served but unfortunately, not in the way they had hoped.

A new inmate arrived at HMP Portland—an inmate who took an instant dislike to David. This inmate had been transferred from HMP Wakefield and was a nasty piece of work. He was serving three life sentences for multiple murders, so there was no chance of him ever getting out, but he had never hurt women...

David did his best to keep out of his way but every time he saw him, he threatened David. It didn't take too long for the beating to come in the shower block one morning; unfortunately, David took a fatal blow to the head and never recovered.

Annabel was distraught when she found out that she had lost her future. It had been snuffed out by some prison bully, and she wanted revenge.

She turned up at the prison one afternoon demanding to know who had killed her future husband; she wanted to come face to face with the bastard.

The officer at reception advised her to calm down and that he couldn't disclose any information to her.

Of course, Annabel did the opposite, no amount of meds could keep her calm at this point and she exploded in a fit of rage.

The reception guard received three stab wounds to the abdomen and needed emergency surgery. He survived, but Annabel was now serving a 15-year sentence in HMP Holloway.

There was no wedding and no one at David's funeral.

Edna, Abby, Gina and Neil were all very shocked by the news but secretly, they were all a little relieved.

Edan knew where Annabel was and she also knew that she couldn't be causing any more innocent people any trouble.

Gina was a little saddened by David's death; she didn't wish that on anyone but also a little relieved that she didn't have to worry about him coming looking for her when he got out.

When everyone got over the shock, they went back about their lives knowing they were safe from any future aggravations.